MESSIN' UP

A novel by

LATONYA Y. WILLIAMS

Q-Boro Books
WWW.QBOROBOOKS.COM

An Urban Entertainment Company

Published by Q-Boro Books
Copyright © 2008 by LaTonya Y. Williams

ISBN-13: 978-1-933967-33-2
ISBN-10: 1-933967-33-1
LCCN: 200792373

First Printing March 2008
Printed in the United States of America

10   9   8   7   6   5   4   3   2

*This is a work of fiction. It is not meant to depict, portray or represent any
particular real persons. All the characters, incidents and dialogues are the
products of the author's imagination and are not to be construed as real.
Any references or similarities to actual events, entities, real people, living or
dead, or to real locales are intended to give the novel a sense of reality. Any
similarity in other names, characters, entities, places and incidents is en-
tirely coincidental.*

Cover Copyright © 2007 by Q-BORO BOOKS, all rights reserved.
Cover layout/design by Candace K. Cottrell; Photo by Ted Mebane
Editors: Candace K. Cottrell, Maria Delongoria, Brian Sandy

Q-BORO BOOKS
Jamaica, Queens NY 11434
WWW.QBOROBOOKS.COM

Acknowledgments

I am so grateful to God for blessing me with the gift of writing. I want to take time to thank those who continue to help me through this journey. This book would not be complete without the insights from **T'Ronda, Kimberly, Tamika, and Tabitha** for reading the manuscript and providing valuable feedback. Thank you, ladies!

Shawn, my husband, I love you so much. Thanks for being a wonderful husband and father.

Shawn, Christopher, and Brandon, my adorable children to whom I dedicate my life, hoping you'll make great contributions to the world in the future.

Avis, my mother, our long talks help me get through each day. **James**, my dad, thanks for your patience and kindness.

My sisters, Cabrina, T'Ronda, Natalie, Ashley, Lisa, Shatia, it means a lot to have you in my corner.

My brothers, thanks for reading my books and sharing your comments. I know you're going to love Daneisha's story.

Dr. Rudolph McKissick, Jr., my pastor for life, whose name appears in three of my books, as I attribute you for not only changing my life for the better, but you saved my entire family. Your spiritual guidance has been immeasurable. Thank you for providing answers to all of my questions and practically writing your sermons throughout this book. I look forward to reading your books in the future, as I believe they will heal many hurting people.

Mark Anthony at Q-Boro Books, you're one of the nicest men I know. Thanks to you and **Sabine** for your faithfulness to make great writers achieve greatness. My editor, **Candace**, I appreciate your patience. It's been a struggle each time to get the manuscripts in your hands. Thanks for not giving me a hard time.

Thanks to my publicist, **Torrian Ferguson**, one of the hardest-working men, who never gave up on me. Thanks for burning the midnight oil. **Belinda Williams**, you've been there for me since the beginning. Keep doing your thang!

To my family and friends, thanks for continuing to promote my books, keep the boys, and everything necessary so that I'm able to continue writing.

I can't say enough to thank the **book clubs and readers.** I appreciate the emails, reviews, and your personal testimonials. It encourages me to work hard to give you my absolute best.

Peace & Blessings!!!

This book is dedicated to my husband, Shawn,
who I have the deepest love and respect for.

Prologue

I got my skills from my mama. One time, I snuck in her room and watched her fucking her boyfriend from her own closet. Tate had a big dick and he used to make my mama scream. I used to hear her all the way in my room. So, I decided to find out how good she really was. I watched her technique and tried it on my then boyfriend, Chris. When I made him howl at the moon, I knew I had my shit down.

She makes me sick. I'll be so glad when I get away from here. Getting my own apartment in Arlington, my old neighborhood, is going to be so good. That's where we used to live, until my mama married a doctor, who moved us into a lily-white neighborhood. I don't know what happened. Me and her don't get along. And I can't stand Mike's punk ass. Always trying to act like he's my friend and he care about me. His faggot ass lets my mom boss him around all day. And my brothers act like puppets.

I don't know what got into me, all I know is one day I decided not to go along with the LeQuisha-do-what-the-hell-I-tell-you-and-don't-ask-me-no-more-questions-or-I'll-beat-your-ass program.

Men been begging for this stuff ever since. I used to give it away for free. Until my best friend, Kendall, showed me how I could make a lot of money selling my goodies instead. I rebelled, got kicked out of school, and Mama moved me to country-ass Middleburg to live with my grandma and her boyfriend Leroy.

It was hard for a while. I went to school, did as I was told, and started making good grades again. Finally, I borrowed this white girl's cell phone and called my girl, Kendall. Then the white girl showed me how I could buy a prepaid cell phone. By this time, Kendall had a car, so she agreed to pick me up on the paved highway about two miles from my house, which was down a dirt road. I learned how to sneak out and be back before anybody even noticed I was gone.

The night I met Lamium was the best and worst night of my life. We were at the club, and Kendall's car broke down. We asked these guys to give us a ride. No, we weren't old enough to be in the club, but our fake ID's got us wherever we wanted to go. He dropped me off, and even walked down the dirt road with me while his boys waited in the car. I gave him my cell phone number. My stupid grandma still didn't even know I had one.

Drunk-ass Leroy walked in the laundry room as I was sneaking in through the back door. He was tipping in the house, too.

"Uh-huh. Wait until I tell Gayle. You know she gonna beat your ass." He laughed, showing his big, gapped teeth.

"Come on, Leroy. You know I'm going to the detention center if I get in trouble again." I pulled out a stack of hundreds.

Leroy's pop-eyes got big then.

I smiled. "Yeah, that's what I thought." I handed him three bills.

"Now, get out my way." I tried to push past him.

"Not so fast, li'l gal."

"Huh?"

Leroy pulled down his pants and whipped out his dark, wrinkled, old dick. No wonder my grandma be eating women's coochies out. Her man ain't have shit to work with.

"Won't you . . . ah . . . give me a li'l head, too?" he asked. He breathed his stank breath in my face.

I turned up my nose. "Hell no. You better go buy a trick with that money I just gave you."

He shoved my face into the wall. "Suck my dick."

When the numbness left, my nose felt broken. As blood ran down, I wiped it away.

He brushed his dick across my lips. I stroked Leroy's dick to try to get it hard. It was limp.

He slapped me again. This time with more force. I could taste the wood and paint on the wall.

"Don't play with me." The look on his face warned me if I didn't do it, the cops might find my dead body in the woods somewhere. It's not like he hadn't killed a nigga before. Served nine years in prison. My grandma knew how to pick 'em.

I put his nasty penis in my mouth. It tasted like sweat, dirt, and it smelled like a sewer. I almost gagged.

He swelled up in my mouth. Forced his way down my throat. Pulled on my thousand-dollar weave.

"Yeah," he grunted.

Oh no. It got harder. I pulled back, and he rammed harder. Deeper.

His cum tasted like rotten eggs.

Leroy zipped up his pants and closed the laundry room door.

I ran to the kitchen sink and threw up. As I purged, everything I ate that day came up too.

I'd had it! I packed up my shit and hitchhiked a ride out of Middleburg. I didn't even know Lamium all that well, but I went and stayed with him anyway. I loved me some Lamium. He was always in control, and treated me to any and everything I ever wanted. We had so much fun together, doing shit like getting high and talking for hours. Not to mention Lamium had a high sex drive. We were in perfect sync with each other.

Well, Mama found out where I was and dragged my ass back to her house. She saw the bruises on my face and told everybody Lamium beat me up. Since she thought Leroy was so good to my grandmother, I didn't have the heart to tell her Leroy beat me and raped me. She thought she knew every damn thang.

Mama tried to get me back in school. I had to be retained because I missed sixty-five days. Boy, was she mad at me! I didn't even care, I didn't have time for no school. I was all about making that paper and spending time with my man.

More bad news . . . I was pregnant.

Lamium was scared, thinking Mama would have the authorities charge him with statutory rape. He begged me to get an abortion. For once, Mama and Lamium agreed on something. I didn't need to have no baby.

What about me! I wasn't about to let anyone tell me what to do. And I wasn't having no abortion either. I took that money and got me a manicure and pedicure at the spa. Mama kept me prisoner until I had my baby.

Now I can't wait until I get the hell up out of here and settle into my own place. Lamium says he's going to buy me all new furniture. We already picked it out at Warehouse Furniture. My man treats me very well. He says when he has saved another $20,000, he's through dealing for good. He's going to start him up a barbershop, you know, like the movie. And I'm-a be strutting up in there with my fresh gear and hairdos, making all them stank bitches who want my man jealous. I know they be wondering what a thirty-year-old man see in me anyway.

Anywayz. My bags are packed and my man is pulling up in his money-green Mercedes. We're going to have a ghetto-fabulous life!

I'm still making my money. One thing I learned from watching my mama's stupid ass is to gets mine. Okay. If Lamium knew, he would kill me. But, he don't have to know everything.

Lamium's car was so loud, I was hoping it wouldn't wake up Mike. Their bedroom window faced the driveway.

I dragged two garbage bags full of clothes.

"Lamium, turn off the ignition," I said as I handed him my stuff.

"For what?" Lamium opened the trunk. "Your nosey-ass mama ain't here."

"Yeah, but I still don't want to wake my brothers up. They have school in the morning." I snatched his keys out of the ignition and tossed them to him. "Now, I need to get LJ's stuff. Just wait for me in the car."

Lamium's voice went deep as he raised his eyebrows. "Who you bossing around?"

"Nobody." I turned and walked away.

"Bring your ass here. Right now."

I stopped in my tracks. "I need to get the rest of the stuff and get LJ. What do you want?"

Lamium grabbed my breasts from behind and rested his dick on my behind. "I was admiring how good you look from the back. And I'm glad you're my girl." He kissed the fold in my neck.

I felt myself want to melt right there. No man ever made me feel the way he did. "Wait until we get to our apartment. Lamium, it's gonna be muthafucking on then!"

Lamium licked his lips. "I'm counting on it."

I ran inside and picked up LJ from the crib my mama bought me. I didn't need it anymore because I was getting all new stuff from Lamium. One more garbage bag later, and I had everything I came to her house with.

I strapped LJ in his car seat and plopped down beside Lamium in the front.

Lamium peeled down the street.

"You're mine now. You know that." He ran his hand down my leg.

I always loved it when he did that. I reached over and kissed him on the cheek. "No, you belong to me."

Chapter One

September 2006
(Four Years Later)

Surrounded by the St. Johns River on its west end and the Atlantic Ocean on the east, Jacksonville is one of the most beautiful cities in the country. Originally named Cowford for the cattle lines that passed through, it was renamed after President Andrew Jackson, who was one of the first military leaders in Florida. Home of the NFL's Jaguars, Jacksonville is both massive in its urban appeal and gorgeous coastal waterways. Proudly, Jacksonville citizens will boast about living in the largest city in America, but the Florida weather is enticing enough for tourists to lay out on the sunny beaches.

Walking along the Landing or Riverwalk, many enjoy the shopping and restaurants, which serve the best Southern food to one's heart's delight. Ask anyone, and he or she will tell you the friendliest people live in Jacksonville. Hospitality, in the best sense. The kind when a gentleman will open the door for a woman, then wish her a good day.

At night, a drive downtown along I-95 is breathtaking. The view captures the neon-lit skyline along the tallest buildings in the city, and the crossover Main Street Bridge is lit in the brightest topaz blue imaginable.

Just like any other city, there exists the ghetto, where blacks, whose people traveled from Alabama and Georgia in search of work at factories like Maxwell House Coffee live. There, these former slaves found good-paying blue-collar work and settled in the downtown areas if they didn't own cars, and the Northside, which was fully integrated at the time. As more blacks purchased homes, the whites moved out in search of their own utopia, better known as suburbia.

On the Northside, and further east to Arlington, resides the heart of Black Jacksonville, the beat of the city. Beating to a slower drum than one would find in New York, the people are very laid-back in most ways. On Saturday, married men are tending to their green carpeted lawns, and young, single brothers are standing in line at the barber waiting for a fresh cut, so they can wash up their cars to take them for a drive around the neighborhood and hit the club that night. Married women and mothers are getting the children ready for a cultural festival in the Metro Park, full of old-school music, food, and art. The single women sit up in the beauty shop, while the stylists are hooking them up with the latest styles out of the magazines. Later, they plan to hit the Regency and Gateway malls to pick out the perfect outfit to wear out with the girls and hit the town.

And then on Sunday, the churches are filled to capacity. Preachers giving hope that better days are ahead. Cadillac Escalades, Honda Accords, BMWs, and Mercedes Benzes are lined outside after service, headed to Grandma's house for an early dinner of collards and mustards with neck bones, cornbread, macaroni and cheese, and fried chicken—

enough fat and grease that will need to be worked off during the week. That evening, work clothes and school clothes are ironed up, and little girl's heads are done at night for a quick brushing in the morning.

Monday through Friday, the hardest working people leave their homes, dropping off the children to school, headed to the workplace. In the evening, mothers and fathers are home helping the children with homework, eating dinner at the table, preparing for another day on the job. No matter the socio-economic status of black people, the values and traditions are very much the same.

Still, there are some that are more GHETTO than others.

That was how you would've described her four years ago. Classy-sophistication-with-a-streak-of-ghetto-fabulousness was the new Daneisha Harris. As Lamium's business grew, so did her standards. She may have been living in a roach-filled apartment in the beginning, but now she was enjoying a taste of the good life.

Your girl had arrived, enjoying her days in Village Walk Apartments, one step away from the mansion Lamium promised he would purchase within the next two years. Yes, Daneisha was sitting up in a 1600-square-foot, three-bedroom, two-bath apartment in the prestigious St. John's Bluff area. Indonesian Crust walls, another word for beige, was accented with crown molding along the ceiling. There were tall maple cabinets in a top-of-the-line, upgraded gourmet kitchen, which she never cooked in. That's what she had Valerie for.

In the living room, there was a built-in entertainment center with a movie theater audio system that would make anyone jealous. That was for Lamium, since Daneisha wasn't really into movies all that much. Unless, you counted the Tyler Perry "Madea" videos, of which she owned the entire collection.

Surprised?

I know when you last heard from Daneisha, she was a buck wild teenager causing her mama, LeQuisha Stocks, all kinds of hell. She heard all your comments. That fast-ass Daneisha. Like her mama, she kept her head held high and handled her business. Since then, Daneisha has grown up.

Today, it was Daneisha's turn to host a luncheon for her friends. This was something they did once a month, each sharing the duty of hostess. It was a special time for them to take a well-deserved break from their hectic schedules, to talk about the men in their lives, the children, money, and whatever they wanted to pretend was so damned perfect. Even though they were probably one moment away from breaking the hell down.

Kay was Daneisha's best friend. Kay was Daneisha's girl from back in the day. Her full name was Kendall Jane Harms, but for the past two years she's wanted to be called Kay. They've been inseparable since they were little girls growing up in Arlington. Kay still lived at home with her mother, while going to school to become a paralegal. In the meantime, she worked at a downtown law firm as a receptionist.

Those other bitches, Angel and Myra, had to be there. Their husbands worked for Lamium. And as his wife-to-be, it was Daneisha's job to keep up the his flashy, show-off, make-the-people-think-you're-large-and-in-charge image. Part of that was socializing with the top half of his organization. The key players.

"Alright, Daneisha, what are we going to do for your birthday?" Myra asked as she leaned back on the couch.

"Whaaaattt?" Angel smiled. "Are you finally going to be legal?"

Kay snickered.

"Yes. Ladies, I'll be twenty-one years old," Daneisha responded. She took a sip of her lime margarita and crossed her freshly shaven legs.

"Gimme that drink." Myra playfully grabbed the glass out of her hand and spilled a little on the carpet. "You're still wet behind the ears," she teased.

"Oh no, you didn't, bitch!" Daneisha stood up from her chaise lounge and took her drink back. "I'm trying to get my buzz on." She cackled loudly.

"In the afternoon?" Angel asked in a disapproving tone, shaking her head in judgment.

"Oh, shut up." Daneisha waved her hand as she didn't have a care in the world and plopped back down at the edge of her seat. "Everybody can't be perfect like you heifers." She took another sip.

She burped and tried to cover her mouth afterward.

Angel laughed. "Did you hear that? And she has such class too."

Feeling aggravated, Daneisha pointed in Angel's direction, then waved her hand around. "See, I'm about to put y'all asses out already."

Kay rubbed her stomach. "I know you're not even thinking about putting me out and you haven't fed me yet. Please, you better get Hector out here with them chimichangas." She clapped her hands twice. "Oh, Hector, you have three starving ladies in here!"

"What was that?" Hector yelled from the outside balcony. His accent was thick.

"You better leave Hector alone." Daneisha glanced at the clock. "Lunch should be ready by now. Let me see what's going on."

Moving down the hall, Daneisha felt a sharp pain below her waist. On the wall, she leaned on one arm until the pain eased up. Earlier that morning, she couldn't even get out of bed. Determined not to be outdone, she swallowed six ibuprofen and got herself together. Daneisha knew her period was due to arrive any day, but couldn't imagine why she had to suffer with severe back pain and cramping days before it came on.

Kay's crazy laugh, probably from one of Myra's jokes, brought her back to reality. Daneisha straightened up her five-foot five-inch frame and walked outside. The smoke from the grill greeted her senses. "Almost ready for us?"

"Yes." Hector kissed two fingers. "I have a wonderful meal prepared for you and the ladies."

"Well, let me see here." Daneisha was pleased at the spread. Chicken quesadillas, with Hector's special guacamole and sour cream dipping sauce, which she could eat by the bucket. Steak fajitas and chimichangas.

Daneisha patted Hector on his muscular bicep. "You did good. I can't wait to dig in." She circled her finger around one of his many tattoos. This one was a cross.

Not resembling the typical chef/ cook, Hector had spent time in prison for drug trafficking. As a cook in the kitchen, he mastered his culinary skills and earned his reputation as the Mexican Don Juan. Upon his release, he was hired by the top restaurant in Jacksonville. Lamium and Daneisha dined at the spot, loved his food, and now he worked solely for her man. Sometimes, Daneisha convinced Lamium to let her borrow Hector for occasions like this.

Hector smiled like a proud uncle. "Thank you."

Before Daneisha could turn around, she heard footsteps approaching.

"Look, she's trying to get a headstart!" Kay yelled back as she leaned against the patio door.

"Some host you are!" Angel chimed in. She gracefully strolled her thirty-year-old frame past them and sat at the table.

Okay. Angel was the snooty, stuck-up one. She was married to Greg Matthews, with one spoiled daughter, who she bragged about all the time. Angel held a doctorate from Howard University, as she grew up in Washington, DC. She worked as a psychiatrist, and lived in a half-million-dollar home in Julington Creek.

Kay sat down and placed the white cloth napkin on her lap. She clapped her hands twice. "Yo, Hector. My meal."

Hector smiled. "Let me give the lady what she wants."

Myra rubbed her hands on his arms. "When are you going to give me what I want?" She puckered her strawberry glossed lips.

The crazy one. Daneisha enjoyed being around her most.

Hector flexed his muscles. "And what would that be?"

Myra whispered in his ear and this time he revealed his dimples. She pinched his firm butt, then took her seat too.

Myra was smart, educated, and creative. Girlfriend could sang! She even sang back-up for gospel recording artist, Lisa McClendon. She was married to Jericho Downs and was working on her own solo project. Her style was Nu-Jazz, and once her album was completed, Daneisha imagined she would be too busy to hang out with them. She was the mother of two boys.

"It smells so good," Kay said with her husky voice. As Hector placed her plate in front of her, she performed the happy dance from her chair.

Myra cleared her throat as her eyes danced in circles. "Yes, it does."

Hector's shoulders went up and down as he chuckled from all the attention he was receiving.

Angel scoffed in her disapproval. "Will you tramps leave this MARRIED man alone?" She lifted her glass in Daneisha's direction. "More tea, please."

Daneisha filled all four glasses with sweet tea. She figured they'd had enough alcohol for the day. They grubbed out on the food, made small talk about life, then the conversation shifted back to plans for her birthday.

"You just seem so much older to me," Myra added.

"Well, I've been on my own since I was seventeen years old."

"That would probably explain your maturity." Myra wiped her mouth with her cloth napkin.

"I was thinking back to the day when I left my mama's house as if it were yesterday. You would think I would've been sad to leave." Daneisha leaned back and crossed her arms. "Honestly, I was so happy." She went back to eating a quesadilla.

"Really?" Angel asked as she raised her perfectly arched eyebrows. "I'm so close to my mother, when I got to ready to move to Florida, I couldn't stop crying."

Myra's eyes lingered on Angel for a moment.

"Well, I wasn't that pitiful. But it wasn't easy to leave home where my mother prepared home-cooked meals every night and baked cakes from scratch," she clarified.

Daneisha finished chewing on a tender piece of chicken. "I have to admit I was pretty stupid. It only took me one week of living with Lamium to realize how hard it was."

"Ain't no way in hell I'm ever leaving home!" Kay spat out with a mouth full of food. "Not until I get married and my man puts me in a house." She straightened her olive plaid jacket. It was something Daneisha would never wear, but Kay pulled it off nicely with flare-leg jeans.

"Oh, I've changed. Becoming a mother had more to do with it." Daneisha took the liberty to fill the empty glasses with more tea. "Especially when it came to raising LJ. My little man can act just as crazy as his daddy."

"Yep, my boys too," Myra responded.

"My Halle is so sweet." Angel smiled and gazed up at the

sky, as if she was thanking the Good Lord for all her blessings. "I don't know why I have such a perfect child."

Kay sighed with frustration. "Where do you come from? I mean, are there others just like you?"

Myra and Daneisha burst out laughing.

Angel gasped. She slid her pewter-gray Gucci sunglasses over her eyes. "I have my hater-blockers on."

Kay clapped her hands. "Good comeback."

"Anyway, I believe we were discussing my favorite topic—ME. Like I was saying, I was miserable! I felt more like a prisoner on lockdown. The warden was this little baby who told me when to eat, drink, pee, and even sleep."

"I felt the same way," Myra chimed in. "With Jason, I didn't think it would ever get better. But now, he's a well-adjusted three-year-old."

"Now LJ is four, it's a little easier. But he's still a bad ass. Last night, he didn't want to take a bath. Lamium sat right there and let that boy cover himself with a red marker, I mean from his hands to his feet. Not to mention, I spotted red marker all over my carpet! It cost me some serious money to have it cleaned two weeks ago."

The girls all chimed a collective, "No, he didn't!"

"No matter how many times I popped him on the thigh, he refused to get in the tub." Daneisha tightened her lips, her hand in a fist to demonstrate the level of "pissoffication" (meaning pissed to the highest degree). "I was about to kill him. That's when Valerie stepped in and kept me from going to jail last night."

"Valerie works nights too?" Angel asked almost immediately.

"Hell yeah! Let me clear something up. Valerie is my personal assistant, which means housekeeper, nanny, cook and anything else I need her to do."

"Excuse me, ladies," Hector interrupted, "are we all done here?"

"Yes."

Hector cleared the table and placed small plates in front of them.

Kay rubbed her hands together. "And now for dessert. What do you have for us today?"

Hector rolled a cart over with the most beautiful cake with fresh strawberries and cream in the middle. "It's called Chocolate Strawberry Dream," he said as he poured chocolate over the top. It ran down the sides.

Myra licked her lips. "Now pour the rest on your chest."

Hector nodded with excitement. "You would like that, wouldn't you?"

Myra leaned forward on the table. "Baby, I would love it."

Angel folded her arms. "Okay, this is getting way too sexual for me. And it's too early for me to do anything about it. Please stop it!" She pulled Myra back down in her seat. "Sit down. You're a married woman."

Myra shrugged her shoulders. "Married, but still looking."

"Myra, you're a nut," Daneisha said.

Angel grabbed Myra's arm. "Oh. Not to change the subject, but is anyone going to see *The Last King of Scotland*?"

"The what?" Daneisha shot Angel a confused look. She was always talking about movies, but none of the good ones.

"Is this another one of those independent films you're always trying to get me to go see?" Myra asked as she stayed focused on Hector.

"Yes. But it's starring Forest Whitaker. Rumor is he'll receive an Oscar nod for this one."

Kay held up her hand. "Well, it's about time we get another one. I remember seeing Denzel's fine ass take his for *Training Day*. It's a shame the brother had to play a bad guy in order to win it."

Myra pointed. "You're right about that."

"With the *Last King*, Forest portrays an African dicta-tor," Angel added.

"Ooops." Kay twisted her lips. "Like I said, another bad guy. I know he's gonna win it for sure."

Myra laughed.

"Now, what I'm going to check out is *Gridiron Gang* with The Rock. I'll watch anything his fine ass is in." Kay snapped her fingers.

"I'm with you on that." Myra and Kay gave each other a high-five.

Daneisha turned up her nose. She didn't care much for the current topic. "I haven't been to the movies in a while. It's just not my thing." She leaned on one arm to avoid the sunlight in her eyes.

"The only thing you do is shop," Kay replied.

A little annoyed, Angel sighed with frustration. "Don't you want to stimulate your intellect just a little?" She leaned in Daneisha's direction.

Daneisha raised one eyelid, higher than the other. Angel was about to get slapped. "No, I don't." She forced a fake smile, wittingly so no one detected her anger. She wasn't about to let her nemesis get the better of her. No, she would keep her cool and pull off this luncheon with-out a sister-girl beat down.

Remember, Daneisha had class.

"So, I take it you haven't read any new novels lately ei-ther," Angel retorted. She was tickled at her own sense of humor.

Kay laughed. "Not unless it's an article in a fashion mag-azine."

"Yes, I read somewhere that if you study a subject for more than a year, then you're an expert in that field."

Daneisha took a long sip from her glass, then swallowed hard. Keeping everyone hanging on her next sentence, she saw Myra and Kay shift nervously in their chairs. "So, that would make me an expert in fashion. And let's say for a minute that I'm an expert, then I would tell you that the navy dress you're wearing is two seasons old, the new blue is cerulean and straps are out, halter is in. And let's talk about your shoes." Daneisha shook her head in disapproval. "Points are out and round toes are in—"

"So, I see you watched at least one movie this summer," Kay chimed in.

"*Devil Wears Prada!*" they shouted in unison.

"My favorite man is back!" Myra clapped her hands as Hector returned with a knife in one hand. The interruption was needed to clear the tension in the air.

Daneisha wanted to use it to cut Angel. She hoped Angel would keep her damn mouth shut for the rest of the afternoon.

Hector cut the cake into perfect slices and placed one on each plate. "Daneisha, if you don't need anything else, I'm going to finish cleaning and leave you ladies to enjoy."

Daneisha smiled. "Okay, that's fine. Thank you for a wonderful lunch."

Kay savored her slice of cake, then took a quick sip of her iced tea. "As usual, Hector showed out."

"You are one lucky lady," Myra added.

"Don't get it twisted. It wasn't always this good. Lamium hired Valerie when LJ was eight months old. Up until then, I was trying to manage it all by myself."

"And you were so young," Angel remarked. "But, that's where you went wrong." She cut her eyes over in Myra's direction. Myra nodded as if she agreed.

"How so?" Daneisha asked, starting to feel a tiny bit paranoid. Had these two hoochies been talking about her behind her back? Maybe Angel was ready for an ass-whooping after all.

"Well." Angel scratched her forehead. "You said so yourself, you were doing all this by yourself. Where was Lamium?"

Kay cleared her throat. "That's a good question."

Daneisha frowned. Kay was supposed to be on her side, and there she was, waiting to be vindicated for her constant criticism of Daneisha's parenting skills. Daneisha believed women with children had no right to criticize, so she never gave Kay's suggestions a moment's thought.

Angel continued. "I mean, why didn't you just ask for his help?"

"Yeah," Myra chimed in. "Make Lamium step up and help you raise LJ?"

"You weren't the only parent." Angel gestured with her hands. "I don't understand why he wasn't around."

Daneisha shrugged. "He was busy. Y'all know how he is."

No one said a word.

"Darling, let me break this down for you. And don't get offended." Angel took a deep breath. "You were too young to take on such a tremendous amount of responsibility and too immature to communicate your needs effectively to your partner."

Now Daneisha was beyond irate. Forget trying to keep up appearances. "Okay, so you're calling me stupid?" She leaned back in her seat, tossing her hair to one side.

Angel held her hand to her chest. "Believe me, I know this is hard to hear."

"She needs to hear it." Kay tossed up her fork. "See why my godson is so hard-headed."

Daneisha glared in Kay's direction. "Shut up, Kay. Ain't nobody even talking to you."

"Whatever!" Kay snapped back.

"Okay, wait a minute." Angel tossed up her hands in an attempt to calm everybody down. "There is good news in all of this. It's not too late to get Lamium involved. LJ's behaviors are still changeable. Daneisha, you know I specialize in these in pediatrics. I believe we can get him on the right path." She whipped out a card from her purse. "Why don't you have LJ come in for a session? It's on me."

Daneisha refused to take the card. "LJ doesn't need therapy."

"Well, think about it. My offer is open." Angel placed the card on the table. Then she stood up to help herself to another slice of cake.

Daneisha stared at the card for a few minutes. Maybe she was taking this conversation a little too seriously. It's not like Angel exactly had it going on. Her husband had to answer to Daneisha's man. Angel knew what time it was. She laughed to herself.

Myra's eyes widened when she glanced down at her watch. "We'll have to finish this discussion next time. Don't forget, I'm hosting."

"Well, where are you rushing off to?" Daneisha asked, disappointed the luncheon was about to end so abruptly.

"I'm due back at the studio," Myra responded, as she gathered her things. "I have to meet with a new producer."

Angel followed. "I need to get back, too. I have appointments lined up all afternoon."

Kay cleared her throat and made a sad face like a small child. "Sorry."

"Oh no. Not you too." Daneisha put her hands on her hips. "Can't you stay for a few minutes and help me straighten up?" She was trying for any excuse to get Kay to stay around, so she could have a little company.

"We can't be like you, Ms. Lady!" Myra shouted as she headed toward the front door. "We all have to work for a living. As for next month, don't be late either, unless you like cold food. I don't have a personal chef, but I'm having lunch catered."

As Daneisha followed them to the door, she noticed Hector was gone. The kitchen was spotless.

Kay shrugged. "I guess you don't need my help after all."

Daneisha frowned. "I guess not."

"As always, this was wonderful." Angel hugged her. "Thanks again."

Daneisha tried to put on her best smile. "Of course. See you soon."

When they were gone, Daneisha racked her brain trying to find something to do, then figured the best cure for boredom was shopping. She called to remind Valerie to get Lamium's suits from the cleaners. She searched in her closet for the perfect hat to match her RocaWear tee and khaki short shorts she was changing into. She pulled down the oversized leopard print hat. Checking out her slamming body in the mirror, she folded the top rim of her hat. Too divalicious!

Tightening the straps to her patent leather platforms, Daneisha put on gold bangles and large hoop earrings. Then she strutted out the door in runway-model fashion, climbed in her Lexus ES 350, and headed to the Avenues Mall.

By the time Daneisha made it home, LJ was already in bed. Valerie gave her the usual disappointing look before she left. At that point, Daneisha was so tired, she could barely keep her eyes open. She managed to take out her laptop and surf from one webpage to the next. She signed in on MySpace.

Dang!

Daneisha had thirty-two more friend requests. The pictures she added of her ass in the black thong did just the trick. Now she had more customers directed to her website and the dollars just kept rolling in. Daneisha was careful to make sure Lamium didn't know anything about her side hustle. Shit, the new members would help her with spending money; she was already making close to $2,000 a month.

That's one tip Daneisha learned from her mother; multiple sources of income. With her two sites, money from Lamium, and an occasional date, girlfriend was doing just fine.

Daneisha shut down her laptop and crawled into bed. She wanted to get up to check on LJ, but decided against it. He was a light sleeper, and the mere sound of her feet gently hitting the carpet would be enough to wake him up.

A second later, Daneisha heard the front door open and the alarm system beeping. Then she heard Lamium entering the code on the keypad.

"Daddy!" LJ screamed at the top of his lungs.

Daneisha threw the pillow over her head.

"Daddy! Daddy! Daddy!"

Daneisha didn't know who she was more angrier with: Lamium for coming home so late or LJ for wanting his dad, when he never once cried for his mother.

She dragged herself out of bed and peered down the hall from the doorway. The light from beneath the bathroom door let her know Lamium had the nerve to take a piss when he knew he heard that boy making all that damn noise!

LJ's screams got louder, so Daneisha rushed in the room to comfort him.

"Is Daddy here?" LJ poked his lips out and folded his arms.

"Yeah, well he's busy right now. You got me." Daneisha wiped the tears from his face.

"No. But I want to talk to him. Daddy!"

Daneisha touched her chest. "You know you hurt Mommy's feelings when you say things like that."

"What's going on in here?" Lamium asked. He entered the room and sat on the floor.

LJ's face lit up with excitement.

"I know I didn't hear a little boy in here crying like a girl." Lamium shook his head.

"I wasn't crying." LJ flashed a cheesy grin, showing all his tiny teeth. "I was using my lion voice so you could hear me. See. *RRRRRRRRaaaawwww!*"

"I can do you one better," Lamium said as he approached the bed and let out an even louder roar. Then he pushed past Daneisha and tickled LJ in the stomach.

"Daddy! I had the best day. My class went to the zoo and Ma . . . I mean Ms. Val went too. And we saw a lion. And he was roaring like this. *Raooraaoow!* It was so fun. Then you know what else, Daddy?"

"What, son?"

While he continued, Daneisha scooted off the bed and eased her way out of the room. No one seemed to notice she was gone.

It was nice Valerie was able to chaperone the field trip with her son, but deep down Daneisha wished she'd gone instead. She'd already had the brunch with the girls planned, and it would've been too short notice to cancel.

Valerie seemed more of a mother to LJ than her. If only she wasn't so tired during the day. Not to mention the stomach cramps. Daneisha needed to see a doctor and get checked out. She hadn't found another one since she got in an argument with her last doctor. She didn't appreciate the way he was always talking down to her like she was his child. Then again, she had the option to see her stepfather, Mike, but she didn't want her mama in her business.

Daneisha was wide awake. She emptied her shopping bags from Dillards that were lying on the dresser. Le Quisha used to work there when Daneisha was younger, and it was still her favorite store. Tracie used to work there when Le Quisha did, and she made a point to call Daneisha when the new stuff came in or a sale was coming up.

Naturally, when Tracie put together the white Melissa lapel jacket with the Antonio flare-leg pant, Daneisha couldn't resist buying it despite the price. While she was in the dressing room admiring herself, Tracie added the Grayce sleeveless V-neck sweater. This was just what Daneisha needed for her fall collection, even though very few people could pull off white like she did.

As Daneisha was hanging her Antonio Melani clothing in the closet, Lamium came in and stripped out of his shirt and jeans. Daneisha admired the way his shirt sleeves hung perfectly on his muscular biceps. She checked out his abs while he faced the mirror. Yes, he was cut in all the right places. She pictured her hands running down the ripples in his chest. How hard his muscles pulsated against her when they made love.

"I'm beat. You showered yet?"

"Yes, earlier." Daneisha almost lied and said no. Sex in the shower was always good. But she didn't want the steam to mess up her thousand-dollar hair extensions. "Since you woke everybody up, I figured I'd get this out of the way."

"That's right. You had such a long day at work today, didn't you? And you need your beauty rest to conquer the world of hairdressers, nail techs, and malls tomorrow," Lamium remarked sarcastically.

Daneisha sucked her teeth wryly. She marveled at his sense of humor. "Oh, please. I do plenty around here."

"No, Valerie does plenty around here." Lamium's voice sounded harsh. "I ask you to run a few errands for me and you can't even do that."

Daneisha fired back. "Why should I do menial things like pick up your dry cleaning, when you have Keysha to do that for you?" She raised her index finger. "Oh, but I had to ask Valerie to do that too. So, I guess you have two women that don't wait on your behind."

Lamium's face turned red hot. "You're my woman." He slapped his chest forcefully. "Not no damn Keysha. Show me some appreciation every once in a while for all I do. I get out there and bust my ass every day."

Not the slightest bit afraid of his caveman dance, Daneisha climbed in bed, hoping that would be the end of their small tift. "And I love you for it. Can you turn the light off please?" she asked sweetly.

Lamium shook his head. "See, that's what I'm talking about. You have no problem telling me what to do."

Daneisha kept her voice soft. "Baby, I know you're not getting pissed at me for asking you to turn off a light."

"No. It was an example of how you asked me to perform a menial task, when you yourself admitted you can't do the same for me."

Daneisha laughed. "Whatever!"

Lamium turned off the light. "Unlike you, I don't have a problem with doing things for my woman." He went in the bathroom to shower.

Daneisha tried to fall back asleep, but she tossed and turned, unable to find her groove in the mattress.

Lamium came out of the bathroom humming a Luther Vandross song. Not that Daneisha personally owned a Luther CD, but she recognized it from her mama's CD collection. Pretending to be sleeping, she watched him slide a pair of boxer briefs on. She even let out a snore or two to sound convincing.

He snuggled up close to her. His wet body pressed against her night gown.

Daneisha sighed.

Lamium ran his hands along her backside. "I know you're not 'sleep."

Damn!

Her eyes popped open. "Look, I'm not trying to have sex with you tonight," she whined.

"What?" Lamium sounded surprised.

"You heard me," Daneisha said sharply. "I'm tired."

"Shit, I've been working all day and night." Lamium's voice filled with conviction. "I came home to you and you don't want to give up no ass?"

Daneisha sat up. "I haven't even seen you since Saturday. You call that coming home?"

Lamium threw up his hands. "I was away on business, and you know it!"

"Not one time did you call to check up on me or LJ," Daneisha said, adjusting the scarf on her head. She tucked the loose hair strands back inside.

"Yes, hell I did!"

Daneisha sucked her teeth in disbelief. "When, Lamium? You need to stop your lying."

Lamium peered in her face. "When I fucking called, your ass wasn't here," he said, his vein rising in his neck. "Before you start trying to put together a lie, I called your cell phone too. It went straight to voicemail. I need to turn that shit off. I could be asking you where the hell you was, but no. I chose not to walk up in here and start interrogating you about your whereabouts. Don't let Daneisha hear a rumor about me doing something. You want to cut all my shit up and throw it on the lawn and shit for everybody to see."

"That was a long time ago." Daneisha slammed her fist into the mattress. "When are you going to let that go? And I had every right to be mad at you. Lamium, you fucked that bitch in my apartment and in my bed!"

"See, that's your problem. You believed what that ho told you. I'll admit I'm not perfect. But can you honestly tell me, right now, you believe I would stick my dick in that nasty girl?"

Daneisha's eyes lingered down at the floor for a moment. "Okay, so she was lying."

"Finally, you admit it. It's about damn time."

Lamium was on a roll, and not about to back off.

"I was young and stupid back then," Daneisha defended. "How was I supposed to know she lived in the apartment before I did? Plus, it doesn't diminish the fact that you've slept around. Lamium, you know you haven't been faithful to me."

"Let's not get into this. Because you know I can get in your shit too. So don't sit here like your shit ain't stank! I can easily turn this right back around to where you was on Sunday." He rested his hand on the bed and locked eyes with her.

Suddenly Daneisha felt a yank in her stomach. She rubbed her side, but it wouldn't ease up. "Lamium, I was out. I had to run some . . . do something for Kay."

Lamium turned away from her as he felt enraged. "I don't have time for this. You better hope I don't ever catch your ass. Daneisha, I will break your ass in two!" He punched his hand into the wall by the door.

The sound made her jump. When he left the room, the imprint in the wall made a lasting impression in her head. It took Daneisha a few minutes to get herself back together.

Okay, so that was messed up.

Daneisha knew she was wrong for not being home on Sunday. But when was she ever home? Usually, she had a good excuse, but Lamium caught her off guard. Valerie didn't tell Daneisha that Lamium called, so she wasn't prepared with an airtight alibi. She was usually better on her game.

Daneisha wondered if Valerie was setting her up. Valerie was the fool. Surely, Valerie had to know if it were up to Daneisha, she wouldn't even have a job. And if they split, she would fire Valerie quick as a heartbeat. And Daneisha knew she couldn't find another job making $800 a week. It looked like Daneisha needed to have a serious talk with her. Let her know who was running things up in here.

In the meanwhile, Daneisha needed to put out the fire that was burning right now. She knew exactly what her man needed. She went into the living room, where Lamium was sitting on the couch drinking a Corona. She wrapped her arms around him and kissed him on the neck.

"Okay. I'm sorry. I was jealous about what happened with LJ earlier. I shouldn't have taken that out on you." Daneisha grabbed his face and kissed him. As her lips met his, he invited her tongue inside. She savored the taste of his beer for a moment. "As for Sunday—"

"I'm through talking. I'm past it."

"I just want you to know that—"

"Shhh." He put his two fingers on her lips.

Daneisha stood up and led her man back to the bedroom. It was time to reaffirm his manhood. As he locked the door, Daneisha sat down on the bed. She pulled him close to her, ran her hands down his arms.

In a whisper she said, "I'm sorry, baby."

As his tongue entered her mouth, she sucked on it.

Roughly, he grabbed her ass and lifted her up in the air.

Then he plopped Daneisha back down on the plush duvet comforter. No, she didn't want to mess it up, but right now she was really feeling him. When Lamium showed his heart, she couldn't stomp on it.

Like her mama, Daneisha believed in pleasing her man. He was very forceful. Rough, the way she loved it.

Lamium put her ankles around his neck as his tongue stroked her pussy. She shuddered as he went deeper.

"Uuuhhhmmm."

His tongue licked faster, then swirled around.

Daneisha sang a sweet melody.

He lifted her higher, her arms barely touching the bed.

He gripped her thighs tighter, and she pulsed out a hard orgasm.

Lamium's lips worked backwards. Then he lay her back down. He bit his bottom lip. "Your nectar is like honey, baby."

Daneisha grinned and looked away, embarrassed. He was so poetic.

Dropping his briefs, Lamium revealed his erection. Daneisha knew she was in trouble.

He snatched Daneisha's scarf off, letting her hair fall. Then he entered her, pushed himself with all the strength he could muster.

"Ooooohhh. Baby, your pussy is so tight."

As he eased in and out, he wrapped Daneisha's hair up in his fist. Her eyes tightly shut, straining to hold it all together, when suddenly she felt another one coming. Daneisha swayed her hips as he pulled her closer.

"Oh shit!" His dick worked faster as he released his juices inside of her. When he finished he wiped the sweat from his forehead. He rested on top of her body. Each breath labored for a moment, then became shorter.

Oh no.

Daneisha clinched her side. The pain came as swiftly as

her orgasm a few minutes ago. She pushed Lamium's life-less body away and limped to the bathroom. Once she shut the door, doubled over in agony wanting to yell out in pain. Instead, Daneisha kept silent, not wanting to ex-pose her problems to Lamium. She wanted him to think she was healthy, ready to have a baby when he was ready. Also, if Lamium thought she had some kind of STD, he would accuse her of cheating and probably beat the hell out of her.

Once Daneisha could get herself together, she reached in the medicine cabinet and swallowed four Percocet. She was going to have to see a doctor about this, because it seemed to be getting worse. When she came out of the bathroom, Lamium was nestled under the sheets, sleeping like a baby. And her comforter was on the floor.

Damn!

The cleaners charged her sixty dollars to clean it last time. She slid beside him and hoped the pills would kick in soon.

Chapter Two

The next morning, Lamium woke Daneisha up to finish what they'd started last night. Fortunately for her, there was no cramping. She almost threw her back out trying to satisfy him. She'd hinted that there was more to come, hoping it was enough to make him come back.

Daneisha spent the afternoon with the travel agent, ironing out the details for her birthday plans. She'd been dying to stay in Cabo San Lucas since her mama went last year. Mike was always whisking her off to remote places. Even though Daneisha knew her mother deserved it, she was still jealous, especially when LeQuisha returned with a beautiful tan. When Daneisha saw the few pictures they managed to take, because she guessed they spent more time in the bedroom, she fell in love with the island.

Ever since, Daneisha begged Lamium to take her. For her twenty-first birthday, he finally agreed to pay for the trip. Lamium got jealous when he heard how much fun she was going to have. Then he decided he would come and bring his friends too.

Now, the trip had turned more into a task, with

Daneisha having to take care of travel plans for eight people. It didn't help that Lamium wasn't answering his cell
phone, so she had to do it herself.

On Wednesday, it was the same situation. She needed to
remind him about the parent conference. Daneisha hadn't
seen Lamium since Tuesday morning, and she was blowing up his phone. Frustrated, she lowered herself to call
his assistant, Keysha.

"Hello," she answered with a Jay-Z song playing loudly
in the background.

"Keysha."

"Who is this?"

"You know who the fuck this is, bitch." Daneisha rolled
her eyes.

Keysha hung up the phone.

"No, she didn't!" Daneisha stared at her cell phone in
disbelief. She pressed *send* once more.

"Heeeellllo."

"Keysha, this is Daneisha."

"Oh, you the one that just called here?" She laughed.
"My bad. What's up, girl?"

Daneisha took a deep breath. What she wanted to do
was track that nasty whore down and slap the shit out of
her. Don't even get it twisted. Just because Daneisha was
petite, weighing 110, she could still throw down and tap
some ass.

Taking a few short breaths, Daneisha calmed down. She
realized Keysha had the upper hand right now.

"I need you to tell me where Lamium is."

"Oh." Keysha sucked her teeth.

Daneisha could picture her cleaning out her teeth with
a rolled-up piece of paper. She scrunched up her face in
disgust.

"Well, I ain't seen him since last night, when him and

Greg dropped off a shipment. But, if he stops by, I'll be sure to tell him to call you."

"Sure you will." Daneisha hung up.

Lamium would leave her hanging like that. He'd promised Daneisha he would attend the parent conference. She didn't want to walk in there by herself. It was bad enough that Valerie was always there instead of her; LJ's teacher probably judged her as a lousy parent already. She massaged her temples to clear her head from an oncoming migraine.

Daneisha turned up her XM radio when "Fergalicious" by Fergie came on. She rocked her shoulders to the old-school beat. When Daneisha stopped at the red light, she broke out in full dance mode. Catching a glimpse of the man beside her in his silver Mercedes, she flirted with him and danced even harder. With his dark hair slicked back, he looked Italian.

Daneisha winked in his direction and threw her hair off her shoulders as she gripped the steering wheel like a supermodel in a music video. He signaled for Daneisha to pull over. Daneisha shook her head and sped off as the light changed to green.

The Mercedes quickly whipped behind Daneisha's Lexus and tailed closely on her car's bumper. Daneisha wasn't sure if she should she be scared or flattered. Nervously, she smiled at him as he pulled alongside her car, desperate to get her attention. As Daneisha came up to Starbucks, she drove into the parking lot.

As predicted, he followed.

Still nervous, because he might be a serial killer, she said a quick prayer. She glanced in the mirror to make sure her hair was tight and her nose was clear.

All clear.

As the strange gentleman walked up to her Lexus,

Daneisha let down the window. He was of medium build with big arms, obviously from hitting the gym. He was dressed very well in a white silk shirt and chocolate brown dress slacks.

"How you doing?" he asked, sounding like Joey from *Friends*.

Daneisha grinned. Her lips quivered. "Fine."

He leaned inside the window. "I can see that."

"Do you mind?" Daneisha cocked her head to one side in an arrogant manner. She didn't want him to take her for a skeezer.

He backed up, holding both hands up like he was about to be arrested. "Oh, I'm sorry, Miss. I couldn't help but notice how beautiful you were, and I said to myself, 'Self, you've got to get this woman's number.'"

Daneisha tried not laugh out loud. "Oh really?" She licked her lips. "Well, why don't you give me your number instead. Maybe I'll give you a call."

"No problem." He reached in his pocket, then extended his hand for hers. He placed a card inside her palm. "I'm Chris."

In a seductive manner, Daneisha slowly tucked his card inside her pink lace bra. "Okay, Chris, I'm Jennifer."

Chris showed his approval with one nod, letting her know everything he liked was right before his eyes. And Daneisha knew he would be the most eager and willing sponsor. When she was through with Chris, his whole world would be turned upside down.

"Nice to meet you, Jennifer. Hey, you want to have a cup of coffee or something?" Chris pointed in the direction of Starbucks.

"Sorry, I'm in a bit of a rush." Daneisha leaned on the steering wheel, careful to squeeze her breasts upward. She wanted him to get a good peek. "But I'll call you."

His eyes danced as he eyed them. "You do that."

"I will." Daneisha put her car in reverse and drove away.

It wasn't her thing to meet perfect strangers in that manner, especially on her way to LJ's school. What you don't know about Daneisha was, she had to take care of hers. Like her mama always told her, she had to handle her business. Yes, Lamium had been her man for over four years and took good care of her for the most part. He still liked to keep a woman on a tight leash, meaning, Lamium liked to withhold funds when he didn't get what he wanted.

Like that tantrum he pulled at Daneisha's apartment the other night. If she was tired and didn't give up the booty, Lamium probably would've disappeared for a few days or even a week. Then she would resort to calling up all his females, like Keysha, the bitch you met earlier, or maybe even get desperate and call white girl Becky.

Seeing that Daneisha didn't have a job, except for her small business on the side, Lamium wanted to keep his reign over her. So, Daneisha saw an opportunity to meet someone who would help a sista out every now and then. You know, take a date or two. That way she could keep her savings up. At present, the balance was very low due to a few ridiculous shopping sprees. Maybe Chris would be just the kind of man to sponsor a few trips to New York or even Miami to build up her fall wardrobe.

At LJ's school, the parent-teacher conference didn't go well. Daneisha was so mad at Lamium for not showing up. The teacher complained that her son was rude and didn't comply with the rules. Mr. Murdock, the school's director, sat in too. He threatened if LJ's behavior didn't improve, he would have no choice but to expel him from school.

What Daneisha really wanted to tell Mr. Murdock was to kiss her ass. But she didn't. She sat in her chair like a classy woman, tapping her silver Jimmy Choo's on the dirty carpet. As the discussion continued, Daneisha pretended to pay attention, but she focused her thoughts on Cabo. Picturing the teal blue water and her perfectly manicured toes digging into the hot sand helped her remain calm.

Since LeQuisha had pulled strings just to get LJ in that school, Daneisha broke down and told them she would make sure LJ behaved properly. It was against her better judgment to enroll LJ in a private academy with all them rich white folk to begin with.

The second Daneisha got in her car, the cell phone rang. It was Lamium. She rejected the call. If she talked to him right then, he was liable to get the cursing out of his life. She waited until she was back at home to return his call.

Lamium apologized and made up some lame excuse as to why he neglected to show up. He must've felt guilty, since he came to her place around 10 PM, which was early for him.

They were in the bedroom. That's where they spent the majority of their time together. Daneisha hated the fact they never did anything. Even though it sounded corny, it would've been nice for Lamium to take her to a movie or dinner.

Lamium wasn't the type to dine in a restaurant, unless there was a bar. Since she wasn't twenty-one yet, that was his excuse not to take her anywhere. No, her man's idea of having a good time was hanging in a titty bar, kicking back with boys, getting drunk out of his mind. Just thinking about him getting a lap dance from some enormous-breasted, thick-thigh, stank-breath stripper made her insides hurt.

"I'm going to need to put a five-thousand-dollar deposit on the trip."

As Daneisha sat there and watched him place his Blackberry on her jewelry armoire, she wanted to tell him how she felt. Voice her frustration.

Reaching in his wallet, he pulled out a blank check and
signed it. "Don't you go adding more than five to it either."

Daneisha curled up her lips in disgust. "Please."

Lamium left the room. "I called LJ's teacher too!" he
yelled from the hall.

Daneisha got out of bed and followed him to the
kitchen. She didn't want his yelling to wake up LJ.

"I told you not to. I had it under control."

"I'm a grown-ass man." Lamium held her eyes angrily as
he took a sip of Corona. "And that's my son. If I want to
call his teacher or anybody else, I'll do that."

Daneisha wanted to snap back, but she was cramping
way too badly to fight with him.

"I'm not trying to shut you out, I just didn't want you to
be bothered. That's all."

"Well, we ended up discussing you and your attitude
more than LJ's. How you gonna call the woman a butch?"

Daneisha looked up. "She told you that?"

"Yeah."

As Daneisha headed back to her bedroom, Lamium followed.

"I mumbled that under my breath. I didn't know she
heard me."

"She did."

Daneisha crossed her arms. "Now you've seen her, and
you know she does look like one."

"LJ is doing good at that school. Now, don't you go and
mess it up," he ranted. "I'm-a take LJ to school in the
morning, so I can explain how I expect him to behave in
that classroom." He cut his eyes over in Daneisha's direction for a response. She didn't give him one. "Most men
don't have to do this, but you don't seem to have the tini-
est bit of mothering skills in you."

His words hurt her like a slap in the face.

"How could you say that?" Daneisha went in the bathroom and plugged in the flat iron. "I'm a good mother."

"That's a muthafucking lie, Daneisha. How does it feel to know that Valerie is doing a better job than you?"

Daneisha shut the bathroom door to block him out.

"I don't even know what to call you!" he shouted through the door.

After the frustrating day she had, she didn't need his criticism. She felt bad enough as it was. She wiped the tears from her face, while continuing to iron out her frizzy ends. If she didn't feel good, at least she could look damn good.

Fake it 'til you make it. That's what Mama used to say.

Daneisha heated up the curlers and placed them back on the counter. She used the comb to part her hair, then grabbed the curlers and rolled it up. Then counted to ten, and released them.

She stared back at her reflection in the mirror. As much as she didn't want to admit it, maybe Angel was right. It *was* Lamium's fault LJ was so bad. He was constantly talking about her, when he never stepped up as a father. All he wanted to do was be LJ's friend.

In all honesty, Daneisha knew Valerie was more of a mother to LJ. But to hear it from Lamium added insult to injury, considering he was hardly ever there. And still, LJ loved his father more than her.

Chapter Three

Daneisha moved from her bedroom and bathroom, trying to get ready to meet her mama for lunch. Her iPod was docked in station, playing all her favorite jams. Kay downloaded all the songs for her, and she was tearing up a rendition of Janet Jackson's "Miss You Much." She performed in the mirror, wearing nothing but panties and a bra.

A call from her brother interrupted the show.

"I need to get my hands on some money fast," Dante said.

"No, I think I should let Mama get a hold of you for spending all your money."

"Now why would you even play with your baby brother like that?"

"Because I love to make you shit in your pants." Daneisha giggled. "I'll give you the money, but don't ask for nothing else. Lamium has me on a budget now, and I ain't got time to give up my spending money for someone who blows his monthly allowance on buying a PlayStation 3."

"Thank you!" Dante took a sigh of relief. "When are you going to send it?"

"As soon as I go back online."

"When is that? You don't necessarily live on the internet like I do."

"I have to take care of my bills online today, so when I do that I will make a small transfer into your account."

"Well, can I call you later today?"

"No, you may not. Look, I don't have to do this for your behind. So don't be blowing up my cell phone today. Plus, I'm having lunch with Mama in an hour. And you know she can sniff you out so easy."

"That's true." He paused. "You know how much I love you, right?"

"Yeah. Yeah. Save it."

"And I can't wait to see my little nephew when I come down in a few weeks."

"Yes, I know LJ can't wait to see you. Well, I gotta go. I need to finish getting ready."

They said their final good-byes, and Daneisha slipped into her Tracy Reese black wrap dress. Since the temperature was slightly chilly, she decided to put on her Gucci leather boots.

When Daneisha arrived at the restaurant, her mama's car was nowhere in sight. Since she was always late (operated on CP Time), Daneisha went inside to put their name on the list. She placed the plastic pager in her Gucci handbag.

Daneisha couldn't believe it when her mama parked her black Acura RL and got out sporting a similar dress to hers, except for a fuchsia pink belt around the waist. Her boots had rhinestones and gave her a more Southwestern flavor. Funny how it was more Daneisha's style than hers.

"I know you're not trying to look as good as me." Daneisha leaned along the hood of the car.

"Daneisha, as fine as I am, you wish," LeQuisha said as she removed her sunglasses. She flung her hair back; it was a fresh-styled bob cut. Blessed with a body that wouldn't quit, LeQuisha's oval-shaped face made her even more attractive. Although she was in her forties, she looked at least fifteen years younger.

"Mama, we're twins. See?" Daneisha twirled around in a complete circle.

"Yes, except my outfit probably cost less." LeQuisha wrapped her arms around Daneisha and gave her a peck on the cheek. "I missed you. How are you doing?"

"Fabulous as usual." Daneisha gleamed.

"Oh yeah. Well, let's get inside. I'm cold and hungry. How long did they say the wait would be?"

"Ten minutes or so. It's long enough for you to get all up in my business."

"Listen to Ms. High Society." LeQuisha stepped back and tossed her hand up. "And you know I intend to."

Hand in hand, they entered Olive Garden, LeQuisha's favorite place to eat. It didn't matter how much money Mike earned as a doctor, she insisted fine dining was Olive Garden, Red Lobster, and just about any of the Darden Restaurants. Not to mention, LeQuisha made good money herself, working as an ER nurse at Florida Baptist Hospital. That's where she met Mike.

Mike no longer worked in the ER. He ran his own family practice closer to their home in Mandarin. Daneisha's oldest brother, Donny, was finishing up his residency at Baptist Hospital. Mike planned to hire Donny when he completed his studies.

Daneisha's mother made her feel like she was a disgrace because she was supposed to follow in their footsteps and become a doctor or lawyer. Any prestigious profession where she earned a six-figure income would've been acceptable on her terms. To Daneisha that meant having no life, and working more than seventy hours a week just to please her mother. Daneisha decided she didn't want that and rebelled as a teenager, dropping out of high school and earning her GED instead.

As Daneisha chowed down on the Seafood Alfredo, LeQuisha enjoyed the Asiago Chicken. Their conversation was short and casual. Daneisha broke a piece of breadstick and dabbed it in Alfredo sauce.

"How did the meeting at LJ's school go?" LeQuisha asked.

Daneisha chewed long and hard on her bread, then swallowed. "Oh, it went fine. Lamium took him to school this morning. I know he was hurt that his daddy had to get on his behind."

"That's exactly what LJ needs. That's my only grandson, and I should be the one to spoil him. You and Lamium took care of the spoiling all by yourself. When he comes to my house acting the fool, I break my belt off on his butt."

Suddenly, Daneisha felt a knot in her throat.

"Mama, I told you not to spank LJ. That's why I don't send him over to your house now."

"Better not. 'Cause I'm not afraid to tear his behind up. The Bible says not to spare the rod. You know I don't play." LeQuisha gazed around the room at the other guests. She had a habit of checking them out to see if they were checking her out. "That reminds me, write down all LJ's sizes, so I can pick him up some clothes and shoes when I go to Burlington today."

Daneisha sucked her teeth. "Mama, they don't hardly sell Sean John and Phat Farm at Burlington. Why don't you stick to buying him books and toys?"

"Yes, they do." LeQuisha defended. "And how do you know what they sell? You don't go there, too busy flying off to Miami. My daughter can't be bothered with these nickel-and-dime stores here in Jacksonville."

"Mama, I'll have you know I shop at Dillard's every now and then."

"Oh please," LeQuisha said wryly. "Don't remind me about that place."

"Why do you say it like that? You act like you don't want to remember the times when you had to work two jobs. That's when I had the most respect for you."

"I can tell. Anyway, I'm not completely proud of my past. What you didn't know was how I had to get my hustle on, just to make ends meet most of the time. However, I'm saved, sanctified, and filled with the Holy Spirit. God has forgiven me for my ways. And if you had any sense, you would drop to your knees and do the same thing I did."

Daneisha shook her head. "I'm not ready for all that. I'm young and enjoying my life. I ain't got time to spending it all up in the church."

"Uh-huh." LeQuisha stretched her arm across the table to scratch it, obviously annoyed by what her daughter said. "Having fun and wasting your life away. What you need is a job!"

Daneisha took a deep breath. "Mama, I have a job. I'm a housewife, remember?"

LeQuisha snapped, "Ha! You need to be married to be a wife anything. And you and Lamium are just happy shacking up. But you don't want to listen. I don't know why you became so stubborn and hard-headed and had to do things your way." She sighed heavily. "Lord, I just pray my daughter gets it together before it's too late."

Daneisha closed her eyes and shook her head. "Mama, can we enjoy this lunch and not get into how I turned into an embarrassment to you?"

"I never said that."

Daneisha stared down at the table, refusing to make eye contact with her mama.

"I love you." LeQuisha grabbed her daughter's hand.

"No matter what. You're my baby girl and you mean the world to me. Yes, I'll admit I wish you would've gone to college like Donny and Dante, but it's not too late. And you know me, I believe whatever you do, do your best. If all you want to be is a mother, then be the best mother you can be. Read some parenting books, take a class, and do not let Valerie raise your own child. Now, that's something I couldn't do."

"Is that what you think? Valerie is not raising my son." Daneisha pointed her index finger on the table with each word she spoke. "I'm there for him every single day."

LeQuisha rolled her eyes in disbelief. "If you say so."

The waitress came back and asked if they wanted dessert. As always, her mama ordered the raspberry cheesecake.

When she left to place the order, Daneisha took the opportunity to change the subject.

"Lamium is taking me to Cabo San Lucas for my birthday."

LeQuisha leaned forward. "Oh, you're going to love it." Her face lit up as she continued. "I keep asking my honey when we're going back, but he won't say. You know he loves to surprise me."

A beautiful butter golden complexion, LeQuisha was a double threat with her pretty face and a nice body too. Not to mention, she had a butt J-Lo would be jealous of. When Daneisha was in school, she used to get so mad when the boys she liked commented on how fine her mother was. Here she was, trying to get a boyfriend, and they were too busy noticing her mother. It ruined Daneisha's self-esteem.

"Well, it's your turn to be jealous of me. We're renting a villa for a week and even hiring our own private cook, so we don't have to go out if we don't want to."

The waitress came back with LeQuisha's dessert. Before she took a bite, she offered Daneisha a taste. "You want some?"

Daneisha shook her head.

"Well, the trip sounds nice." She pointed her fork at her daughter. "Just make sure Lamium don't try to sneak no drugs through that airport. With the tight security, you'll end up spending your birthday in jail."

"I know, Ma. Lamium isn't stupid."

At least, Daneisha hoped he wasn't. It was well known that Lamium was on his way to becoming the next drug lord as he worked out this new deal with the Coast Guard. His new guy Rowan worked for the Coast Guard and was helping him finalize the details. Lamium never included Daneisha in on his business affairs, but he did hint that if he pulled off that account, he would be "big time." She wouldn't have to live in an apartment anymore, but a million dollar home. She was looking forward to that.

"When was the last time you heard from your baby brother?"

"I spoke with him this morning."

LeQuisha raised an eyebrow. "He didn't ask you for no money, did he?"

"No."

"Uh-huh." She twisted her lips suspiciously. "You answered that a little too quick."

Daneisha glanced back at her. "Okay. He said he was broke."

LeQuisha's face got hot. "I can't believe it. You know I'm depositing five hundred dollars in that boy's account every month, on top of paying his rent and utilities."

"No, I didn't know that. I thought Dante had a scholarship."

"That covers his tuition and books. Meanwhile, I'm scrimping and scraping to take care of everything else. Plus, I took him shopping the last time I was up there, and you mean to tell me that boy is crying broke?"

"Why are so upset? Mama, you're the one that spoiled him."

LeQuisha took a shallow breath. "He was my baby. And yes, Dante got a little more attention than you and your brother. But this is ridiculous. That boy is taking advantage of me and your father, and I won't have it."

Daneisha's throat tightened. She couldn't stand it when her mama referred to Mike as their father. It's like she was living in a fantasy world, where she wished the only man she'd slept with was Mike. However, her mama used to get around, and Daneisha could name many others before Mike.

"I'm thinking a surprise visit is long overdue."

"What's that going to solve?"

"Oh, once LeQuisha gets all up in his stuff, I'll know exactly where my money's going."

"I'm sure."

They said their good-byes, and Daneisha headed home. She didn't want to say anything during lunch, but the cramping was back and more painful than the last time. Her right leg went completely numb with a tingling sensation. She wondered if she would be able to drive home.

On her way home, she dialed her brother's number and placed her Bluetooth in her ear.

"This is your handsome brother, Donny," he said in his deep voice.

"Hey. I need you to do me a favor."

"Let's do this again. Hello. This is your handsome brother, Donny."

Daneisha took a deep breath. She really didn't have time for his dry sense of humor. Since she needed him, she humbled herself and played along with his corny game.

"Hello, handsome brother, Donny. This is your cute and sexy sister, Daneisha."

The spitting image of Daneisha, Donny could pass for

her identical twin. Donny was four inches taller with gorgeous green eyes. Unlike Daneisha, Donny made it his mission in life to take care of their mother. He catered to her every whim. When they were young, Donny was in charge of the house. He made sure Daneisha and Dante finished their homework and cleaned up around the house. Daneisha always resented him for being the golden child, but she had to admit: no matter what, he was there for her when she needed him most.

"Why, Daneisha. I haven't heard from you in a very long time. How are you?"

"Just great." Daneisha gritted her teeth. "How is your residency going?"

"Wonderful. I haven't slept in . . . let me see . . . oh yes, in twenty-six hours, four minutes, and twelve seconds. Other than that, life is grand."

Daneisha poked out her lips. "I'm sorry that baby is so tired. It will pay off when you begin to earn your huge six-figure salary. And then you can help take care of your wonderful sister."

"You know I'm not in it for the money. I want to save lives. And I only help those that work but need a small boost every once in a while."

Daneisha sighed heavily. "I work. Every single day. And you will take care of me because I'll whip out the promissory note you signed last year when I loaned you that ten thousand dollars."

"To my recollection, I think I remember something along the lines of a small loan—"

"Yeah, that's what I thought—"

"Let me finish," Donny interrupted. "It's going to my handsome nephew's future college account."

"Enough of this." Daneisha placed her hand on her forehead. She felt a migraine coming on.

Donny snickered. "Something wrong?"

"You're making me crazy. Damn. I'm in so much pain. I don't need this shit!"

"What can I do for you?"

"I need you to call in a prescription for me."

"I just called in a prescription for you last week," Donny argued. "What are you trying to do to me?"

"Look, this is the last time I'm asking you to do this. I'm going to see the doctor, and I'll get him to write me one next time. I promise."

With more coaxing, Donny agreed and called in the prescription. It helped to have a brother that was a doctor to write a prescription for her. Before hanging up, Daneisha did promise him she would see a doctor. Kay recommended her gynecologist, so Daneisha scheduled an appointment for next Thursday.

As soon as she got home, she swallowed four Vicodin and went straight to bed. She took a nap, because she planned to spend some time with LJ when he came back from school. Although Daneisha pretended not to care what her mama thought, she really did. She wanted the perfect relationship with LJ, but he seemed to hate her from the moment he was born. She remembered the nurse asked her if she wanted to try breastfeeding. When Daneisha pulled LJ's mouth close to her nipple, he pushed it away and screamed like she was trying to murder him. Daneisha and the nurse tried for the rest of the day to get LJ to breastfeed, but he wasn't having it.

LeQuisha even came to check on her daughter and tried to help LJ nurse. It made no difference; he rejected his own mother's breast. Nobody could understand it. It didn't help that he always cried when Daneisha tried to hold him. LJ was more content laying in his crib or bouncer seat than being held by his own mother. When it came to LJ, Daneisha never got to experience what it was like to be a real mother.

That's why she wanted to have another child. She thought she would get it right next time. At seventeen, she wasn't in the proper mind frame to deal with a pregnancy. She worried a lot, wondering how she would care for a baby. Lamium put her at ease, promising to support her every step of the way. He always wanted a son, and he was so happy when LJ was born.

When Daneisha came out of her bedroom she expected to find LJ in the living room. All she found was a note that Valerie left on the counter. She took LJ to soccer practice.

Daneisha held both hands on her forehead.

I forgot all about my baby's first soccer practice. Now, Daneisha felt worse. She went in the kitchen and made an ice cream sundae and drowned it with caramel. Stretched on the couch, she enjoyed every spoonful. She remembered the last time she and LJ shared one together at Dairy Queen. It was one of the few times they actually spent quality time together.

What a shame!

Daneisha decided to make a sundae just for LJ. She knew he would love it. Two scoops of peanut butter ice cream, covered with fudge, lots of whipped cream, and nuts. Then she put a cherry on top and covered it with Saran Wrap.

Valerie and LJ arrived home about an hour later. Daneisha was plopped on the couch listening to her iPod. She took her earpiece out.

"Hey, LJ." Daneisha ran her hands through his curly head. "How did soccer practice go?" she asked as she kissed him on the cheek.

"Yuck!" LJ wiped his cheek like his mother had cooties.

"LJ, answer your mother's question," Valerie scolded as she pointed her finger in his direction.

"It was okay," he said in his whiny voice.

"Did you score any points?" Daneisha grabbed his arms and sat him on the couch beside her. LJ's chocolate brown

face was the exact replica of his daddy. He was so handsome. Daneisha loved his strong cheekbones.

"No."

"They just went over the basics today," Valerie added.
"I'm going to run his bath while you two chat."

"Yeah, you need your bath. You stink." Daneisha held
her fingers up to her nose. "P-U."

LJ laughed. "What does that mean?"

"It's just what we used to say when I was a kid and a little
boy like you smelled." Daneisha tickled him in the side
and made him laugh until he begged for mercy. Then she
jumped up from the couch. "Oh, I almost forgot. I made
something for you."

"*You* made something?" LJ shot her a confused look.

"Yes. Why do you seem so surprised?" Daneisha put her
hands on her hips. "I make stuff all the time." She went in
the kitchen and opened the freezer door.

"No, you don't." LJ shook his head.

Daneisha gasped. "LJ. Yes, I do."

"Mommy, what is it?"

Daneisha took the sundae out and placed it on the
breakfast bar.

LJ licked his lips. "Uuhhmmm."

"Here, try some." Daneisha handed LJ a spoonful of
whipped cream with fudge.

"This is good, Mommy." LJ smiled. "Thank you."

Valerie stormed over to the counter. "LJ, I know you're
not eating that before your dinner." Her Jamaican accent
was only thick when she was angry.

LJ dropped the spoon on the counter. "Sorry, Ms. Val.
Mommy said I could have it." He pointed at Daneisha like
Valerie was going to whoop her ass.

"Yeah, he's my son. I can give him whatever I want to."

Valerie waved her hand. "Daneisha, you need to grow
up. What this boy needs is a hot meal to stick to his ribs,

not dessert. You should be ashamed of yourself. Now, come on here and get in this tub, LJ."

Valerie took LJ's hand and walked him to the bathroom.

By this time, Daneisha was infuriated. She couldn't believe Valerie just did that. That bitch had gone way too far! Because Daneisha didn't want to raise hell in front of her son, she let that shit slide. She intended to give Valerie a piece of her mind once LJ was in his room. Daneisha realized, now more than ever before, that Valerie thought she was LJ's mother. If Daneisha wanted a chance to turn it around, she needed to get Valerie's bossy ass up and out of her son's life.

"Lamium, I need you to write me a check to give to Connie. I'm stopping by first thing in the morning to pay the remaining balance for our trip," Daneisha said as she placed his plate in front of him. When she had lunch with her mama, she ordered the Asiago chicken to eat later. Since she wasn't hungry, she'd decided to fix it for him instead.

Lamium took a fork and dove into the chicken and savored the first bite. "I know you didn't make this." He sliced another piece of chicken. "This shit is good."

"No, I didn't make it." Daneisha rolled her eyes. "Did you hear what I said?"

"Yeah, I heard you. Stop your bitching. I just got here."

Daneisha stared up at the clock above his head on the wall. That was exactly the problem. He couldn't come home any earlier. It was bad enough days would come and go without a word from him, then he bust his behind up in her apartment like a muthafucking king or something.

"Just give me your wallet, I'll write it out myself."

Lamium reached in his back pocket and handed it over. "Turn that shit up." He pointed toward the TV.

Daneisha grabbed the remote control so he could catch the ESPN highlights. "You know we should get married while we're in Cabo. It's the perfect setting, and all of our friends will be there with us." She crossed her legs in the chair and stuffed in a mouthful of buttered popcorn.

Lamium raised his eyebrows and turned to face her. "No, that's not gonna happen. Daneisha, I don't want to marry you."

"What? Since when?"

"Since you stopped doing what the hell I ask you to do. You're not wife material."

Daneisha wanted to throw him out of his chair. "I can't believe you're telling me this shit right here to my face."

Lamium started laughing. He reached over and pinched her waist.

"It's not funny." Daneisha tried to push him away.

"You know I'm playing with you. It's not the right time. With this big deal I got going, I don't need my personal life fucking it up." He kissed her on the cheek. "But I do love you, baby."

"Just don't take too long, or else I just might be taken. And LJ will have another daddy."

Lamium went back to eating his food. "See, that's what's wrong with you. You play too damn much. You better be glad I didn't knock your ass against that wall for saying that shit."

Daneisha shrugged her shoulders. "Whatever!"

Daneisha wasn't about to make Lamium think he got to her. Hell to the NO! She flipped the script on his punk ass and gave him something to think about. She loved Lamium, but it wasn't like she couldn't get somebody else.

Daneisha closed her bedroom door and slipped the check in her Gucci bag. Then she grabbed her cell phone to call Kay.

"I got the money, so it's all set."

"All right. I can't wait to be chillin' by the ocean in Cabo San Lucas!" Kay giggled.

"Me too," Daneisha added as she used a nail file to fix a nail. She broke it earlier when she went to get a plate out of the dishwasher. It was so sharp, she scratched herself on the arm. "We're leaving next Saturday morning and returning Wednesday night. Hopefully, everyone will be on time."

"Now, who is going?" Kay asked in her husky voice.

"It's me and Lamium, of course. Then Angel and Greg and Myra and Jericho."

"And me."

"Yeah, you, and I'm going to make sure you and Rowan hook up too."

"Are you sure he's not bringing someone with him?"

"All I know is, if Rowan is bringing some bitch, she ain't flying with us."

"I can't wait. But you think we'll hook up?"

"Oh, hell yeah!" Daneisha held her nail up to inspect it. It would have to do for now. "He just doesn't know you yet. Please, give him some time. I guarantee you, you and Rowan are going to fuck before the week is over."

"If that's all I get out of it, I'll be satisfied. My year-old dry spell will be over."

"So happy I could help." Daneisha went in the bathroom to pee. "Anyway, I'll call you tomorrow."

"Okay. Bye, Princess."

Daneisha smiled. "Bye."

The next morning Daneisha went over the trip details with Valerie and discussed LJ's schedule. LJ's scrimmage soccer game was Saturday morning, and she needed Valerie to take him since their flight was due to leave at the same time. Also, Valerie needed to understand LJ was to sleep in his own bed every night. Daneisha didn't want him staying at Valerie's house, especially with her two grown sons still living at home with her. Daneisha knew Valerie had raised two good sons who were in college, but it didn't look right.

"Are you going to make LJ's play group today?" Valerie asked.

It was important to Daneisha that LJ hung around kids his own age, being an only child. That's why he met with a play group twice a week after school at a different location. This week it was at a nearby park.

"No, I have too many stops to make already," Daneisha lied. She never made a single play date, because she knew Angel would be there. Her daughter was just like her, and she got on Daneisha's last nerve too.

Valerie opened the refrigerator and took out a salmon to prepare for dinner.

"It's a shame. I know LJ doesn't like it when all the other kids have their mothers there, and he has me. I look more like his grandmother."

"I'm not asking you to be his mother," Daneisha snapped.

"No need in getting all bent out of shape." Valerie flipped her gray locks of hair to one side. "I'll take care of it as I always do."

"That's what I pay you for. To do all the shit I don't have time for. Don't you forget it."

Valerie cut her slant eyes at Daneisha. "Oh, I didn't forget. LJ is a sweet boy. He just needs his parents. You and his father never seem to have time for him. He misses you, you know."

Daneisha put her hand on her stomach. "I'm cramping way too much. I don't have the patience to deal with LJ today."

"And when are you going to see a doctor?" Valerie asked.

"I made an appointment for next Thursday."

Daneisha watched her drizzle olive oil and base down the salmon. It looked like something she could do; if only she did what Lamium suggested and put forth a little effort.

"Good. You're way too young to limp around in pain like that."

Daneisha grabbed her purse and performed a balancing act to step into her shoes.

"It sure don't stop you from strutting around in them there heels. You need to put on more comfortable shoes."

"They are comfortable," Daneisha replied and walked out the door.

On her way to the hotel, Daneisha stopped by Connie's office to deliver the check. They had it worked out where she would cash the check for $8,000 and give Daneisha half of the money. One of her many hustles. Lamium was stingy with her allowance, and he left Daneisha no choice but to become creative.

Chris called her other cell phone, which she named J-Lo, four times this morning. He wanted to meet at the Embassy Suites on Southside. Quickly, Daneisha strutted through the lobby as if she was there for business and took the elevator up to the fifth floor. When she knocked on the door, the Italian Stallion greeted her at the door dressed in nothing but a towel.

Chris kissed her cheek, then whispered in her ear. "Jennifer, you're so hot. I can't wait to stick my big dick up your ass. Are you ready for me, baby?"

Daneisha smiled coyly. "Oh, yes."

She laughed to herself as she pictured him trying to force his three-inch dick up her ass. Just like last time, she planned to bury her head in the pillow and fake each orgasm. All that fun and entertainment for the sweet price of $500.

Chapter Four

*H*ow could someone even drink a cup of coffee after looking at this nasty shit?

Daneisha stared up at the brown water stains on the ceiling. Wearing nothing but a tacky, faded-out gown, she was told to leave it open to the front. All so the doctor could do a breast examination. She always wanted to ask Mike if he sometimes got turned on when he felt on a woman's breast.

Who was she kidding? Like Mike was going to admit any lustful thinking to his stepdaughter, the one who couldn't stand him and made his life pure hell while she lived in his home. But still she wondered. Not a small-chested person like her, but the big-breasted women that had huge nipples that even she sometimes thought about licking.

In no way did she consider herself a lesbian by anyone's standard, but there were women like Tyra Banks or Angelina Jolie, that made her think, *Damn! I wish I could suck on those.*

Daneisha wondered if her breasts were supple and hard like theirs, maybe LJ would've taken to breastfeeding. She laughed to herself when she remembered even though her newborn baby's vision was blurred, he took one glance at her flat chest and seemed to ask, "Where's that fucking bottle?"

Of course, she could ask Donny too, but he was going to be a pediatrician. As far as she knew, Donny never worked with anyone over the age of 16. And she hoped to God he wasn't turned on by any of his patients.

Daneisha impatiently let out an exaggerated sigh as she stared at her Movado watch to check the time again. It seemed like she'd been on that hard table for close to an hour, but only fifteen minutes had passed. The system of making a patient wait in the front for almost forever, then sit in the freezing cold exam room seemed ridiculous.

Half an hour later, Daneisha tore out of Dr. Baldwin's office. After receiving devastating news, she tried her best to contain her emotions. Even though she wasn't quite sure what endometriosis was, she knew by the doctor suggesting surgery meant it was pretty serious.

She dialed her mother's phone number. Daneisha knew her mother was at work, but she always made a point to answer her phone when it came to her children.

"Mama, are you busy?"

"Never busy for you, Sweetie. What's wrong with you?"

"Do you know what endometriosis is? Is it bad?"

"Of course I know what it is. It's when the tissue lining the uterus spreads to other female organs. It causes extreme pain for most women. Why are you asking?"

"Well, I didn't want to tell you because I knew you would be worried. But I've been having strong pains and cramping, especially with my period. The pain was so bad, I couldn't even get out of the bed most days. I kept putting off going to the doctor, but I wanted to go before I left the country and went to Mexico. I know they don't have good medical care. Anyway, he thinks I have endometriosis."

"What doctor did you see? Hold on, I'm going to call Mike."

"Ma, please don't—"

Before Daneisha could finish the sentence, she clicked over to put Mike on three-way.

"Daneisha."

"Ma, I was trying to tell you not to call him."

Mike's voicemail came on. Daneisha was glad, because she really didn't want to discuss this with him.

"Well, I'm going to leave a message anyway. And when he calls me—"

The beep sounded.

"Honey, I need to ask you a few questions about something our daughter is concerned about. Talk to you soon."

The phone clicked.

"I'm so glad he didn't answer. Mama, you're always doing this to me. Now I wish I hadn't called you."

"What? I'm trying to get a professional to answer all of your questions. Who better than my husband, your dad, to do it?"

"He's not my father. My father is Don Harris."

"Daneisha, don't make me reach through this phone and slap the taste out of your mouth. I know who your father is."

"Mama, I didn't mean it like that. I'm sorry. I guess, I'm more upset about this than I thought I would be. He wants to schedule this laparoscopy when I get back from my trip."

"That soon?"

"Yes, he sounded very serious. And I'm too young to be dealing with all of this. Not to mention, we want more children."

"What? Daneisha Harris, I know you're not talking about more children."

"At least one more. Mama, I'm not trying to have a tribe."

"You're not even raising the one you got. All you should be concerned about is your health. Is Lamium pushing you into this?"

"Well, he just said it. And it's what I want too."

"I think before you think about getting pregnant, you need to take care of your health first. Next, get married."

"Me and Lamium are going to do that."

"Whatever. I need to see about these new arrivals in the ER. I will call you back in an hour. I'm sorry you got the news. I'm proud of you for seeing a doctor and finding out what the problem was. No matter what, we'll get through this. I'm there for you. And I love you."

"I love you too. Bye, Mama."

By this time, Daneisha was an emotional wreck. She tossed the phone into her purse. She decided not to tell Lamium about the surgery. She knew her mother was probably right about trying to get pregnant. It was too soon. Still, she held on to the hope it was possible to have at least one more child.

Daneisha overheard Lamium one time, talking on his cell phone with Greg, who was probably bragging about Halle and how wonderful she was. When it came to that girl, Greg was just as pathetic as Angel. Lamium commented that he wanted a daughter. He laughed as he said he always pictured himself having a daddy's girl.

Daneisha had to admit, she wasn't exactly thrilled about the idea of another pregnancy. If she wanted to be Lamium's wife, she had to give her man what he wanted. And that was another child. She couldn't risk one of his tramps getting pregnant by him. After she invested four years with him, she needed to seal the deal and become his wife.

Once the Coast Guard plan was in the works, Lamium would be worth millions. Daneisha overheard Rowan saying that his men alone seized over a million dollars in cocaine and cash. However, that's what they reported. The actual amount was more like ten million dollars. Rowan had his own drug ring set up from Miami to South Carolina. He had the entire East Coast on lock, and he was using Lamium to distribute along the East Coast markets.

Jericho was Lamium's right-hand man. He was in charge of logistics, coordinating shipments from the docks, and getting it in the hands of the area dealers, who then got the product to the street dealers. Greg was third in command, and he handled all communications. He was always setting up new accounts and bringing in new money, which was how he orchestrated this new deal with Rowan.

Well, that was Lamium's stuff to figure out. Daneisha had enough going on in her own life to get caught up with every single detail. Still, she made it her business to keep up with who was who and what was what.

What she needed to focus on was her relationship with LJ. Daneisha had to prove to Lamium she was a fit parent.

Daneisha dug around in her purse, found her cell phone, and let Valerie know she was picking up LJ from school. The surprise in Valerie's voice let her know she had that old cow stumped for words. She knew she was on the right track.

As Daneisha entered her Lexus into the long line of cars leading up to LJ's school, she immediately wished she could turn around. By now it was too late. She was stuck in the concrete loop and there was nowhere to drive but forward. She counted at least ten cars behind her. Glancing at the time on the dashboard, it was 12:30, and she was ten minutes early. All these so-called soccer moms in their SUV's and mini-vans really got on her last nerve. Then again, Daneisha had to put her attitude in check.

She heard the bell ring and loads of little kids resembling herds of cattle charged to the pick-up area. Slowly, her car approached a woman wearing an orange vest and holding a bullhorn in one hand. Her athletic build made

Daneisha think she was the PE teacher. She announced each student's name being picked up.

Daneisha rolled down her window. "I'm picking up LJ, I mean Lamium Jackson."

She shook her head. "Where's your decal?"

Daneisha took off her sunglasses. "My what?"

"Your parent decal. She pointed at the car behind her. See, every parent has a sticker in the window identifying who you are and the student's name."

"Well, I don't have one of those. My nanny, Valerie, usually picks up my son."

"Oh yes, Valerie. Where is she today?"

Clearly annoyed that she was being interrogated about her own son, Daneisha decided to play along for now.

"She's at the house."

"Well, I gotta call this in. It's for security reasons. I know you understand."

"Oh sure." Daneisha tossed up her hands in frustration.

The woman called in the tag number from her walkie-talkie. Daneisha could see LJ standing in front, being held by another adult. Finally, she saw his teacher yelling over to the bitch with the bullhorn that it was okay to release LJ.

Bullhorn Lady nodded. "Okay, I advise you get a sticker. That way you don't hold up the line next time."

Daneisha smiled. "I sure will. Thank you."

"Sorry about all the confusion. We're just doing our job."

Why is this bitch still talking?

Daneisha really felt inclined to give her a piece of her mind, but she was proud of herself for keeping her cool. She already had a bad reputation with LJ's teacher, and didn't want to make matters worse.

"Hey, Mama." LJ climbed in the backseat.

"Hey." Daneisha drove away from the school. "How was your day?"

"It was okay. Where's Ms. Val?"

"She's at the house. Aren't you happy to see me?"

"Yes." He blew her a kiss.

Daneisha pretended to catch it. "I missed you. That's why I came up here to get you."

"Mommy, you have to get a sticker."

"Okay, I'll get the sticker." Daneisha wondered if he was repeating what someone else said.

Daneisha caught a view of her son from the rearview mirror. LJ was staring out the window. Sometimes, he was so serious. And smart. She couldn't believe how well his vocabulary improved. Before he started school, LJ whined all the time, so much that he sounded more like a baby. LeQuisha intervened and had LJ tested for speech and language classes at three. Early intervention made a huge difference.

"Well, me and your daddy are going on a trip this weekend."

"Ms. Val told me."

"That's good. We'll be back Wednesday."

"Okay."

"Do you want me to bring you back something special?" Daneisha asked.

"I want a new video game."

"Which one?"

"*SpongeBob Battle for Bikini Bottom.*"

"Okay, I'll get it for you when I get back."

"I don't want to wait," LJ pleaded in a whining tone. "Can't I get it now?"

"Only if Valerie gives me a good report."

"Please, Mommy. I promise, I'll be good."

"Nope. Sorry."

Daneisha turned into Village Walk Apartments, finding a parking space close to the stairwell. Her timing was perfect.

Daneisha opened the door for LJ to get out.

"Do you want another sundae?"

"No, Ms. Val won't let me eat it. She says I have to eat foods that are good for me."

Daneisha knelt down to LJ. "Let me tell you something." She pointed to her chest. "I'm your mother. And you're my son. If I say you can have a sundae, then guess what?"

"What?"

"You can."

LJ put a huge grin on his handsome face.

"Now, who wants a peanut butter-fudge-whipped cream-with-nuts-cherry-on-top sundae?"

"I do!"

"Well, let's go make one together."

LJ threw his fists up, like he was the champ. "Yeah!"

Daneisha picked up LJ's backpack and followed him inside. She felt better already.

It was Saturday morning, and Daneisha was sitting at the hair salon getting her hair done. She was pressed for time, knowing her flight was leaving in less than two hours. Lamium had been blowing up her cell phone, but she couldn't be bothered with him right now. She was already upset.

"Is Grandma going to be all right?"

"Yes, she and Leroy got home this morning," LeQuisha responded. "She said her back was sore, but other than that she seems fine."

Damn.

Daneisha was hoping a funeral for Leroy was in the works. No such luck. The nasty bastard was still alive. Ever since he'd raped her, the hatred she kept for him stayed deeply buried. She never thought of herself as a murderer, but she would kill that muthafucka. If ever there was a person she wanted to stab in the chest and watch him bleed to death for her personal satisfaction, it was Leroy.

Daneisha never went to her grandmother's house after that. Of course, she called to check on her and sent her money every month. She would still see her grandmother from time to time, but never at her home. Daneisha didn't want to risk running into Leroy.

For a sixty-year-old woman, Gayle Stocks had it going on. She was a beer drinking, cigarette-smoking, curse-you-out-in-a-heartbeat kind of grandma who loved to hit the bars and could dance her ass off.

"Is Grandma right there next to you?" Daneisha asked. She shifted a pink roller to make room for the blue one that was pulling a few strands of her hair. "I want to talk to her."

"I gave Ma a few pain pills and she fell asleep."

"Okay, my flight is leaving soon. I will call you when I get to Cabo San Lucas. Hopefully, I can speak to her then."

"Don't you worry yourself over this. It was just a little fender bender. But, I'll let Ma know you called to check up on her."

"Well, my head is getting cold. I need to stick it back under the dryer."

Daneisha said good-bye, adjusted her phone to silent, and tossed it in her new Cole Haan bucket tote. Leaning back, she pulled the dryer over her head. Flipping through the pages of the October issue of *People* magazine, she imagined the water mixed with sand and shells running in between her toes as she stood along the beach. When she closed her eyes, the sound of the dryer reminded her of the crashing waves rushing against her ankles. Just the escape she needed.

Sebrina hooked up her blonde hair weave, even though

she preferred to call it "Sebrina's Champagne Signature Color." It hung down to her waist, as she decided on the Beyonce look. Rushing home, Daneisha changed into a Liz Clairborne denim jacket with the sash and tan mini-skirt.

When she slid in her seat beside Lamium, she knew he was pissed off. He didn't speak one word until the plane was about to take off. Only then did he mouth the words: "If I die and you live, make sure my son remembers me."

When they arrived at the Villa Golondina, Daneisha was impressed that it was gated to provide guests with privacy and seclusion from the cheaper resorts. The drive up the hillside gave them a spectacular view of the Sea of Cortez. The water was the darkest blue—more like indigo. The beach's sand was brown and yellow, with cacti and rocks surrounding it. With the desert and island feel, it was like the best of both worlds, seeing that they were from Florida.

The Villa of Golondina was a marigold building with columns that reminded Daneisha of pictures she'd seen of Italy. The limousine dropped them off in front of the paved entrance, and two men in white suits welcomed them and loaded their bags on a cart. Daneisha checked in at the counter, while everyone else relaxed on the couches in the lobby. An escort showed them to the villa, and everybody was blown away by the oceanfront view from the beautiful foyer with vaulted ceilings.

Everyone voiced their approval of the four-bedroom villa. The gourmet kitchen was stocked with plenty of American food, and Daneisha was told the chef was going to prepare dinner very shortly. Angel and Myra made an appointment with the private yoga instructor. As far as Daneisha was concerned, they could have that!

Lamium and his boys asked where the bar was and left without even checking out the rest of the place.

It didn't take Daneisha longer than ten minutes to

dress in her black bikini to meet Kay in the foyer for a poolside massage. Afterwards, they lay on their stomachs, enjoying the cool breeze blowing on their backs. Daneisha felt so relaxed, she was damn near close to falling asleep.

"I see you and Rowan set up in the same bedroom."

"Yes, well he called me last night."

Daneisha turned on her side and rested her head on her hand. "Are you serious?"

"We talked for hours." Kay grinned from ear to ear. "And you didn't tell me he was so smart."

"Well, I figured the less I said, the more you'd like when you met him in person."

"I like him very much. And he's so gorgeous. I mean, when I was listening to him over the phone, he sounded sexy. I kept saying to myself, please don't let this man have some serious issues."

"Now, you know me better than that." Daneisha lowered her Baby Phat sunglasses, olive-gold to complement her new hair color perfectly. "Have I ever let you down before?"

"No, but I didn't want to get my hopes up too high. When I was struggling to get my luggage through the double doors at the airport, this fine-ass man asked if I needed any help."

"What a gentleman!"

"I know," Kay added. "Immediately, I recognized his voice, so I asked in my sweetest voice, because you know I was so nervous."

Daneisha lay back down and flipped her hair off her neck. "Oh my God, what did you say?"

"I was like, 'Are you Rowan?' "

"I bet you sounded corny as hell. I know your ass."

"I have to admit, I did. Anyway, he said yes and he even said he recognized me in the elevator."

"You mean to tell me you rode in the same elevator together?" Daneisha saw Angel and Myra engaged in heavy conversation and laughing as they walked down the steps leading to the pool. She was hoping they didn't see them and would find chairs on the other side.

"Yes, but he was standing next to another black woman with kids. So I assumed he was with her."

"Wow! This sounds like a scene from a movie." Daneisha was trying to pay attention to Kay, but she saw Angel and Myra getting closer.

Shit.

"What does?" Myra asked. She and Angel stood in front of them.

"When me and Rowan met earlier at the airport."

Myra laughed. She plopped down at the end of Daneisha's lounge chair. "You should've seen your girl looking all bug-eyed at Rowan. It was love at first sight."

"Oh, shut up!" Kay leaned on her elbow and tossed up her free hand.

Angel pulled up a chair. "More on Kay's part though. I don't think Rowan was feeling you in the same way." She tied her wrap skirt around her waist and sat down.

"I disagree. Rowan is kind of shy. I think he likes you too. I overheard him talking about you to Lamium right before we left. That's why we were late getting down here," Myra said.

"What did he say?" Kay asked in a schoolgirl voice.

"That he hopes y'all get together tonight. Oh, and by the way . . ." Myra looked at Daneisha. "Your boy is already tipsy."

Daneisha frowned. "I'm not surprised."

"Oh, that could mean a booty call with no strings attached." Angel rolled her eyes then looked at Kay. "Please, don't be so anxious to give it up to a man you barely know."

"Angel, we're in Mexico." Daneisha butted in. "Let my

girl get her some sex tonight, just like I know you and Greg will be doing."

"That's right," Myra chimed in. "Mind your business. You're off the clock, remember? No therapy sessions please." She lifted her braids and leaned back in the lounge chair.

Angel grabbed Kay's hand. "Kay, you'll be wishing you took my advice."

"The only thing I'm wishing for is some good dick." Kay stood up and started freak dancing.

"Whoa!" Myra giggled.

"Exactly." Daneisha gave Kay a high-five. "Get your groove back, Stella!"

"I mean," Myra added, "well, I want to get my dance on tonight."

Angel leaned back, pulling her straw hat forward to block out the sun. "Yes, we heard about this club called Melia Cabo, where there is plenty of good food and salsa music."

"I don't know about dancing to no salsa music, but I'm going anyway." Daneisha flung her hair and wiped the sweat from her glistening shoulders.

Myra snapped her fingers and swung her head back. "I'm definitely in."

All three were silent for a moment, waiting for the last response.

Kay smiled coyly and shrugged. "I don't know."

"Excuse me?" Daneisha asked as she leaned closer to her best friend. "Oh, you're coming." She held her eyes, letting Kay know there was no way in hell she was going to leave her to hang out with these two bitches all by her damn self.

Kay waved her hands in a frenzy. "Okay. But I'm coming back early."

After dinner, Kay bowed out of going to the club. Daneisha wanted to kick her ass for abandoning her for a man. However, she couldn't fault Kay. Her last boyfriend ended their two-year on-again-off-again relationship with a text message. A week later, she heard Anthony was engaged to Denise, her co-worker. It took Kay a long time to get over the betrayal. After Anthony and Denise married, a baby boy was born six months later. When Denise came to work to show off the baby, Anthony Jr., Daneisha thought her best friend was capable of a mental breakdown.

Still, Kay never told Denise about her relationship with Anthony. That couldn't have been Daneisha. No, that bitch would've found out right before the wedding. When Daneisha got through with that heifer, she would've been searching for a new job.

They went over to the nearby resort, which housed the night club. Myra, Angel, and Daneisha were getting their dance on with some sexy-ass white guys from California, there for a bachelor weekend. Daneisha hooked up with the bachelor, blonde with blue eyes and resembling Kiefer Sutherland. They were bumping and grinding, and she had way too many drinks to even care that she was with Lamium on this trip. If his cute self wanted to invite her back to his room, she wouldn't have said no.

When Daneisha felt some cramping coming on, she had to cut her grind fest short. She was furious that she couldn't even enjoy a trip without having to deal with this shit. When she told white boy she had to leave, he was disappointed. But she didn't have time to worry about him. She even forgot to get his room number just in case they wanted to hook up later. Daneisha struggled to get back to the villa, but she knew relief was within reach. Then she remembered she couldn't mix prescription pills with alcohol. Frustration set in and she felt like a ticking time bomb was set to go off, knowing she would have to wait until she sobered up to take anything.

When she laid down in the bed, Lamium came in, wobbling from side to side.

"Hey. Where you been?" His voice was slurred where she could barely understand him.

"Out," Daneisha snapped and pulled the covers up to her ear.

"I know. I was looking all over for you."

"Just go to sleep." Daneisha took a deep breath. "I can't believe you. I thought this trip was supposed to be for us to be together."

Lamium lost his balance and fell on top of her. "Just where I want to be." He laughed, hinting that he wanted to have sex.

As much pain as Daneisha was in, she wasn't feeling it. But she was a little horny from the white boy rubbing all up on her coochie.

Daneisha climbed on top of Lamium and straddled her thighs. His dick got hard.

Lamium grunted. "That's what I'm talking 'bout. Do that shit, D."

She leaned over and placed his penis inside her. Then she slid down nice and slow.

She rode him hard.

"Slow down. Damn." Lamium's face scrunched up.

He leaned to one side and pulled out. His cum squirted all over her stomach.

"Lamium!" she shouted.

"What?" Lamium shot her a dumbfounded look.

Daneisha pointed at the white cream on her body. "This is what! You shot that shit all over me."

She used the flat sheet to wipe herself dry.

"Oh. My bad." Lamium grabbed a pillow and closed his eyes.

Daneisha stared at his crusty toes all curled up on the bed. She wanted to kick his muthafucking ass!

Like an old woman, she limped to the bathroom and showered. Two minutes later, the water turned ice-cold.

"Are you fucking kidding me?" Daneisha shouted as she grabbed a towel and quickly dried herself off. When she dressed in pajamas and walked in the bedroom, she saw Lamium passed out, taking up the entire bed. She didn't even want to bother with pushing him to one side of the bed. Besides, Lamium's snoring was so loud, she knew there was no way she would be able to fall asleep in there. Frustrated, she left the room to find something to eat.

When Daneisha passed by Kay and Rowan's room, she heard the two of them going at it like dogs in heat. She wanted to be happy for her girl, since she hadn't fucked in close to a year, but she was caught up in her own misery.

Her stomach was feeling funny, so she decided against eating leftovers. Daneisha called home to check up on LJ. Since his time was an hour ahead, he should've been getting ready for school. It hurt that LJ didn't seem to miss his own mother. But he was upset when she told him he'd have to wait until after school to talk to his father. Daneisha tried to call her mother to find out if her grandmother was doing okay. When LeQuisha didn't answer her cell phone, against her better wishes, Daneisha decided to call her grandmother's house instead.

Leroy answered. As Daneisha went to hang up, he started talking.

"Hey, Daneisha."

She sucked her teeth. "Where's Grandma?"

"Oh, she's laying down."

"Is she doing okay?"

"Yes, we're both doing as good as we can."

I wish your dirty ass had died!

"I was just checking up."

"Yeah, Gayle is doing fine. Me, on the other hand, probably got it the worst."

"Oh yeah? How you figure?"

"Well, my back is messed up. You should come over and see about me."

"I ain't never coming over there after what you did to me. With your nasty ass!"

Leroy chuckled. "Maybe I should tell your grandmother how you tried to come on to me. You think she would like that?"

"If she had any sense, she wouldn't believe it. I don't even know why she is even fooled up with you."

"Same reason you sucked on my dick and swallowed my cum. It's good to the last drop."

Daneisha felt her head fill up like a balloon about to pop. "You muthafucka! I'm-a kill you!"

She closed her cell phone.

As the tears rolled, she wiped them away quickly.

How could you be so stupid! That's what you get for calling over there.

Daneisha slapped her face, the same way Serena Williams did when she messed up in a heated tennis match. She closed her eyes and took several deep breaths.

No way was she going to let an ignorant old man ruin her trip. She decided once and for all she was going to tell Lamium what Leroy did to her. It was time that bastard paid for his sins.

Chapter Five

"It sounds serious."

"No, we're just kicking it. But I stayed at Rowan's apartment last night."

"Was it the first time?" Daneisha asked.

"Yes."

"I'll admit, I'm a bit surprised. After the way y'all carried on in Cabo, I thought you were going to move in with the man."

"Apparently, I wasn't the only one getting over a dry spell."

"Really? Fine as Rowan is, you mean to tell me he wasn't getting any ass either?"

"Shocked the hell out of me!"

Daneisha's line had a beep, and she saw LJ's school number show up on caller ID. Although, she knew it could've been an emergency, she wanted to finish getting the scoop first. Kay rambled on about how she was falling for Rowan.

"He's such a nice guy. I can't believe he's a bad boy."

"He's with the Coast Guard."

"Yeah. I just don't know how this would play out in the

end. I'm almost finished with school, and I don't want to risk losing my job at the firm. Besides, I'm seriously considering earning my law degree."

"All the more reason to keep seeing the man. I think Lamium has room on his payroll for an attorney." Daneisha laughed.

"You don't get what I'm saying."

"Yes, I do." Daneisha adjusted her position on the bed. "That was just a little jokey joke."

"Okay."

"Really."

"I believe you. Enough about me, how are you feeling?"

"I'm in the bed now as we speak."

"When is your surgery?"

Daneisha crossed her legs. "Next week."

"I'm so glad you finally listened to me and went to see Dr. Baldwin, with his pretty-boy self."

"I know. You didn't tell me he was so cute."

"Yes, honey. That's why I be rushing up there for my yearly inspection," Kay cooed. "My bad . . . I meant check-up."

"You're so bad!"

"Sometimes." She cleared her throat. "Let me stop. On a more serious note, I'm praying for you. I'm believing God that after your procedure, you'll be back to yourself again. I hate that you're going through all of this. What does Lamium have to say?"

"To be honest, I haven't told him anything."

"I guess he's very busy with everything he has going on right now. I can understand you not wanting to add more stress."

Daneisha sucked her teeth dryly. "Too busy for his family."

"That reminds me. Are you going to Lamium's club opening this weekend? Rowan asked me if I wanted to go, since my best girlfriend never invited me. Myra's supposed to be making her singing debut."

Daneisha cocked her head to the side. She didn't know what the hell Kay was talking about. "Kay, there you go, giving the wrong information and shit. Lamium ain't got no club."

"Okay. Because I was like, why didn't Daneisha tell me about this? Then I thought you might be preoccupied with other stuff and just forgot to mention it."

"Not to leave something like that out. Kay, you know me better than that."

Daneisha racked her brain trying to remember if Lamium mentioned anything about wanting to open a nightclub. But she couldn't. Lamium was always throwing out one crazy idea after another, none of which he ever brought to fruition. When she and Lamium first hooked up, he'd promised he was getting out of the business and opening up a barbershop. That never happened. And Kay was always getting her facts wrong. She wondered how her best friend managed to survive working in a law firm.

"Anyway, I know the part about Myra singing at the nightclub is right. You want to come with us?"

"No, I'm not trying to rain on your parade. If Myra personally invites me, maybe I'll show up to support her."

Daneisha's phone beeped again. "Look, it's LJ's school again. I gotta take this."

"All right. Feel better."

She clicked over to the other line. "Hello."

"Yes, I'm sorry to bother you, Daneisha." It was Sister Ford, the school secretary. She went to Bethel and was friends with her mother. "They're having a problem with Lamium this morning."

"What's wrong?"

"Well, he was in trouble for losing his temper and hitting another child."

"Oh no."

"Yes, and he was out of control. Security is in there with him right now."

"What! My son is not a criminal. What the hell is a security guard doing putting his hands on my child—"

"Wait a minute. You need to calm down. This is standard procedure for a situation like this. Also, I'm not supposed to be calling you, but the school has been trying to reach you for the past hour."

Daneisha thought back to her house and cell phone ringing several times, and she'd never bothered to answer it.

"Your mother is on her way up here. But I wanted to try and reach you on your cell phone."

"I thank you so much, Sister Ford. I'm on my way."

As Daneisha tried to get out of bed, the pain below her stomach hurt so much, it felt like her insides was about to drop to the floor.

She sat back down.

Daneisha was so upset, she wanted to scream. Here her baby was in trouble, and she couldn't even get her lazy ass to answer the phone when the school called. Not to mention, she sat on the phone talking to Kay, like she was more important than her own son.

Knowing there was no way she could get out of bed, Daneisha dialed Valerie's phone number.

Even though her mother was going to the school, Daneisha knew how important it was for her to be there for the meeting too. If not her, then Valerie would have to do. Her mother would give her hell about it, but Daneisha didn't have time worry about that.

"Valerie, I need you to go pick up LJ from school. He's in trouble. And I can't get out of bed."

"I'm sorry. I'm at the doctor's office," Valerie responded flatly.

Daneisha's face grew hot. "What! You never told me you were taking the day off."

"I told Lamium."

Daneisha wanted to reach through the phone and slap her. "What the fuck! You don't work for Lamium, you fucking work for me."

Daneisha heard the dial tone. She stared at the phone in utter disbelief.

No, this bitch didn't.

She pressed *send* once more.

Valerie answered.

Daneisha yelled into the receiver. "You're so fucking fired! Don't ever come back to my house again!"

She heard the dial tone again.

That was fine. I told her everything she needed to hear.

Daneisha dialed Lamium. No answer.

"Oh my God!" she screamed in agony.

Daneisha dialed his number once more. When the voicemail picked up, she cursed his ass out from left to right, up and down. Every word she knew, she used for his black-sorry-terrible-excuse-for-a-man-wannabe-husband-father ass!

Daneisha threw her cell phone against the bedroom wall. Instead of shattering to pieces, it landed in her purse. At least she wouldn't have to search for it later.

Struggling to get to the bathroom, Daneisha swallowed six pain pills. She didn't even know which ones. She struggled to put on the same clothes she wore the night before, which were laying on the floor next to the bed. She slipped on a pair of slides and headed out the door.

A few times, Daneisha pulled over to the side of the road. It felt like she was in labor all over again with LJ. When she reached the school, she spotted her mother's Acura and pulled up beside it. Then she tried to call her on the cell phone. It wasn't working. She used her backup cell phone instead.

Mama answered on the second ring.

"Hello."

"Mama, I'm outside."

"Whose phone is this you're calling me from?"

"Mama, I'll tell you later."

"I was trying to figure out—"

"Forget what the caller ID says! I can't come inside. I'm in way too much pain. What's happening to LJ?"

"He's been expelled from school. I'm with the principal right now."

"I can't believe this." Daneisha's voice drifted off. She dropped the phone and passed out in the car.

Next thing she knew, her mother was leaning close to her face. Like she'd just performed CPR.

"Wake up, Daneisha."

"Huh?" Daneisha's speech was slurred.

"Baby, wake up."

"Should I call 911?" a strange voice asked.

Daneisha opened her eyes again. She was in the back seat of her car. She didn't remember being taken out of the driver's seat.

"Did you take something?"

"Yes."

"What did you take?"

Daneisha could hear the sirens blaring loudly. As the sounds came closer, she saw the red lights. Then she passed out again.

Later that night, the attending emergency room doctor dismissed Daneisha from the hospital. He explained her body went into shock from taking so many prescription drugs within a relatively short period of time. LeQuisha stayed at the hospital with her daughter.

"When I talked to Mike on the phone, I was so embarrassed that I didn't know what doctor you've been seeing all this time," LeQuisha said. She was driving, headed to Daneisha's apartment.

"Like it matters anyway," Daneisha responded.

LeQuisha cocked her head to one side. "Yes, it does matter. And I want his name and number."

"For what, Mama?" Daneisha asked in a defiant tone.

"I want to know what doctor has my daughter taking so many different drugs at the same time." She raised her voice. "He should be arrested. Now, what's his name?"

"Mama, I told you he didn't prescribe all of those for me. Some of them were old bottles I'd kept from way back."

"I still want his name. I need to give him a piece of my mind. Daneisha, you don't understand that you could've died in that hospital. It's a good thing I work at Baptist and can get you the best medical care. I'm not one for suing doctors, because I think this medical community is all messed up from bogus malpractice suits. We can't keep good doctors in the ER as it is. For one, they can't afford the insurance. And, second, one little mistake can cost them their license."

"Mama, it's not like that." Daneisha took a deep breath. She didn't want her to know that her beloved son wrote those prescriptions. Even though they were grown, there was still a natural fear. She knew that once her mother was through whooping up on Donny, he would never hook her up again. "It was an honest mistake. I've just been in so much pain."

"I'm still waiting."

"Dr. Baldwin." Daneisha pretended to cry. Once she really let her emotions go, the tears were real. "I don't want that man to get into any serious trouble."

LeQuisha rubbed Daneisha's shoulder. "He's not. Mike and I just think it's important for—"

"What does Mike have to do with this?" Daneisha asked, more frustrated than ever. Just the mention of his name, and she was ready to explode.

"He's just as concerned about you, like I am," LeQuisha defended.

"Mama, you're always telling me to grow up! And every time I try to handle my business, then you want to step in and take over. Why can't you just let me do this?"

LeQuisha raised her eyebrows. "Because you're my daughter. If something happens to you, then I'm the one that everyone is going to look at. Suppose you had died in that hospital." She hit her chest. "Then I would've been planning a funeral. I would be raising LJ. It definitely wouldn't be Lamium. That's for sure!"

Daneisha leaned her head back on the head rest. "Here we go again. Let's dog out Lamium while he's not here to defend himself."

"No. The problem is he's never around. I just pray one day you'll see the light."

"Just admit it, you've never liked Lamium. That man has done so much for me. It's never too good for you. You're always dogging on him."

LeQuisha shook her head. "I'm not dogging on that boy."

"Why are you calling him a boy? He's a man. Mama, he's a good man."

"Your definition and my definition of a good man is way off. I'm sorry, but someone that sells drugs and could end up in prison is not a man. Someone who sleeps around with any tramp that will spread her legs, including your best friend, isn't a man in my book."

Daneisha's jaw dropped. "I can't believe you went there. Mama, I'm-a tell for the last time, Kay didn't have sex with Lamium. It was just a rumor."

"Whatever!"

"It's not like you've never been with dogs. What about Tate?" Daneisha folded her arms. "He dogged you out so bad. And you're still in love with him!"

LeQuisha pursed her lips tightly and shook her head. Then she slapped her daughter so hard, Daneisha felt the taste leave. She pulled her car off the road and put the car in park.

LeQuisha turned to face her. "Daneisha, don't ever disrespect me like that again." She pointed. "Or I swear . . . you'll never have to worry about me meddling in your business another day. You're my daughter, and I love you more than life itself. I've made so many sacrifices for you and your brothers. And, yes, I did some things I'm still asking God to forgive me for. But I won't ever let you use it against me, just so you can defend that sorry son of a bitch!"

Daneisha cried out, saliva dripping. She truly felt bad for what she said. She knew she struck a nerve when it came to Tate. "Mama, I'm sorry."

LeQuisha threw up her hand. Daneisha flinched, fearing she would be slapped again.

LeQuisha took a few minutes to regain her composure. Then she whipped her Acura back on the road. The rest of the ride was completely silent.

A few tears rolled down Daneisha's face. She couldn't believe what had just happened. It was like the slap heard all around the world. When she heard the chime on her J-Lo cell phone, it was the distraction she needed.

Daneisha had four voicemails. It was Chris. He was pissed she hadn't returned any of his calls. Since he held offices in New York, Jacksonville, and LA, he was out of town most of the time. He wanted a steady girl, which would be her, to be at his beck and call when he arrived in town for three days a week.

Daneisha tried to tell him that she couldn't do that. She had other priorities. Dumbly, he continued to make future plans with her. He even went so far to offer to buy her a house in Jacksonville and free access to his pad in South Miami Beach. Daneisha wasn't sure if he was that stupid or just used to having his way. However tempting the offer was, she was nobody's fool.

It was bad enough she had to deal with that bullshit from Lamium. Plus, she knew Lamium would have her ass on a chopping block if he ever found out about Chris. So far, she was doing a pretty good job of keeping her business ventures undercover. One mistake would cost her everything. That's why she couldn't slip up.

When they arrived at Daneisha's apartment building, her mother helped her climb the stairs.

"Now, let me get my keys." Daneisha dug deep in her purse to find them.

"Girl, we don't have all day," LeQuisha said impatiently. "It's cold out here."

"Hold on, Mama. Here they are." Daneisha struggled to hold her balance and pull out the keys.

"Oh, forget this." LeQuisha rang the doorbell.

A few minutes later, Valerie opened the door. Daneisha shot her mother a crazy no-you-didn't look.

Now, I know I'm not stupid. I fired that bitch!

Valerie held out her arms. "Come on in." She wrapped her arms around Daneisha, who kept her arms at her side in defiance. "LJ was so worried about you."

"Where is *my* baby?" Daneisha asked in a nasty tone.

"He's sleeping," Valerie responded. "I was just washing these dishes. I left two plates on the counter in case you were hungry. They're covered in aluminum foil."

LeQuisha followed Valerie to the kitchen. "Yes, I'm hungry. What did you cook?"

"Not much. I just threw a little something together. Smothered pork chops, rice, green beans, and corn bread."

"Just a little something? Sounds like you threw down to me!" Excitedly, LeQuisha grabbed the plate and plopped down at the table.

Not the slightest bit interested in eating, Daneisha limped down the hall to her bedroom. She peeked in on LJ, who was in bed sleeping soundly.

As Daneisha tried to close the door behind her, LeQuisha tapped on the door.

"What is she doing here?" Daneisha asked.

"I called her and asked her to pick up LJ. She told me she didn't think it was a good idea, since you fired her."

"That's right." Daneisha sighed. "You couldn't ask one of my friends?"

"I don't know them. Besides, I couldn't get a hold of Kay or Lamium. So I called Valerie back and told her she was rehired."

"I want you to make her leave. Right now."

LeQuisha put her hands on her hips and rolled her neck. "I don't think so."

"Well, if you don't, then I will." Daneisha stood up from the bed.

"No, you won't either." LeQuisha shot her daughter the now-sit-down-before-I-drop-your-ass look.

Remembering how her mother slapped her in the car, Daneisha sat back down.

LeQuisha pointed. "You need help around here. You got surgery next week. If you want to be mad at someone, be mad at me, not at the woman who takes better care of your son than you do."

Daneisha poked out her lips. She knew her mother was right. She really couldn't count on anyone else.

"And you're going to apologize to Valerie."

"Mama—"

"Daneisha." LeQuisha gave her daughter the staredown once more.

Daneisha's face was still stinging from the last slap. "Yes, ma'am."

Daneisha was days away from surgery. Anxiety kicked in overtime, as her mind continued to picture the absolute worst scenarios. What if she bled to death on the table? Who would there be to raise LJ? Boys needed their mothers, and the thought that she couldn't be there really became depressing.

Refusing to answer the phone or call anyone back, Daneisha didn't want to be bothered. She lulled around the apartment in her silk pajamas. Her pink fuzzy slippers dragged across the carpet. Since Valerie was out grocery shopping and running errands, she decided to watch a movie. Searching through stacks of movies, she settled on *Something New*, featuring her favorite actress Sanaa Lathan. Plus, the white guy from *Devil Wears Prada* was the boyfriend, and she loved him already in that movie.

With her back leaning on an oversized pillow, Daneisha plopped her feet up on the couch. Then she grabbed another pillow. She ran her fingers along the walnut tapestry pattern, while waiting on the menu to appear. Once the movie started, she tried to focus, but her thoughts continued to wander.

Daneisha tried not to think about the surgery, because her fears were starting to get the best of her. LJ kept coming to mind. He was in a new school, and she prayed he would act right and avoid expulsion this time around. LJ's new teacher was young and pretty, and there seemed to be a mutual attraction between the two of them. Daneisha liked the way Ms. Hope had a "keeping it real" attitude. She thought that LJ was used to women like her.

Then Daneisha prayed about her relationship with Lamium. She hadn't seen him since Monday. She didn't even waste her time trying to call. It's not like he would answer the phone anyway. As Daneisha continued to watch the movie, she couldn't help but feel the emptiness. She loved Lamium, and she was committed to keep her family together. She just wished they had what every other married couple had.

Daneisha couldn't stand the fact that her mother was so happy with Mike. There were so many times Lamium would compare Daneisha to her mother, and that would infuriate her even more. Again, she reminded herself that if she wanted to become Lamium's wife, she had to prove to him that she could be an excellent mother.

Sitting in one place and praying to God put her mind at ease. Instantly, she knew what she needed to do in order to make the proper changes in her life.

When the movie ended, Daneisha turned off the DVD player and went in the kitchen to fix something to eat. As she laid out a package of sandwich meat on the counter, she remembered Myra was hosting the next luncheon. She decided to call and offer her services if needed. Myra had a habit of waiting until the last minute to do stuff.

"Hello, my darling!" Myra sang.

"How are you doing?"

"Great. We're in the studio recording 'Tell Me Now.'"

"Oh. You know I love that jam." Daneisha smiled.

"I know." Myra was talking to someone sitting next to her. "Sorry about that. I have this new producer, Jillian, and she demands nothing less than perfection. It's mad crazy around here. The label has us on this ridiculous deadline."

"I understand."

"Jericho was telling me you needed a job. We could use you down here at the studio. I could get the manager to pay you a nice salary."

Daneisha turned up her nose. "What is your man doing telling you I need a job?"

"Don't get snotty with me, Daneisha. I'm only relaying what Lamium told Jericho."

"Lamium told your husband I needed to get a job?"

"Uh-huh. I was only trying to help one of my sisters out."

"Well, don't. I don't need it." Daneisha took a deep breath. "Anyway, I was calling about our next get-together. Do you have a venue picked out? Also, I know a caterer you can call."

"I meant to call you about that. Look, I have too much going on right now. I have my career to consider. No offense, but I don't think Angel and Kay can take the time off either."

Daneisha chopped up an entire head of lettuce. She only meant to cut a few pieces. "First you speak for my man, now you're speaking for my best friend," she said as she held the knife in the air as if she wanted to stab Myra. "What the fuck is up with you?"

"You can't be serious," Myra said, sounding confused. "Why do you have an attitude?"

"No, just answer my question." Daneisha's voice was unsteady as she paced back and forth across the kitchen floor.

"Who do you think you are?" Myra asserted. "I don't have to answer anything."

"Yes, you do have to answer to me," Daneisha corrected. "Myra, don't forget your man works for my man, okay? I head up this shit here."

"Daneisha, you're deluded. And if we're really going to

be honest here, Lamium is not your man, just in case you hadn't noticed."

Daneisha grew more livid. Myra's condescending attitude drew the final straw. "Okay, now I'm about to come down there and bust your ass."

"There's the ghetto queen rearing its ugly head." She laughed. "I'll repeat, I don't have time for this. Unlike some people, I have work to do."

She hung up.

What was her problem?

All the years Daneisha knew Myra, she never acted that way. She knew there was something going on with Myra. Not that Daneisha really cared all that much, because she had her own personal drama to deal with.

Daneisha tried her best to calm down. Looking at a perfectly made turkey sandwich with provolone cheese, she had no desire to eat it. The only way to remedy the situation was to relax her nerves. She went in the bedroom dressed in a gold wrap-style top and white Express jeans, slipped into her Colin Stuart platform sandals and was ready to hit the factory outlets in St. Augustine. Searching all over for her cash envelope, Daneisha discovered it in the panty drawer, which was strange, because she always kept it hidden between two shoe boxes in the closet. When Daneisha counted a measly $300, she knew somebody had been in her shit. The only person that came to mind was Valerie.

Uh-huh. And she thought she would put it back before I noticed it was gone.

Daneisha couldn't wait to confront her ass. But she remembered what her mama said. With her surgery date coming up, she needed someone to watch LJ. Hopefully, her money would be back and she wouldn't have to tap that ass for now.

Good thing Daneisha had her J-Lo stash tucked into a

private savings account. On her way to the bank to make a withdrawal, her phone sang "Rich Girl" by Gwen Stefani.

It was her mama.

"I'm so frustrated right now, I can't talk," Daneisha said.

"What's wrong with you?"

"Everything. But nothing I want to talk about right now."

"Your name came up as a missed call. I was in surgery. Sorry, I couldn't get to it."

"It's okay. Mama, are you going to take me next week?"

"Yes, I have cleared my schedule. Dante will be down to help out with LJ too."

"Oh, for real?" Daneisha turned up her nose. "I need to check up on baby bro."

"Did I tell you Mike and I went up there while you were gone?"

"No, I can't believe you didn't tell me."

"I couldn't, because I had to deal with bad behind LJ getting expelled from school. Then you almost overdosing on prescription pills." LeQuisha sighed. "Lord Jesus. I tell you, I thought I raised better children than this."

"Mama, please." Daneisha held her forehead as she shook it from side to side in frustration. "It was an honest mistake. It'll never happen again."

"That's what you say."

"Mama, just get to what happened with Dante."

"Well, we bust up in his place. He wasn't there, so you know me, I gots to inspecting."

Daneisha snickered. "Mama, what were you hoping to find?"

"What was wrong with my son! That's what. Well, I didn't find no drugs, but I found some used condoms in the trash."

Daneisha scrunched up her face in disgust. "Mama, that's nasty."

"Whatever. He better be using them."

"Was that it?" Daneisha asked, almost relieved her baby brother didn't get murdered.

"Well, the boy got thousands of video games in there. That's where most of my money is going."

"Better the video games than something else."

"That's true," LeQuisha said slowly. "He was so scared when he saw us chilling on his couch watching a video from his porn collection."

"He's a boy. What do you expect?"

"No, let me back up." LeQuisha spoke each word slowly, careful that her daughter didn't miss anything. "Dante was the one doing the filming. He had DVD's he's selling called *FAMU Girls Gone Buckwild*."

Daneisha almost ran her Lexus off the road.

"Mama, I know you're lying. Stop playing with me. I almost swerved and hit another car."

"Now, why would I lie?"

"It sounds so crazy." Daneisha shook her head. "Well, I know he's out."

"You better believe it. Mike and I are headed up there tonight to help him pack up his stuff. He's coming home. I am not paying for my son to be involved in all kinds of extracurricular activities when he supposed to be busting his behind on them books, not working on the next porn series. I don't think so."

"Mama, I know he's been asking for a lot of money lately, but I would never have suspected that. Maybe Donny."

"And why Donny?" LeQuisha snapped.

"I know you think Donny is your angel son that can do no wrong, but he has a weakness for women."

"Well, I have to agree with you on that. Nevertheless, he has made me proud by becoming a doctor. I do want him to get his personal life together. I want all my children to be successful. When y'all were little, I worked two, sometimes three, jobs to make sure you had what you needed. Most of all, I stayed on y'all about them books."

"Yes, you did. You kept us on the right path."

"Somewhere along the line I went wrong. That's why I stay in prayer mode. I'm not giving up. No, I'm sticking with what the Word of God says."

Daneisha rolled her eyes. She braced herself for what was next to come out of her mother's mouth.

"Daneisha, you were so smart. You have got to get back in school. I'm proud of you for earning your GED. But even you know that's not enough. Do something with your life while you're still young and only have one child," LeQuisha pleaded.

Daneisha saw her J-Lo phone light up.

"Mama, I gotta go. I have to take this call."

LeQuisha sighed. "Yeah, you got your hoochie phone ringing. I hear it. Daneisha, I answered that phone of yours while I was in the hospital for you. There were so many nasty men calling you."

Daneisha's jaw dropped. "Mama, what did you say?" she asked anxiously. She knew there had to be a reason why she hadn't received any new calls.

"I told them you were a married woman, and to please stop calling my daughter," LeQuisha responded sharply.

Daneisha sucked her teeth. "Mama, you need to stop! See there, you out there telling lies. You better pray the Lord don't strike you down right where you're standing."

"No, I didn't lie. You're the one out there claiming to be married. I just used your words."

"Mama, you need to stop meddling in my business." Daneisha shook her head. "You had no right to do that."

"I'm-a tell you this, then I need to get back to work. You're playing a very dangerous game, out there hustling these men for their money."

"No disrespect, but I learned it from you," Daneisha snapped.

"None taken," LeQuisha responded quickly. "And the next time I see you, I'll remember to knock you out. So, listen to this lesson. The same men you taking money from will eventually take your life, just like your Aunt Rhonda. Now keep on messin' up like you been doing."

"That's never going to happen," Daneisha said adamantly. "I ain't no crackhead."

"Rhonda wasn't always like that. She was a track star before she became a crack star. She was offered a full scholarship to University of Florida. But she decided to run behind a baby daddy, just like I did. Does this ring a bell to you?"

J-Lo rang again. She was grateful for the interruption. The last thing she wanted to talk about was her Aunt Rhonda, who was shot and killed in their home six years ago. It didn't help that it was during Daneisha's birthday party. Many times, she'd blamed herself for her aunt's death. If only she hadn't insisted on having a party, her only aunt would still be alive to this day. And her cousins, Pee-Wee and Tank, would have their mother.

"I gotta get this."

"You go ahead," LeQuisha said in a reluctant tone. "Bye, baby."

"Bye, Mama."

It was Chris. He was in town and wanted to meet at Embassy Suites. Daneisha told him she would be there around one PM. She had to make a quick stop to Frederick's of Hollywood first. One turn onto Southside, and she was cruising to the Regency Mall, where she made two small purchases. Then, she stopped by her apartment to shower and change. For some reason, Daneisha wanted to project a professional image, so she dressed in a gray business suit. The skirt had a high split in the back.

As Daneisha entered the hotel, she picked up the key from the front desk and headed toward the elevators. While waiting on one of the four doors to open, she caught a glimpse of a hotel worker staring intently in her direction. Daneisha shot him a what-the-hell-are-you-staring-at look. He turned away and continued mopping the floor.

The doors on her right swung open, and she stepped in. Pressing the PH key, Daneisha inserted the key, and as the doors were about to close, the weird guy stepped in. He pressed the button for the third floor. Then he took a spot on the opposite side of her, almost drooling at the mouth as he eyed her sexy physique from head to toe.

Clearly annoyed, Daneisha continued smacking on her gum. She prayed he wouldn't try to make a pass, because his short and chunky butt didn't stand a chance. She checked out weirdo with a closer eye and noticed he wore a beige company polo shirt. So she guessed he was safe.

"Are you from around here?" he finally asked in a slow country drawl.

Daneisha popped her gum. "No, I'm not."

"Oh." He pointed as he poked out his bottom lip. "You remind me of this girl I went to school with."

She forced a fake smile. "No, it's not me. Sorry."

Daneisha tapped her foot as she grew more impatient. Finally, the doors opened for him to get out.

"Well, I'm sorry."

"Don't worry about it," Daneisha responded. She rolled her eyes.

"Anyway, enjoy your stay here. It's a real nice—"

Daneisha pushed the button to close the doors. God knows she wasn't trying to be rude, but he was just too much.

When Daneisha reached the penthouse, she used the key to enter. She braced herself as she expected Chris to grab her as soon the door opened. To her surprise, he was nowhere in sight.

"Chris," Daneisha called out.

No answer.

When Daneisha tiptoed in the bedroom, she saw his collection of sex toys on the nightstand. The jelly beans and bullets were laid out. However, she noticed a pink fixture with a light bulb at the end of it. It was like some kind of dildo. Daneisha picked it up and squeezed it, as it was very soft, probably made from acrylic. Knowing Chris, he wanted it shoved as far as it could go for another backdoor experience.

Poor Chris, he was this rich guy that had so much going for him. But Daneisha pitied the woman he would eventually marry. He was into some kinky shit.

Daneisha took off her clothes and spread out on the bed in her pink ruffled cami and crotchless panties.

She heard the door swing open.

"I'm in here!" Daneisha yelled out.

"I'm coming in a hot second."

Five minutes later, Chris walked in wearing nothing but a cowboy hat and boots.

Daneisha laughed to herself.

This fool is crazy!

He climbed in the bed and pulled Daneisha by the arm.

"Come here, baby." He kissed her on the neck.

"I've missed you," Daneisha whispered as her hot breath entered his ear.

"Missing this big cock, were you?"

Daneisha forced a naughty smile. "Oh, yeah."

"Did you see my new toy?" He pointed at the night stand.

"Yeah. What is the pink thing?"

"It's called an anal arc. I want you to use it on me."

"It will be my pleasure." Daneisha ran her hand over her hair.

"Okay, now I want to feel all ten inches of that bad boy."

Daneisha deepened her voice. "You will. I'm going to hurt you so bad."

Daneisha rubbed his hairy back and delivered soft kisses on each shoulder, all while running her hands down his back. When she inserted her index finger up his ass, his butt muscles clenched tightly.

"You're making me so hot," he grunted. "Give me all four."

Daneisha rammed her entire fist inside.

"Uh!" he screamed.

"Can't take it?" Daneisha screamed and spit on his back.

"Yeah, I can take it. Anything you got, baby. I can take it."

She picked up the anal arc and pushed the button underneath. It started to vibrate. Lubricating him lightly, she aimed it inside forcefully—all ten inches at once.

Chris screamed like he was a small infant.

Just then, she felt a strong pain in her side.

"I'm sorry, I can't do this," Daneisha cried out and ran into the bathroom. As she washed the jelly from her hands, she caught a glimpse of herself in the mirror.

You're a whore!

Chris pounded on the door. "Baby, what's wrong?"

Daneisha tried her best to sound calm. "I'll be out in a second."

Ten minutes passed and Daneisha was still staring at her reflection in the mirror. She was completely disgusted with herself. By now her face was covered with black mascara, and her eyes were bloodshot red.

When she finally willed herself out of the bathroom,

she grabbed her clothes to make a quick exit. "I'm sorry. I can't be with you anymore."

Chris wrapped his arms around her. "Jennifer, what's the matter with you?"

"It's not you. It's me. I'm having some problems, and I have to have this surgery to get it fixed."

Chris looked concerned. "So, these are like female issues?"

"Yes, something like that."

"Well, all you had to do was tell me." Chris cleared his throat. "I wanted to see you, but not if you weren't up to it. I apologize."

"No, you don't have to be sorry. It's my fault, and I guess I thought I was up to it. But, the truth is, I'm in a great deal of pain. Sometimes so bad, I can't get out of bed."

"This is terrible. When is the surgery?"

"In a couple of days. Then I have to wait a few weeks after that. What I'm saying is, I won't be able to have sex for a while."

Chris held her chin and gazed his gorgeous blue eyes into hers. "Don't you worry about anything. I'm going to take care of you."

"No, I'm not asking you for anything."

"I know." Chris kissed her on the lips. "What you've done for me is phenomenal. No other woman as classy as yourself has been there for me like you have. I'm very appreciative for everything you do. These fucks are some of the best fucks I've ever paid for. And believe me when I tell you this: I've paid more money for some bimbos and gotten much less."

Daneisha scrunched up her face. "Are you supposed to be paying me a compliment?"

Chris shook his head. "Okay, this isn't coming out right.

Let me just say this . . . you call me when you're feeling up to it. And I'm going to take you somewhere real nice."

Daneisha's mind wandered as to whether he was serious or not. "Like where?"

"It's my surprise. Of course, you have to trust me."

He looked her squarely in the eyes.

Daneisha nodded. "I trust you."

"Okay."

As he hugged Daneisha, she felt her pussy aching for the feel of his dick. She reached down and started to massage it until it became hard. She laid down on the bed and spread her legs wide. Chris worked his tongue inside her clit, causing her to have a sweet orgasm.

His fingers stroked her clit as he put on a condom. He eased in and out of her like he knew how to work those three inches. He pumped quickly and hit it from the side.

Daneisha shuddered, asking him to go faster, deeper.

"Jennifer!" he yelled out over and over.

Daneisha felt bad, knowing he still didn't know her real name. Maybe it was time to be completely honest.

As he kissed her ankles, he grabbed a dildo and inserted it underneath his penis for more pressure. It did just the trick! She came so hard, so often.

Chris wasn't stupid. He knew he didn't have enough to please her, but he made up for it in other ways. In the end, Daneisha enjoyed it better than four years of mindless good fucking with Lamium.

Chris made love to her all night long. And in the end, she walked out of his penthouse suite with $3,000 and one satisfied pussy.

Chapter Six

Dr. Baldwin performed the laparoscopy. He not only confirmed she had endometriosis, but the worst case he'd ever seen in his professional career. Daneisha didn't know if she was supposed to be proud or depressed. She chose the latter and lay around in bed like a helpless victim.

The weather was horrible; it rained like cats and dogs. Watching the news was depressing as the forecasters predicted another hurricane might be headed their way. Her mother already claimed the victory over all hurricanes for 2006, so she believed not another storm would hit Florida. After all they suffered in 2004, Daneisha hoped her mother was right. There was a serious fear of hurricanes after Katrina kicked ass over in New Orleans the year before.

It was Thursday. Daneisha didn't know why it should've mattered, except for the mere fact that another week had come and gone without a word from Lamium. Daneisha knew that Lamium made a point to call the house when he was sure she wasn't there. Daneisha was glad Lamium took time to talk to LJ. Even so, she felt so dejected that he never bothered to check on her. She knew Valerie or LJ mentioned to Lamium that she had surgery. She wondered if he ever cared about her.

Earlier that week, Greg stopped by to bring her rent money and some extra. Although she appreciated him for continuing to support his family, it was no substitute for her man being there, present in her life and her son's life, whom he claimed to love so damn much. Daneisha stopped calling Lamium's cell phone, seeing as how it went straight to voicemail each time.

This wasn't the first time Lamium fell in love with some other female, only to realize she wasn't going to put up with all of his crazy demands and controlling ways. Sooner or later, Lamium would come back to her. For his sake, Daneisha hoped it wasn't later.

Hell, she had it going on! And one thing Daneisha never had a problem with was getting a man. For now, she needed to focus on her health. Then there was LJ, who was her little man. She loved him, and needed to spend more time with him. Daneisha knew he was missing his daddy, and she was going to do her best to help fill that void.

LeQuisha helped her daughter in the bed. She was in pain, like she'd given birth to another baby.

"Okay, I'm leaving to pick up your prescriptions. Do you need me to get anything else while I'm out?"

"Some orange juice," Daneisha murmured, as she fell fast asleep.

When Daneisha woke up, it was dark out. She realized she slept with her duvet comforter clenched up to her chin, and now her body felt as hot as an oven. She sat up in her bed and wiped away the sweat on her neck and face. She needed to pee, but as soon as she tried to turn over on her side, shock waves shot up her spine.

Daneisha yelled out in pain.

Kay came in. "Nurse Kay to the rescue of a young damsel in trouble," she said.

Daneisha shook her head and laughed at her silly friend. "Where's Mama?"

"She had to leave. She mentioned something about Dante having a girl up in her house and took off. I didn't know your brother was back from college."

"I have to pee." Daneisha raised her hands, signaling for Kay to help her up. "Dante was trying to set up a *FAMU Girls Gone Wild* porno movie deal, and Mama wasn't having it."

"Ooohhh." Kay held both arms under each of Daneisha's shoulders. "I can't believe sweet Dante would get involved in something like that."

Daneisha grunted as Kay lifted her up. "I can. Dante has always been sneaky. And you know Mama can sniff out a liar in a heartbeat."

Daneisha squealed as another pain shot up from her thigh.

"Just a few more steps and you're there."

"Yeah." Daneisha tried her best to concentrate on picking up each leg, but it was more of a drag-then-limp movement.

"Your mom told me the doctor has never seen a case of endometriosis as bad as yours."

"Yeah." Daneisha sat down on the toilet and let her urine flow like Niagara Falls. "Dr. Baldwin said the tissue is wrapped around my organs, completely twisted, and squeezing them."

"That's why you've been in so much pain."

Daneisha wiped the sweat from her forehead. "I'm done." She lifted her hands for Kay's assistance. Once she washed her hands, Kay helped her back to bed.

"Do you know he told Mama I should have a hysterectomy?"

"That's what she told me. Don't you think you should?"

"At the age of twenty-one?" Daneisha took a deep breath. "Besides, me and Lamium want to have at least one more child. He wants a girl, but it doesn't matter to me." She rambled on with such confidence. While in her heart, she was breaking. Judging by his actions, she had to assume he didn't care about her anymore.

"Well . . ." As Kay's lips shivered, she hinted there was bad news coming. "If your health is at stake, then I wouldn't take the risk. At least not for Lamium."

"Okay, so what's going on?" Daneisha balled her hand up in a fist, getting herself geared up for the worst.

"Lamium opened up that nightclub, just like I told you. And there was a reason why he didn't want you to know about it."

Daneisha adjusted her position on her right side. "Somebody else?"

"Yep. Lamium is dating this woman . . . I think she's some music exec or something in the music business. Anyway, she works with Myra."

"Myra . . . our Myra?" Daneisha was shocked.

"Yes, I guess anyway. Don't quote me on any of this stuff. I'm doing my best to put it all together."

"I know." Daneisha's voice went stiff. She wasn't so sure she wanted to hear the rest. "What's the name of the club?"

"Club Sensations."

"What?" Daneisha burst out in laughter. "That shit sounds corny as hell."

"Just like Lamium. You know he's corny."

Still, curiosity got the best of her. "Yeah, did people show up at the opening?" Daneisha didn't know why she should care, but she did love the man. Nothing would change that. And she wanted him to be successful. Hell, he had bills to pay and a child to support for another fourteen years or so.

"He had a few people show up. You know it's just a front business anyway."

Daneisha squinted. "Still, he should've asked me to help him come up with the name."

"Are you going to let me finish?"

"Yes, go ahead. Tell me about the skeezer. What does she look like?"

"She's gorgeous."

"I didn't ask for your opinion," Daneisha mumbled as she fought back the tears.

"Oh, I'm sorry. I didn't mean to hurt your feelings." Kay put her arm on Daneisha's shoulder.

Daneisha threw up her hand. "Save it, okay? I can't believe you didn't tell me. You're supposed to be my best friend. How long have you known about this bitch?"

"I just found out. I met her at Myra's luncheon on Monday."

"Luncheon . . . the one Myra supposedly cancelled?" Daneisha was infuriated at this point. Her last conversation with Myra came to mind when she hinted that Lamium was no longer her man.

Daneisha was ready to kick some serious ass.

"No, she didn't cancel. I was wondering why you weren't there, and when Jillian showed up I was like, what's up with this?"

"What's up is Myra had that bitch up in my spot. That's what."

"Basically." Kay nodded in agreement. "Anyway, Jillian is a music producer or something. I missed when she was giving all the details of how she first met Lamium because I had no clue who she was talking about at first. I started to pay more attention when she mentioned how Lamium started to flirt with her while he was there at the studio one day."

"How come I'm just now hearing about this? That was damn near four days ago. Kay, are you on my side or what?"

Kay put her hands on her hips. "How you gonna ask me some stupid junk like that? You know we go way back. What did you want me to do? Kill them hoochies?"

"Something," Daneisha snapped back.

"Those are your supposed-to-be friends, but I never liked them anyway. Especially that Angel, she gets on my very last nerve. I thought you were going to be there. I did my best to keep my cool and gather as much information as I could."

"That's true. But you still didn't answer my question."

"You were having surgery. That's why I waited. A few days weren't going to make that much of a difference. Hell, you said Lamium was probably fucking somebody else yourself."

"Saying it and knowing are two different things. It still hurts." Daneisha turned away and stared at the wall. "Like I've been stabbed in the heart." She buried her head in her hands.

Kay walked around to the other side of the bed.

"I'm so fucking pathetic. Lamium doesn't give a damn about me. And here I am crying over him."

Kay rubbed Daneisha's back.

"Do you want to hear the rest?" Kay asked in a soft tone.

Daneisha used the comforter to blow her nose. "There's more?"

"Well, I remembered when I went to the club with Rowan this past weekend. It was clear from jump that Jillian was in charge. But I thought she was the club manager at the time."

"It's all so embarrassing." Daneisha's face scrunched up in disgust. "I can't believe he hasn't called me! He doesn't give me the courtesy of telling me he has kicked my ass the fuck out of his life!" She wiped her nose once more with her comforter. "He's a no-good piece of shit, that's what he is."

Kay nodded and handed her best friend a Kleenex from the nightstand. "It's obvious Lamium has fallen for her big time."

"So, what does she look like?" Daneisha asked, knowing she must have it going on.

"Oh, she's tall. Probably a few inches taller than you. So, probably about five foot seven, maybe."

"Of course," Daneisha added.

"Not skinny though, she's athletic. Kind of shaped like Serena Williams."

"With the big ass too?" Daneisha asked in frustration. At this point, she might as well forget she even knew Lamium.

"Well, you had to know Lamium would fall for a big butt and a smile."

Daneisha laughed a little, careful not to cause more pain. "Good one."

"Anyway, Lamium is a dog. Look at the way he was messing around with them other girls. And you just put up with it."

"That's because I had my own thing going," Daneisha explained. "Did I like that he was fucking Keysha and white girl Becky? Hell no. But if it kept me from having to suck his dick, then I went along with the program."

"Yeah, Lamium does have a big one." Kay's hands trembled. Then she laughed nervously.

Daneisha stared at Kay blankly. "What the fuck! I thought you didn't want to talk about that. And here you are bringing it up."

Kay shrugged. "I know I didn't. I was embarrassed to be in something like that."

"A threesome?" Daneisha turned over on her back. "I can't believe I let Lamium talk me into doing it either."

Kay sighed. "I can't believe I let *you* talk me into it." She rolled her eyes. "The things you're willing to do for your best friend." She lay on her back and slid close to Daneisha.

"I'm sorry." Daneisha looked up at her with sincere eyes.

"I know." Kay crossed her legs mid-air.

"I just wanted me and Lamium to be in a real relationship. You know, married. I was willing to do whatever it took to make him love me. LJ is going to be so hurt by all of this. You know he worships his daddy."

"Yes, he does. But it's going to be okay." Kay smiled. "You're going to find someone else to make you happy."

Daneisha thought about Chris. Before she left him the other night, he said he wanted to set her up in an apartment. Maybe she would consider it, at least for the time being.

"I do have Chris."

"The white boy with the small dick?" Kay frowned. "No, baby."

Daneisha popped Kay on the arm. "Stop talking about my friend. He has money and he can take care of me."

"See, that's where you went wrong with Lamium. It's time for you to stand on your own two feet. Why don't I move in here and help you pay the rent? I've been thinking it may be time for me to move out of my mama's house."

"I thought you would be moving in with Rowan."

Kay ignored the comment and continued. "And I can help you get a job at the firm with me."

"Don't get offended. But what kind of work would I be doing?"

"Filing. You do know your ABC's, right?"

Daneisha popped Kay's arm again. "Shut up!"

"How come I haven't seen you in two weeks?" Daneisha asked as she approached Lamium in the kitchen. She stopped a few feet short of him. He smelled awful, and his clothes were stained like he'd been working all day in the fields. The stench reminded Daneisha of her grandmother when she used to catch the work bus to pick potatoes and cabbage in Hastings. She would leave early in the morning, while it was dark out, and not come back until it was dark night.

"I've been busy." Leaning against the counter, he finished his beer and tossed the bottle in the trash can.

"Well, I hear you've opened yourself a nightclub and didn't bother to tell me anything about it."

Lamium's piercing eyes met hers in a way that gave her a slight chill. "So what?"

Daneisha cocked her head to the side. Here the man she'd spent almost five years with started a business and didn't bother to mention it. And he had some nerve to just waltz up in her apartment like he actually lived there.

"I guess all the rest I've heard must be true also."

Lamium tried to brush past Daneisha, but she leaned forward so he couldn't leave. Uncertain of what might happen next, she held her breath.

He checked her out from head to toe. Then he pushed her shoulder back and made his way past her. "Don't even start confronting me about some shit you heard from your friends either."

Lamium staggered down the hall. Daneisha followed him to the bedroom, where he was in her closet turning shoe boxes upside down. She eyed the box with her new pair of Bandolini sandals on the floor.

"Why are you tearing up my closet?" As Daneisha kneeled down to pick them up, another shoe box hit her in the back of the head. She turned up at him. "Lamium, you hit me in my fucking head! What the hell are you looking for?"

Not paying her any mind, Lamium tossed every box on the floor. "I'll let you know when I find it." He snatched down her jewelry box and opened it, tossing all her old gold chains over her clothes hanging in the closet.

"Lamium, I know good doggone well you ain't put no drugs up in my apartment."

Lamium lunged toward Daneisha and pushed her up against the wall. "Would you shut your muthafucking mouth for a second? Damn! This place might be bugged." He whispered in her ear.

His funky breath was so strong, she could taste it. Daneisha turned her head away.

"And you giving them all the evidence they need to lock me up."

Daneisha freed herself from his grip, allowing him to rip part of her nightgown. "What are you talking about? Lamium, you promised me I wouldn't have to deal with none of this."

Lamium pulled a black case down from her closet. Inside was a laptop. He sat down and placed it on the bed. When he lifted the keyboard, there was a wad of cash inside. Even though his hands were shaking, he managed to count out the stack of hundreds.

Slowly, Daneisha walked up behind him. When she touched his back, it was cold as ice.

"What's wrong with you?" she asked.

"I'm sorry," he said. Then he handed her some money.

Daneisha put the money in her purse. Then she rubbed her hand across his bald head. "Baby, what's wrong?"

"Nothing." Lamium grabbed her arm forcefully, almost pulling her down. She struggled to keep her balance. "There's some shit going down. That's all."

"You took that money from me, didn't you?" Daneisha asked. "And I blamed it on Valerie. I thought she was stealing from me."

"Daneisha, I got to put you on a budget. You're spending way too much money. Now, this deal with Rowan, baby, it's pretty much sealed and delivered. All I gotta do is get my crew in place."

Daneisha nodded. "I understand." For somebody who thought the apartment was bugged, he sure was giving out a lot of information.

Nervously, Daneisha fidgeted with her hands and tried to decide what her next move should be.

All the years she'd known Lamium, he hardly ever used. Of course, he sampled his product every now and then. But it was evident by his sweaty body that he was fucked up. The paranoid talk let her know he'd been like that for a while.

"What I need from you right now is your trust. If I can't trust you, then we need to just call it quits." Lamium continued to ramble on for another twenty minutes.

Daneisha wasn't listening to a thing he was saying. *Maybe I need to pack up all my shit and get me and LJ the hell away from here.*

"It's been hard out there for a nigga. But I'm working hard. Busting my ass for you, and this is how you want to repay me. Sleeping with some dude. All penned up in the hotel with a white boy."

Daneisha was stunned. How did this conversation go from Lamium talking about himself to her sleeping with a white boy?

"What the fuck are you talking about? I *ain't* sleeping with nobody."

"Quit with all your lies. Your ass is caught. One of my boys has a cousin who works at the Embassy Suites. He saw you there."

Damn it.

Daneisha wanted to shit in her panties. That little punk-ass boy she saw with the mop. For the life of her, she had no clue who he was. In Lamium's circle, she came across so many guys. But they all knew who she was. She wanted to kick her own ass for being so careless.

Daneisha laughed nervously. "Please. Ain't nobody seen me nowhere."

Lamium grabbed her by the neck and threw her across the room. Daneisha's head was inches away from hitting the dresser. "I know everything about you. Daneisha, you was a whore when I met you, and you ain't nothing but a nastier whore since I been with you."

Daneisha stumbled to the floor, unable to see clearly. As Lamium came closer, she held her hands up to defend herself.

"Please. Stop it," she whimpered.

Lamium pressed hard on her left shoulder and lowered her to the floor.

"Yeah, I did some searching. I know about your My-Space, your websites where you showing your pussy and tiny tits for all the world to see."

"Lamium, I—"

"Shut the fuck up!" He punched her in the mouth. Then he stood up and kicked her in the stomach. "I'm taking LJ with me."

Daneisha tried to scream, but nothing would come out.

"No," she said in a soft voice. "You can't."

"I can't? What did you say?" He leaned down toward her

face. "I thought I told you to shut the fuck up." He kicked her once more.

Before Daneisha realized what she was doing, she reached under the bed and pulled out her knife. The one she stashed for security. She never thought she would be forced to use it.

"Lamium, I don't know . . ." Daneisha spit out a mouthful of blood. "I don't know what you've been smoking." She pointed the knife in his direction. "But you better get the hell away from me. Get the fuck out!"

"Mommy!" LJ screamed from the doorway. "Don't kill Daddy!"

As she turned to face LJ, Lamium pushed her on the bed. He tried to make her drop the knife, but she held onto it tightly. She wouldn't let go.

Daneisha kneed him in the groin. Once he kneeled over, she tried to run, but he grabbed her leg. She swung the knife wildly in Lamium's direction so that he would release his grip. That's when she heard a ripping sound.

Her hands covered her mouth in horror, as she felt her chest expand with huge breaths.

"Aaaahhh." Lamium fell face forward on the bed. As the blood gushed out from his neck, she stared at the bloody knife and dropped it to the floor.

Without hesitation, Daneisha grabbed her purse. She snatched up LJ and ran toward the door. Not once did she look back. Barefoot and wearing nothing but a torn nightgown, she held onto LJ's hand as they got closer to the car. She tossed LJ over to the passenger side and turned on the ignition. As the brake pad bruised the bottom of her bare foot, she ignored the pain and pressed the gas. Daneisha raced out of her complex like a NASCAR driver.

"What happened to Daddy?" LJ asked in a low voice.

Daneisha looked over at him in the passenger seat. "Put your seatbelt on."

LJ tapped her shoulder to get her attention. "You're bleeding."

Daneisha ran her fingers across her face. They were covered in blood. In the mirror, she could see what her son saw. And she felt sorry for him.

"Hand me some napkins." Daneisha pointed toward the glove compartment.

LJ struggled to open the glove compartment, but did as he was told.

"Thank you, baby."

Aunt Rhonda's bloodied face popped in her mind. Daneisha shook her head to get rid of it. She didn't want to think about it.

I don't want to go to jail.

Lamium wasn't dead. He was breathing. He was alive.

As Daneisha drove, she did her best to clean her face. A vision of her Aunt Rhonda's dead body lying on the carpet flashed in her head.

A part of Daneisha wanted to turn around, but she was too scared. No, he was high. She knew when he came to, he would remember that she had no choice. As far as Daneisha was concerned, when it came to their relationship, it was over. He knew about Chris. And her sites on the Internet. Lamium was never going to forgive her.

Constantly checking the rearview mirror, Daneisha searched for Lamium's car. It was nowhere in sight. Still, she wasn't sure if he had one of his boys following her.

Daneisha's hands wouldn't stop shaking. She kept telling herself the worst was over, but she was so frightened. In all the years she'd known Lamium, he never once laid a hand on her. He'd threatened on more than one occasion, and she knew he was capable of it. Something was not right with him.

Daneisha dialed her best friend's number. When Kay finally answered, she was so relieved.

"What's up, Princess?" Kay asked in a slumber voice.

"I'm outside. I need you to come out."

"What's wrong?"

Daneisha took a deep breath. She exhaled a few times, then broke down in a small cry. "I just need you to come to my car."

"Okay."

LJ's huge eyes peered up at her. He grabbed her hand. "It's okay, Mommy. Don't cry."

Daneisha shook her head and wiped away the tears.

"You're right, baby."

Kay walked to the car. As Daneisha got out, Kay saw her best friend's face. Her mouth fell wide open. "What happened to you?"

"Daddy beat up Mommy," LJ said as his eyes welled up. He started to cry. "I hate him! I hate my Daddy!"

That was it. Daneisha tried to suppress her emotions. "Daddy was just drunk. He didn't mean to do it."

Kay helped Daneisha out of the car. "Are you okay?"

"Yeah, I can stand," Daneisha responded.

Then Kay went over and picked up LJ. Daneisha followed her into her mother's house. It was dark and quiet. Kay led her to the guest bedroom.

"I'll get some clean sheets and towels," Kay said as she rubbed her thighs. She disappeared for a minute and came back with a stack of linens.

Once Daneisha got LJ off to sleep, she washed up in the hall bath. She dressed in a pair of cotton pajamas, courtesy of Kay. To Daneisha, they were hideous, but it didn't matter as much as her swollen face and busted lip. Not to mention, her nose felt broken. She rubbed her temples as she felt the beginnings of a severe migraine.

After Daneisha told her what all happened, Kay slowly crouched down to examine Daneisha's injuries. "Are you sure you don't want to go to the hospital? I'm worried about you."

"No, I'm not trying to get the police involved in this," Daneisha said as she waved her arms wildly in the air. "I cut a man, remember?"

"Because that man was kicking your ass!" Kay exclaimed through clenched teeth. She ran her fingers through her curly tresses. "I just think you should get checked out."

"And who do I say did this to me?" Daneisha pointed toward her busted lip. "A woman can't go into a hospital looking like this and not report it to the cops. The laws are made to protect women who get their asses kicked all the time. I know Lamium didn't mean it."

Kay peered into Daneisha's face. "Lamium isn't right. You say you love him, but I don't believe that either."

"I do love him."

Kay leaned in forward while she tossed up her hand. "No, it seems like you've confused love for gratitude. Yeah, he helped you get out of your mom's house and supported you. He also got you pregnant and kept you locked up in the apartment while he fucked every bitch in sight."

Daneisha sighed with frustration. "You don't know shit, Kay. It's more to it than that."

Kay completely ignored what she said and continued. "Then he talks you into having a threesome."

Daneisha cleared her throat. "I thought we weren't going to talk about that. Ever!"

"Well, I'm talking about it. Now!" Kay declared as she marched to the other side of the room. Her head flung way back, in slow motion like Matrix style. When her soft curls dangled, Daneisha knew Kay was about to let her have it. Although she loved Kay dearly, she hated the way she always had a knack for making a point crystal clear.

"Daneisha, don't you hate him for what he did? He

made you sleep with your best friend and kicked back in a chair with a beer in one hand enjoying it. And then he fucked my brains out too."

"It's not like we never fooled around before."

"We experimented. Most girls do. But Lamium . . . with his sick, twisted mind crossed the line. He orchestrated it. Then he bragged to his boys about it."

Daneisha stood up and tried to push past Kay in the doorway. But she held her ground. They locked eyes for a moment, which signaled a temporary truce. Then they hugged.

"I can't stand to see your face like that. I want to kill Lamium myself." Kay shook her head. "I just don't understand."

"I don't either." Daneisha rubbed her left arm, hoping the numbness would leave. "Are you sure Rowan doesn't know anything?"

"Not that I know of. Rowan just said Lamium was stressed out. That's all. We don't talk about the business side that much."

"Too busy fucking each other's brains out."

Kay held a goofy grin on her face. "Yeah."

"I know. I can see it." Daneisha smiled as she reached out for Kay's hands. "You're happy."

Kay's face beamed with pure joy. "I am."

"Good." Daneisha stared down at the floor. "Your life gets wonderful and mine blows the fuck up. What the hell is that all about?"

"Your guess is just as good as mine."

Their hands remained locked for a few minutes. The room was silent, but their dialogue continued. In their minds, they were as close as two people could get.

Kay stared at the clock. "Hey, it's almost four. I have an early class, so I need to crash for a bit. Are you going to be okay?"

"I'm fine."

"Well, help yourself to clothes, shoes, whatever. I'll stop in on my way out."

As the door shut, Daneisha heard J-Lo chime. Somebody left her a message. It was no surprise it was from Chris.

"Two dudes paid me a visit after you left my room today. They told me to stay the fuck away from you or they would kill me. I didn't know your name was Dantesha. Or whatever the fuck it is. Sorry if I mispronounced it. We had some good times. I hate to say what I'm about to say next. Forget you know my number. Have a nice life. By the way, it's Chris. That's my real name, bitch."

No, he didn't!

It was bad enough he fucked up her name. Then he had the nerve to call her a bitch too! Oh, very nice.

When I wipe my ass, I'll be sure to think about how you licked it clean. Too bad your tongue is bigger than your dick!

Knowing she had bigger problems, Daneisha thought about her next move. She calculated her net worth, which was close to $2,000. If she could get Kay to loan her another $1,000, she would have enough money to get out of town. But where could she go? She thought about Mike's two daughters, Tasha and Nicole. They were up at Spelman College in Atlanta. Maybe she could find a job and a place to stay up there.

A job?

Every lecture from LeQuisha hit Daneisha like a ton of bricks. She'd never worked a day in her life. Here she was, twenty-one years old, never had a job, no college degree, and had barely earned her GED.

Daneisha called Tasha's cell phone number. No answer. It was still early. She left a voicemail for her to call when she got the message. She hadn't talked to Tasha since last Christmas. Still, Daneisha hoped she would call her back.

LJ woke up asking if he was going to school. He seemed to be doing better, but he didn't have any clothes to change into. She had no choice. She needed to go back to her apartment. Running away wasn't an option. Yes, she was scared. No, she didn't want her ass kicked again.

But, in a way, I deserved it.

She called Lamium. It wasn't a surprise that he answered on the first ring. When guilty, the conscience always does the right thing.

"Baby, where you at? I've been so worried about you."

He sounded genuinely sincere. Still, she couldn't trust that shit. Not with the way he went psycho on her ass just hours ago.

"Don't worry about that. I have to take LJ back to get him changed for school. You better not be there when I get there, or I'm calling the cops."

"I won't be here," Lamium responded slowly. "I'm going to see a doctor. Did you go to the hospital?"

"No. I'm fine. What about you?"

"The same. That dull knife you used barely broke the skin."

Daneisha was surprised. "But there was so much blood. I was afraid you were going to bleed to death."

"If you thought that, why didn't you call an ambulance or something?"

"I don't know."

"I know I must've fucked you up, huh? I don't remember that shit. I was so messed up."

"Just stop trying to explain," Daneisha said.

"Is LJ mad at me?"

"He hates your fucking ass. And I do too. How could you do this to me?"

Lamium cried into the phone like a baby. "I'm sorry. I know I fucked up bad. Daneisha, I need you to forgive me."

"It's over between us!"

Daneisha waited to hear a response from Lamium. Nothing.

"Did you hear what I said?"

"Yeah."

"You jumped on me for fucking somebody else!" Daneisha shouted into the receiver. She grabbed her jaw as it hurt like hell. "Knowing full well you're eating, sleeping, and fucking somewhere else. We don't even have a relationship. We never even had anything that even resembled a relationship. I can't believe you did me like this."

"Why are you saying all this?" Lamium asked calmly.

"Because I want you to leave me alone. Don't come fucking with me. Only thing between us now is LJ. That's it! Don't you fucking come around. I mean it, Lamium."

"I'm not going to bother you."

"Before you walk out the door, make sure I have enough to cover my bills."

"You don't ever have to worry about that. I'm-a take care of the mother of my child. No matter what."

That's what Daneisha needed to hear. When she arrived at her apartment, Valerie was there and got LJ ready for school. She asked no questions, and Daneisha didn't bother to provide any answers. Daneisha was sure LJ would fill in all the details on his way to school.

She removed the blood-stained sheets from her bed. The black case and laptop fell to the floor. Realizing Lamium forgot to take it with him, Daneisha picked it up.

Searching inside, she found papers with contracts between him, Rowan, Greg, and a few other names she recognized. There were also emails on drug and money trafficking seizures, port schedules, and detailed information on the Coast Guard's employees.

Lamium better be glad I didn't call the cops on his ass. Otherwise, his ass could be locked up for a long time.

Feeling the right side of her face aching, Daneisha put an ice pack on it, swallowed a handful of pain pills, and stretched out on her bed. She was nobody's fool, and she figured Lamium would come back searching for the case later. She decided to open a safe deposit box at the bank to hide her new discovery and pretend she knew nothing.

Valerie knocked on the door around noon. "I took the liberty of calling the locksmith. I figured you wanted the locks changed right away."

"Yes, thank you," Daneisha replied, gazing into thin air.

Valerie took a step forward. She rested her hands on the footboard. "Whatever it's worth, I'm sorry this happened to you."

As the tears fell down Daneisha's face, she was frozen. A nod was all she could muster up as a response.

"If you need anything, just call." Valerie turned around and shut the door behind her.

Daneisha reached over on the nightstand for her cell phone. She'd hoped LeQuisha was back home. She really needed someone to talk to. More importantly, she was ready to admit her mother was right. She was an even bigger fool than her mother had imagined.

Chapter Seven

Is ya man on the flo?
If he ain't
Let me know.
Let me see if you can run it, run it.
Girl indeed I can run it, run it.

Daneisha and Kay were singing to the lyrics with Chris Brown. Kay gripped the steering wheel as she rocked her head from side to side, like she was already on the dance floor.

Daneisha sang while she searched through her purse. She wanted to make sure she had everything she needed. Her palms were sweaty. She rubbed them on the seat to dry them. She didn't want to stain her red halter dress.

Moving with the hot beat, her rose and yellow gold bangles clicked as she held up her compact mirror to apply her lipstick. She checked her face, making sure her foundation was even. Her eyelashes were in tact. She was looking damn good and wanted everybody in the club to know it.

When the song ended, the radio went to commercials.

Daneisha sucked her teeth. "I can't stand all these commercials. That's why you need XM radio."

Kay tossed up her hand. "If you pay for it, I'll get XM."

"That's what you got Rowan for," Daneisha said sarcastically.

Kay shimmied her shoulders to the commercial jingle. "Unlike you, I don't depend on my man to take care of me."

Daneisha rolled her eyes. "Neither do I. I have my own hustle going on too. Thank you very much." She used her brush to even out her Lancome make-up one more time. She wanted her face to appear natural like Gabrielle Union's.

"Are you all right?" Kay asked.

"Yes, as Beyonce would say, I got my freakum dress on." Daneisha pursed her lips together. Then she applied another layer of lip gloss. "Why do you keep asking me that?"

"Because you're acting crazy, that's why. First, you keep looking in the mirror and rubbing your sweaty-ass hands all over my seat. In case you hadn't noticed, this is not a Lexus, and my seats aren't leather."

"I know." Daneisha tried to laugh, but her nerves were getting the best of her. Still, the remark made her loosen up a little. She always made fun of Kay's Nissan Pathfinder. It was modest, with cloth seats and very few upgrades.

That was Kay, simple and modest. Usually, when it came to her choice in men too. Daneisha was glad that she found a true gem when it came to Rowan, and Kay always expressed how happy she was. Even though Daneisha thought Rowan was older with more extravagant taste than her friend, it was good that Kay recognized it as well. Kay seemed to accept the challenge and stepped up her game.

Tonight, Kay was sporting a long weave instead of her curly tresses. She was wearing a black jumpsuit that complimented her somewhat boxy figure, with a burgundy leather jacket. It wasn't quite up to the level of fashion as Daneisha would like, but it was a decent attempt. However, her choice of eye shadow, cheek color, and lipstick was way off. It was time for her best friend to visit the Lancome counter with her, instead of her Mary Kay consultant. With Kay's line of work, she needed a professional to give her a lesson or two on the correct colors to use, and lastly, explain why application was so important, making sure her eye shadow wasn't on so thick.

It was cold outside, as it was early October. And while Daneisha should've been wearing a jacket, she decided to freeze her ass off so that she could show off her sexiness once she was inside. If everything went according to her plan, she wouldn't be there long anyway.

When Kay pulled into the Club Sensations parking lot, Daneisha let out a snort of disgust. First, the huge sign up front was well lit with a busty woman sitting with her legs wide open holding a martini glass. It was distasteful and made the club seem more like a strip joint than a respectable business establishment.

Daneisha was surprised, as she always thought of Lamium of having more class. It was weird, but as of late, she really couldn't wrap her brain around who he was becoming. He had changed, and this whole club fiasco was making it all more evident.

Now she wasn't so sure this place was even worth a few minutes of her time. It didn't seem like it was up to her usual choice of places to hang out. Still, curiosity got the best of her, and she decided not to say anything. Running her fingers alongside her inner thigh, Daneisha checked to make sure her switchblade was still in place. Then she ran her hands along her hair and smoothed down the ends. Her hairdresser, Sebrina, hooked her up with the Beyonce blonde weave. It was supposed to be a temporary hairdo, but the attention gained made it difficult for her to part with it. This time she settled on the wavy hair, which was easier to keep up.

Everywhere Daneisha went, she had to deal with the men hitting on her, and women's jealous snares. To glam up her appearance, she was thinking about getting colored contacts. Her brother, Donny, had gorgeous green eyes. She felt it was worth going more dramatic than ever.

It was hard to explain why Daneisha craved so much attention. Definitely being Lamium's woman brought her all the respect and then some, a bigger ego than she'd imagined. Somehow, being reduced to Lamium's baby mama didn't quite have the same level of power. However, Daneisha credited herself on her creativity, and she would find a way to work the title into getting everything she wanted. Even though Jillian had the man, she had his child, and that would always keep her one step ahead of any bitch who dared to cross her.

Kay flashed her VIP pass to the parking attendant. He waved to another guy in the back, and he flagged them to go opposite all the other cars. Kay explained earlier with VIP access, she was able to get a space in the back of the club, near the private entrance.

Daneisha checked out the dark gray building, where security seemed tight. There were three big dudes dressed in black suits just at the back door alone. For a minute, she thought about aborting her plan and returning back to her comfortable bed, where she left LJ sleeping like an angel.

Kay peered over in Daneisha's direction.

Daneisha shrugged. "What?"

"I know that expression on your face. You changed your mind, didn't you?"

"No, I didn't."

"Well, you know I'm your girl." Kay took her hands off

the steering wheel and leaned back in her seat. "I got your back no matter what."

"I know you do." Daneisha laughed. "I just can't believe how this turned out. This shit is so fucked up." She tossed her head back and rested it on the seat.

"See, that's because you keep looking at it the wrong way. I think it's good you are moving on with your life. Think about all the possibilities. You're only twenty-one, and Lamium had you tied down like a prisoner."

"I never thought of it like that. But I guess it's true." Daneisha took a deep breath. "I'm too young to be tied down. Hell, I'm ready to fucking be me. I just wanted to be Lamium's wife, since we had a child together. Does that make sense?"

"It makes perfect sense. Besides, you're recovering from surgery. All you need to focus on is your health and your son."

Daneisha listened intently to what her best friend was saying. "You're right about all of that shit you just said."

Kay grabbed Daneisha's hand. "You ready, girl?"

"Yep."

As they neared the club, butterflies danced around in Daneisha's stomach. She didn't know why it was so important for her to see this woman, but it would mean closure to her relationship with Lamium. Once she saw that Lamium was committed to someone else, that meant she could move on. The club seemed like the perfect chance for her to do that. And with all the buzz about Club Sensations and the endless commercials on 92.7 FM, she wanted to see what all the hoopla was about.

Even though they would no longer be a couple, they shared a child. A little boy who absolutely adored his father. It was up to Daneisha to make sure they were the best parents to LJ, and that included remaining friends. As far as the finances went, she wanted him to be successful.

That only meant more money for her to spend. And she hoped he wished the same for her.

There was a short line at the VIP door, no more than ten people. The bouncer recognized Kay and waved her in. They skipped ahead of the line and entered. MC Hammer's "Too Legit" was blasting.

Daneisha could do nothing but smile as she thought Lamium must be in charge of the song selections too. She pictured him out on the dance floor doing the running man, as she'd seen him do in their living room years ago. The thought-he-could-dance-like-Hammer-but-more-like-Urkel Lamium she would miss the most.

Two guards checked them, and Daneisha was relieved they didn't find the switchblade. She needed protection, just in case somebody recognized her there and wanted to trip. They entered the dark hallway and passed a few women dressed more like strippers exiting the club. With her head held high, Daneisha clutched her Chanel handbag and strutted up in there like she owned that muthafucka.

All eyes were on her, and it only confirmed she chose the right dress and perfect Via Spiga heels to match. Her attempts to show she wasn't at home crying over Lamium so far seemed successful, as she exuded nothing but confidence, elegance, and class.

Judging by the size of the crowd, Club Sensations was officially the place to be. There wasn't a single place to stand or sit. Once they spotted an empty table, she and Kay pulled up chairs and sat down.

"Over on your right." Kay pointed in the direction of the stage. "See the tall woman wearing the cream pantsuit talking to the DJ?"

"Yeah," Daneisha responded.

"That's Jillian."

Daneisha stared in her direction for a long time. Her

hair was jet black, very curly, similar to Oprah's. Her eye-brows were arched thin and extended past her cat-like eyes. She noticed Jillian's glossy lips matched her coffee-brown complexion. Her curvy figure, medium-sized frame, and tall stature gave her a prominent, professional de-meanor in the pantsuit.

In Daneisha's mind, Jillian was everything that she wasn't. Only a twinge of jealousy surfaced, because Daneisha knew the real truth: she was everything Lamium needed in a woman. In comparison to Jillian, yeah, sister had some game, but she was older. No woman like that would put up with his crazy ways. Daneisha was confident he would realize his mistake and come running back to her. It was only a matter of time.

She had to give the woman her just due, she definitely carried herself well. By the looks of her, Lamium had picked a mature woman. To his credit, Daneisha figured she would probably be better to her son than some of the immature skeezer bitches he usually messed with. Daneisha made up in her mind that when he came begging at her door asking for forgiveness she would make him pay dearly for humiliating her.

Kay leaned over. "What are you thinking?"

"I'm thinking that bitch has it going on. And I'm actu-ally ready to go."

Kay's eyes grew wide. "That was quick."

"I know. I've seen all I need to." Feeling like someone was watching her, Daneisha turned around and caught a glimpse of Jericho staring in her direction.

He was talking to a man with a ponytail dressed in a suit, probably security. Daneisha hoped he wouldn't make a scene and ask her to leave. Sure, she had planned to bust up in the club and kick some ass, but she'd had a change of heart. Now, she only wanted to leave in peace.

Jillian took the microphone and began speaking, just as

the music turned down. "I would like to welcome everyone to Club Sensations. How many of you came to have a
good time tonight?"

As the crowd yelled, Daneisha watched over her shoulder as Ponytail came closer to their table.

"Excuse me, ladies, but compliments of the owner of
the club, drinks are on the house."

Daneisha and Kay smiled back.

"Thank you." Kay spoke loudly so that he could hear
her over Jillian on the microphone. "With that said, I'll
have a lime margarita."

"And I'll have a cosmo."

"Coming right up, ladies."

As Ponytail left their table, Jillian announced that Myra
was about to perform, and the band members started to
set up. Caught completely off guard with the special treatment from Ponytail, Daneisha relaxed a bit.

"I guess we can at least stay long enough to enjoy our
drinks and hear Myra sing." Daneisha leaned back and
crossed her legs.

Kay grinned from ear to ear. "And here you was planning to cut that bitch."

"I was ready to put a can of whoop ass on somebody
tonight. But you know it's not all about that. You were
right, it's time for some things to die and for me to grow.
My relationship with Lamium faded away a long time ago.
And I don't need to be mad with no one; otherwise I'll be
stuck in the same place."

Kay nodded. "True."

"And as you can see, they're going to be all right. While,
I'm sitting up in my apartment mad at them, they could
care less about my ass."

Kay held up her finger. "Okay, you haven't even started
drinking yet, and you're already rambling."

"Oh, shut up."

Ponytail came back with their drinks. When Kay ordered wings and nachos with cheese, Daneisha realized the only thing she'd eaten was a bowl of cereal that morning. The food couldn't get to her table soon enough, because she was ready to get her eat on.

Myra took the stage, dressed in a bohemian-style dress and sandals. An even larger crowd formed around the stage. The cheers echoed around the club, showing her local popularity.

Myra raised her hand to silence her rambunctious audience. She cleared her throat. "I want to thank you all for coming out to support me tonight."

Daneisha patted Kay's hand to get her attention. "Would you listen to that bitch trying to sound all sexy?"

"I know." Kay rolled her eyes.

"As you all know, I've been offered a record deal, and my family and I are moving out to LA."

Daneisha sat straight up and cut her eyes over at Kay. "Did you know about this?"

"No, I didn't," Kay answered as she gripped the arms of the chair. "What the hell is going on?"

"I know Myra has been working toward a record deal, but that seems kind of sudden. I mean, she just finished the demo." Daneisha carefully took a bite of a nacho dripping with cheese sauce.

"Well, I'm shocked."

Daneisha finished chewing. "Me too."

Myra cued the band and sang a song Daneisha recognized, but couldn't immediately recall.

"Damn, I know this song." Daneisha clicked her fingers. "Oh yeah, it's 'Stole My Heart.' "

"Do you know all of her songs?" Kay asked.

"Myra burned a few of the tracks on a CD for me. I used to listen to it all the time in my car, until she pissed me off. Then I threw that shit out my damn window."

Kay burst out laughing. "You're so bad. I don't know how I ended up being friends with you."

"Because your ass ain't as innocent as everybody thinks."

Kay caught a glimpse of Rowan walking in and started cheesing like a schoolgirl. "Oh, there's my man!"

Daneisha turned around to check out Rowan dressed in a charcoal gray suit.

"I'm going to say a quick hi," Kay said. She was gone in all but a second.

Daneisha sucked her teeth. She wondered if Kay would forget all about her and cling to her man, just as she'd done with Lamium in the past. It wasn't good when the shoe was on the other foot. Of all nights, Daneisha needed her best friend to be there for her. It wasn't easy to part from the man she loved, especially the father of her son. By the huge turnout at the club, it was obvious Lamium was sitting on cloud nine and had his new woman to share it with. And she was fucking miserable.

Daneisha hoped he would live up to his promise to continue to take care of her. She had no clue what she would do to make a living, but she was no dummy. It was time she relied on her smarts to help get through the next phase of her life.

Maybe she would go to fashion school, since she had a real knack for it. There was nothing tying her to Jacksonville, so she was open to moving to New York if she had to. Daneisha pictured herself walking down the runway modeling expensive couture. Then she pictured herself as one of the head designers. Her creative designs on the bodies of those skeletal-like models with serious faces, posing on the runways in Milan. Just the thought of it got her excited.

Daneisha waved Ponytail over.

"What can I get for you?" He flashed a toothy grin.

"Can I get a bottle of Cristal up in here?" Daneisha asked. She wanted to get drunk on the most expensive shit.

Ponytail scratched the back of his neck. "Let me check on that for you."

Daneisha curled her finger, signaling for Ponytail to come closer. He knelt down, and she whispered in his ear. "Didn't Jericho tell you to take care of me?"

"Yes, he did."

"Did he also tell you that I'm the owner's baby mama?"

"No, he didn't share that with me." Ponytail held up his hands in surrender. "I'm not trying—"

"You seem like a real nice man. What's your name?"

"My name?" Ponytail pointed at his chest. "I'm Milton, but most people know me as Dirty Red."

Daneisha's bottom lip dropped. "Dirty Red."

"Yeah."

"You're not related to Tony Red, are you?"

"Yeah, that's my brother."

Daneisha's body went numb as her mind took her back to that place. Her ears deafened, and all she saw was her Aunt Rhonda's body stretched out on the living room floor. Tony Red's dead body laid on top.

She remembered her mother's screams. LeQuisha cried over and over. "He killed my baby sister!"

Daneisha closed her eyes to keep the tears from flowing. The scene haunted her dreams for years. Even though she knew it was stupid, in her mind she felt like the death of her aunt was all her fault. If only she hadn't insisted on having a birthday party.

"Are you okay?" Dirty Red asked.

Daneisha opened her eyes and held a blank stare, unable to move.

"I'll be back with your bottle."

Kay climbed up in her stool. "Did you miss me?"

"I . . . I . . . yeah." Daneisha tried her best to pretend like she was fine. She bit her bottom lip and pushed her thoughts of her aunt away from her mind.

"What is wrong with you?" Kay asked with a concerned voice. "Did something happen while I was gone?"

Daneisha shook her head. "No, I'm good. I ordered us a bottle of Cristal."

Kay leaned forward. "What?"

"Why are you looking at me like that?" Daneisha asked as she ran her fingers through her hair.

"I thought you were ready to leave. Now, it seems like you're ready to get tore up."

Daneisha forced a fake smile. "That's right."

Myra finished her first number and the crowd screamed their approval. Then she took a quick bow.

"Thank you. This next song is for one of my dear friends, who is in the audience tonight. This is for my girl, Daneisha Harris."

Daneisha coughed up the spit in her mouth.

"Girl!" Kay slapped Daneisha on the back to make sure she wasn't choking.

"What did you do that for?" Daneisha asked.

"I thought you were having a heart attack."

"As you can see, I'm not. This shit is tripping me out though. How did she know I was here?"

"Don't be cutting your eyes over at me! I didn't say anything. I'm sure Jericho probably told her."

The band began playing "Tell Me Now," and Daneisha swayed her head and hands to the music. It was her favorite track from the CD.

A waiter brought over a gold bucket of ice with a cold bottle of Cristal champagne. "Compliments of the owner."

Before them, he placed two diamond-encrusted glasses and filled them. Daneisha and Kay smiled at each other from across the table.

"This is for a fabulous fucking night!" Daneisha screamed as they clinked their glasses. She swallowed hard and savored the taste of expensive champagne. It didn't taste any better than the berry wine coolers she sometimes enjoyed, but knowing the price made her enjoy it so much more.

A tap on her shoulder made her turn around. In front of her was Lamium dressed in a black suede tuxedo. Daneisha searched for stitches. There were none, only a small bandage. She didn't know whether she should run or give him a hug.

"Now is that how you treat the man who just sent over a thousand-dollar bottle of champagne?" he asked with his arms outstretched.

Daneisha stood up, pulled down her dress, and hugged Lamium. Without a care in the world, she kissed him, hoping Jillian was watching every second of it.

When she backed away, Lamium licked his lips. "Damn, baby."

Daneisha sighed, taking a moment to catch her breath. She couldn't say she didn't feel anything, but it wasn't the fireworks she expected either. With the way Lamium reacted, it was good to know she still had it. Now, she knew for sure she was finished with Lamium and ready for Mr. Right. To her surprise, they stayed until the club shut down.

On her way out of the club, Daneisha jiggled the keys in one hand. She went out to warm up the SUV and wait for Kay to finish sucking Rowan's lips off so they could get home. She adjusted the radio to 92.7 FM and listened to one commercial after the next. She skipped to another station, more commercials.

This is exactly why I have XM, because I can't stand this shit.

Kay's truck was taking forever to warm up. Daneisha

kicked off her heels and snatched her jacket from the backseat. Her ass was completely frozen. The back door to the club swung open. It was Myra coming out with a few of her band members. Daneisha wanted to talk to her and congratulate her on the recording deal.

She waited to see if anyone else was about to exit before she said something. Myra passed the truck and opened the door to her Toyota Avalon.

Daneisha rolled down the window. "Thanks for the shout-out tonight."

Myra jumped backwards. "Oh my God. You scared me."

Daneisha stuck her head out of the window. "I would get out, but I'm too cold."

"You never could handle this weather," Myra said as she approached the car. She reached in and hugged Daneisha. "How are you? We haven't spoken since we had that little tiff. Are you still upset with me?"

Daneisha grinned. "No, I'm over it."

Myra laughed nervously. "Well, I had to ask. Especially since you threatened to beat my ass."

"I was mad, but that's no excuse. I'm sorry."

"It's okay, really," Myra said. "I forgave you the moment we got off the phone. I was a bit harsh too."

"Just a bit," Daneisha said, mocking Myra. "Look, I won't keep you. It's late and I know you need to get home to your kids. I wanted to congratulate you on the record deal. I'm so happy for you."

"Thank you," Myra gasped and smiled warmly. "It means a lot . . . really."

"When are you leaving?"

"Monday."

Daneisha clasped her hands together. "So soon? Don't you have to sell the house?"

"The house sold. It's been on the market for weeks. I

was about to say, didn't Lamium tell you, but then I remembered he's with Jillian now. So, you two probably
don't talk all that much."

Myra's comment threw Daneisha for a loop.

"What do you mean? I thought you were the one that
introduced them."

Myra clenched her perfectly straight teeth together.
"Darling, that's absurd. Who told you that big fat lie?"

"Kay. She said you invited her over for the last brunch,
which I wasn't invited to. Thank you very much for that."

"I don't know what you're talking about. I didn't intro-
duce them. I wasn't going to host anything, until Ms. Jillian . . ." Myra rested her hand on her forehead, then
glanced around the parking lot, as if she was being
watched. "She insisted on taking over. You know, I don't
like this at all."

"You don't like what?"

"I really can't say. Daneisha, you made the right deci-
sion to let him go. He's not doing very well. From what
Jericho has told me, he's out of his right mind. Anyway, I'll
end this conversation like that."

Daneisha wanted to press Myra for more details, but she
knew it wasn't the right place. She could tell Myra had
reservations to share what she did. "I understand. I appreciate you clearing things up for me. I was very confused."

Myra took a deep breath. "I hate for it all to end this
way. I'm glad you understand. In a few weeks, it will all
make sense, I promise you. Personally, I can't wait to get
away from here. I told Jericho if he wasn't coming with
me, then I was taking the boys and divorcing him."

"I can't say I blame you. Anyway, let me get you out of
this cold. Call me with your new address and phone number. We need to stay in touch."

"Of course I will." Myra patted Daneisha's hand.
"You're my sister."

Daneisha stuck her head out the window again. "Oh, where's Angel?"

Myra opened her car door. "At home; she's sick with the flu."

"Awww. That's too bad. See ya later."

Myra waved her hand as she sped off.

Daneisha glanced at the clock on the dashboard. It read 2:50. She was growing more weary, ready to settle down in her bed for the night.

A black Cadillac Escalade pulled up beside her and honked the horn. Daneisha was stunned, not realizing she'd drifted off to sleep. She let down the window.

"Hey, stranger," the guy said.

"What's up?" Daneisha responded.

"You don't know who I am?"

"Not really."

"I'll give you a hint. We used to kick it a ways back."

Daneisha began to feel somewhat uneasy. She pulled out her cell phone and speed dialed Kay's number. She typed in 9-1-1. "You need to get the fuck out of here."

"Hey, I'm sorry."

"I know you are," Daneisha snapped.

"Slow your roll, girl. It's Evan."

Daneisha racked her brain until she remembered him. "Evan Meyers?"

He smiled. "The one and only."

Daneisha leaned on the window. "You have to excuse me, I was knocked out, 'sleep."

Quickly, she placed her cell phone back in her purse.

Although Evan used to work for Lamium, that didn't stop him from hitting on Daneisha. Back then, she was easy, and her standards weren't what they were today. Otherwise, she would've made him a sponsor. The whole situation ended badly when rumors circulated around that Daneisha was seen leaving Evan's house one night. It got back to Lamium, and he questioned Daneisha about it. She lied, but it didn't stop him from firing Evan. Daneisha was so scared, fearing Lamium would kill him. She didn't want another man's blood on her hands, unless it was Leroy's. That bastard deserved it!

Evan parked his SUV on the curb. When he got out, Daneisha checked him from head to toe. He stood six feet four inches tall, and wore a long black leather jacket. His baby face was medium brown complexion, complemented with a low haircut and goatee. His ears stuck out a bit, and Daneisha remembered grabbing hold of them when his tongue moved in and out of her vagina.

Daneisha took a shallow breath as he climbed inside.

"Well, how are you doing?" Daneisha asked. "I haven't seen you since April, outside of the Tyler Perry play."

"Oh yeah." He bit down on a toothpick. "You were with your girl, Kendall."

Daneisha nodded. "Yes, she likes to be called Kay now."

"I think I remember her mentioning that. And how is Ms. Kay doing?"

"She's fine. Actually, this is her truck."

"Okay. So, what is Ms. Daneisha Harris driving now?"

"Who me?" Daneisha pointed at her chest. "A Lexus."

"Oh . . . suky . . . suky now." Evan snapped his fingers in a feminine fashion.

Daneisha burst out laughing. "You're so crazy!"

"Hush your mouth, chile," Evan added, like he was pretending to be Madea. "Naw, let me stop. I don't want you to get any ideas, with all this talk about brothers being on the DL."

"No, I wouldn't think that." Daneisa held a mischievous expression on her face. "If I recall, you were with someone that night."

"Oh, you remember that, huh?"

Daneisha ran her fingers through her weave. "What was her name?"

"I don't know. That was a long time ago."

Daneisha sank deeper in the driver's seat. "So, it's like that?"

Evan raised a brow. "You tell me."

"It's getting hot in here." Daneisha fanned herself. "You're bold to be up in Lamium's club."

Evan straightened his leather jacket. Daneisha admired the way he was always so pulled together.

"I could say the same for you. Word is, Lamium has a new woman."

Daneisha raised a brow. "You know me, bold and bad as hell."

Evan chuckled. "Yeah, well from what I saw in the club, you're right about that. You was wearing the hell out of that dress."

"Well, you know." Daneisha bit her bottom lip. "I try."

"No, you did more than try. You sold that shit!"

Daneisha laughed out loud. "Thank you."

They took a few minutes to catch up. Then Evan entered her number in his BlackBerry.

Evan handed Daneisha his business card. "Why don't you give a brotha a call in a few days?"

Daneisha slid the card in her coat pocket. "I just may do that."

Evan stared at her for a moment. Then he opened the car door. "Take care of yourself."

"Always."

Evan drove off, and Daneisha's mind wandered back to their first sexual encounter. In the beginning, the thought of cheating with one of Lamium's trusted workers seemed too risky, even for her. During the late nights when Lamium didn't bother to come home, she and Evan would talk on the phone for hours. It helped to pass the time and keep her mind off the fact that her man was out fucking another chicken head.

Daneisha liked that Evan was very intelligent, more nerdy than Lamium. She learned a lot about politics from him, and Evan was a willing teacher in every subject. They kept their relationship limited to phone conversations for almost three months. Smiling to herself, Daneisha remembered the first time they kissed.

Lamium threw one of his many parties at the Ocean Club. The music was jumping, and all her girls were there dancing their asses off on the dance floor. Back then, she hung with a different crowd. It was weird that Lamium kept her by his side the entire night, while she was anxious to sneak away and exchange words with Evan.

Wanting to impress both men, she was dressed in a purple printed gypsy top with a very short denim mini-skirt. To accentuate her long, slender legs, Daneisha wore purple suede ankle boots. Her hair was pulled up in a long ponytail; at the time she was going for the Puerto Rican, Jenny-from-the-block look.

Finally, Daneisha caught a glimpse of Evan heading toward the restrooms. Daneisha told Lamium she needed to pee and rushed in that direction. She passed Evan in the hall on her way to the restroom. Daneisha knew he was staring back at her, but she pretended not to notice. Inside, she felt like a million dollars. She stared at her face in the mirror, admiring how she'd applied her make-up perfectly.

A few minutes later, he burst in the door and locked the door so no one else could enter.

"What are you doing?" Daneisha grabbed her chest. "You almost gave me a heart attack."

Chewing on a toothpick, Evan laughed.

Daneisha fidgeted with her hands.

"This isn't funny. I'm not trying to get my ass kicked tonight."

"Would you relax?" Standing face to face, Evan pulled her right hand and kissed it softly. "I just wanted to spend a few minutes with you."

Daneisha shrugged. "I don't know about this."

"Come here, baby." Evan moved in closer and wrapped his arms around her waist.

Her breathing was heavy, and she stared deeply into his huge eyes. He buried his head in her chest, and she rubbed his head.

Then it happened.

His lips locked on to hers for what seemed like eternity. He lifted her up and placed her on the counter, forcing her skirt up to her stomach. Moving her thong underwear to one side, his fingers eased in and out of her hairy pussy.

Daneisha felt shockwaves pulsing throughout her body. A sudden knock on the door startled them both.

Daneisha jumped down and pulled her skirt down. "You see!"

"What?"

Daneisha put both hands on her hips. "Are you really that stupid?"

Another knock.

Quickly, she opened a stall door. "Just get in here." She pushed him inside.

She opened the door for two women who looked at her strangely.

"Sorry about that. I needed some privacy."

The light-skinned one turned up her nose. "Okay."

They were talking loudly while they checked their make-up. Daneisha went into the same stall where Evan was, so that she could wipe her wet coochie dry. He tried to feel on her thighs, but she swatted his hands away. Daneisha waited until the women were gone, and made her exit. She hoped Evan would get out the women's restroom unnoticed.

Their next encounter was a private meeting at Lonnie C. Miller Park off of Soutel and Moncrief Road on the Northside. Evan chose the spot. Daneisha remembered it was June and it was hot and humid because it rained earlier that afternoon. At the time it seemed like one of the worst days of her life, having struggled to get LJ to daycare. He was in his terrible twos and made each day a living hell on earth. It didn't help that Lamium was there to criticize rather than lend a hand to get him dressed.

Daneisha called him up, and within one hour, Evan was there. She loved the way Evan had a way of making her feel important. They were sitting on a picnic table underneath the covered pavilion.

"I don't know why it's so hard for me to get a handle on LJ." She leaned back and rested on her hands.

"My sister has three little boys, and she is having a hard time. And she's a teacher. Now, if anybody can handle kids, it would be her."

"She has three. I'm struggling with only one."

"Well, I remember when she had one. And she was burning up my cell phone to come and get him. I was the perfect uncle to my nephew."

"I believe it. You're always so gentle with me."

"Only when it's required of me," Evan said. He stood in between her legs and stretched his arms around her waist. "I can also be rough when it comes to certain things."

Daneisha wrapped her arms around his neck. "Like what things?"

He winked at her. "Like pulling down these mini shorts you have on and stroking your pussy right here on this table."

"Whoa!"

"Are you surprised or turned on?" Evan moved up closer, his erection revealing he had a lot to work with.

"Both."

Evan unzipped his jeans, and his dick stuck straight up. It wasn't longer than Lamium's, but close to it. And it was fat. She'd never seen a head that thick.

He massaged it.

"Let me do that for you." Daneisha moved his hand and worked his penis.

Evan moaned his satisfaction.

Daneisha searched around to make sure no one was in sight. They had been alone in the park for quite some time, and it was getting darker, which meant the park would be closing soon.

She stood up and allowed him to slide her shorts and panties down past her ankles. Her bare ass sat down on the wooden table.

Evan kissed her.

He worked his tongue down to her flat stomach.

Then he eased his tongue inside the folds of her vagina.

Daneisha flung her head back and sighed.

Evan's tongue flickered faster and harder, causing her to scream as she came in his mouth.

Gently, he slipped on a condom. He held her up mid-air then entered her. With every thrust, he grunted, each one louder than the last.

His fingers made imprints in her ass as he grabbed each cheek tighter. Daneisha wrapped her legs around his muscular thighs, squeezing her vaginal muscles each time he eased inside her.

Evan's thighs tightened as he neared orgasm. She felt his dick get harder inside of her. She gripped her legs as she braced herself for his finale. Sweat rolled down his face.

Then she felt her body tingle as she wanted to—

A knock sounded on the passenger side window. It was Kay. Daneisha rubbed her forehead as she quickly collected her thoughts. It took her a few seconds to gather her bearings before she unlocked the doors.

"Sorry it took me so long."

"Whatever!" Daneisha snapped. She was pissed off at Kay for making her wait. She was even angrier that her best friend interrupted her just before she was about to come in her panties.

Yes. I'll be giving Evan a call real soon.

Evan was the perfect candidate for Mr. Right Now.

The next morning, Daneisha sat with LJ watching cartoons. If only Valerie could see them on the couch eating a bowl of Cheerios, she would go off on both of them like she was somebody's mother.

"I'm getting seconds. Do you want more cereal?" Daneisha asked as she rose from the couch.

LJ shook his head. "No, Mommy."

Daneisha took his bowl. "Okay, now don't be begging for my cereal."

LJ giggled. "I won't."

Daneisha went in the kitchen and filled her bowl. She sang along with LJ the theme song to *SpongeBob Square Pants.* When LJ jumped off the couch to hit the long note, Daneisha clapped for him.

"Thank you, thank you." LJ took a bow for his dramatic performance.

"You're a real star. I need to take you on some auditions." She was interrupted by a knock at the door. "You can make us some money with that smile of yours."

Daneisha looked out the side window. It was Dirty Red. He was holding a huge floral arrangement in front of him.

She figured Lamium sent him.

*Damn! That was quick. I guess the freakum dress worked bet-
ter than even I thought it would.*

Daneisha swung open the door, dressed in silk pajamas.
She was embarrassed that her hair was still up in a scarf.
"Hello."

"How are you?" Dirty Red asked.

"I'm fine." Daneisha's voice went up an octave. She
took hold of the flowers in the vase.

He cleared his throat. "Well, I have a message for you,
Daneisha."

His voice sounded sharp, nothing like the night before
at the club. She couldn't help but notice how his eyes
went cold.

"Oh." Daneisha was suddenly caught off guard. Her in-
stincts kicked in, and she felt her safety was an issue. Her
heart began to beat faster.

"Thanks, but no thanks," Daneisha responded as she
went to close the door.

"Wait a minute." Dirty Red tried to force his way inside
by grabbing for the handle.

Daneisha pushed the door back, but he stuck his leg in
between to block it from closing.

He leaned forward. "I need to tell you something!"

Daneisha pushed with all her might, struggling with
him as he caught hold of her arm. Quickly, she freed herself and slammed the door shut.

"LJ, hand me the phone!" Daneisha yelled as she
leaned against the door and secured the dead bolt.

"Mommy!"

"Just get it, LJ." She waved her hand wildly. "It's gonna
be okay."

LJ handed her the phone and she dialed 9-1-1, but
waited to press send.

"I see you're about to do something real stupid by calling the police." Dirty Red spoke through the door. "I'm trying to help you out."

"Okay, now you need to get the fuck away from my door!" Daneisha shouted.

"Mommy!" LJ ran down the hallway to his room. "I'm scared. Call Daddy!"

Daneisha looked through the peephole, waiting until he was gone. Then she ran behind her son. She closed his bedroom door.

Daneisha grabbed hold of both his hands. "LJ, listen to me." Trying to catch her breath, she tried to speak in a calm voice. "It's okay. No one's going to bother us. He's gone."

"But we need Daddy!"

"No, we don't need him. I can handle this."

The phone rang with the caller ID reading UNKNOWN CALLER. At first, she decided against answering it. On the third ring, she answered.

"Hello."

No response. She was about to hang up.

"You know when I met you last night, I thought you were a nice girl. Nothing like the stuck-up bitch Boss Man kept telling me you was."

Daneisha swallowed hard. "Yeah, right."

"Stay away from your boy. There's a hit on his ass."

"You better—"

The phone hung up.

Trying not to alarm LJ, she continued to speak into the receiver. "Sorry, you have the wrong number."

Although, her hands were shaking, Daneisha managed to hide them from LJ as she dialed her mother's phone number.

Within an hour, LeQuisha was knocking on the door.

Daneisha let her in, embracing her with a big hug. "Mama, I'm so glad you're here," she whimpered like a small child. She was never happier to see her mother.

LeQuisha's eyes wandered around the living room. "What happened in here?" she asked as she removed her white shawl and laid it on the arm of the couch. She was dressed in a burnt red pantsuit she wore to church. Before her mother arrived, Daneisha managed to change into a two-piece athletic suit.

By the door, a small table was turned over. Daneisha's expensive Chinese vase was broken. The area rug was rolled over on one side.

"I was fighting with this dude who was trying to bust up in here."

LeQuisha shot her a confused look. "What in the world is going on, Daneisha?"

While her mother helped her straighten up the living room, Daneisha caught her up on everything that happened from the night before until that morning.

"Mama, I know it sounds crazy, but there is something wrong with Lamium," Daneisha said, throwing the broken vase in the trash.

"Probably." LeQuisha's arms were folded as she tapped her foot on the living room floor. "Now, Daneisha I know you better than to try and get involved with all that mess."

Daneisha closed her eyes, trying to fight back the tears. "Mama, I just want to know what's going on. In all the years me and Lamium have been together, nothing like this has ever happened to me before."

"Yes, but it was bound to happen at some point." LeQuisha tossed her hands up in the air. "I mean, get a grip. You're going with a drug dealer. I can't believe you sitting up in here like you're some kind of victim."

Daneisha stretched her neck forward. "What?" She couldn't believe what she was hearing.

"It's not like I haven't tried to tell you." LeQuisha's eyes grew big as she emphasized her frustration. "And you never seemed to care before. After all this time, Lamium's been nothing but dirty and you went right along with it, always quick to defend him before." She turned up her nose.

Daneisha gasped. "Mama, I can't believe you."

LeQuisha ignored her daughter and continued. "As long as the money was right, all you wanted to do was spend it. Now, when this man has dumped you for another woman, you want to get all up in his business."

"Whether I'm with Lamium or not, he's still the father of my son."

LeQuisha shook her head in disbelief. "I think you're just trying to stay attached to Lamium. You're my daughter, and I love you. But right now I'm not buying your act, sweetheart."

Daneisha pointed at her chest. "I have a right to know if someone wants him dead. For all I know, LJ's life could be at risk too."

LeQuisha walked up to her daughter and got close to her face. She waved her index finger. "That's the chance you took when you decided to have a child from a drug dealer."

Daneisha rolled her eyes. "Mama, please."

"So, what are you saying?" LeQuisha asked as she turned away. She sat down on the chaise. "Do you want to leave town?"

Daneisha rubbed the back of her neck. "No, I'm not going anywhere. I'm not running from nobody."

LeQuisha took a deep breath. "You can stay at the house if you want to."

"Thanks, but I'm staying here."

"Well, I want you to know, you can't keep calling me every time you get scared. I mean, what am I supposed to do?"

At this point, Daneisha regretted even calling her mother. She pretended to pay attention, out of respect, but she wasn't listening to another word. Right now her mother sounded like a straight-up hypocrite. Everything Daneisha knew about hustling men for money, she'd learned from the woman right in front of her.

When Daneisha was growing up, her mother paraded all kinds of men in front of her. It didn't matter the marital status or the job choice, all her mother seemed to care about was whether or not that man was going to give her rent money. She hated the fact that while her mother worked hard to put food on the table, she had little respect for herself when it came to men. Especially when all the kids in the neighborhood knew it too.

One day in particular stood out in her mind. Daneisha was in elementary school, and the bus was late picking them up from school. Daneisha always grew uneasy because a late bus guaranteed a fight would soon break out. Donny was holding her hand, as he always did, protective of her.

"What you holding her hand for?" Foots asked. "She must be your girlfriend?"

"No, you idiot. She's my sister!" Donny shouted.

"Yeah, you didn't know that?" Javon said.

Both boys were in Donny's class.

"She's pretty. I want her to be my girlfriend then." Foots started pumping from his mid-section. "Then I can stick my ding-a-ling in her."

All the kids started laughing.

"She'll give it up for free," Brontae responded. She was a bully to everyone at school and never liked Daneisha from the first day of kindergarten. She used to talk a lot of trash, but no one ever challenged her because of her size. Brontae was dumb as hell and had stayed back at least twice.

Daneisha snatched away from Donny. "What did you say about me?"

"I saaaaiiid you give it up for free." Brontae put her finger in Daneisha's face. "Your mama is a ho, and that makes you one too."

Daneisha held up her fists. "You better get your finger out my face, before I knock you out."

"What if I don't?" Brontae touched her nose.

"Fight!" someone yelled.

Then a circle formed around them, each one chanting, "Fight, fight, fight, fight . . ."

Daneisha pushed Brontae.

Brontae pushed her back.

Before Daneisha knew it, she was pulling Brontae's hair and they were falling to the ground.

"Who's on top?" a kid asked.

Daneisha's eyes were closed, as she launched punch after punch. When she opened her eyes, she realized Brontae hadn't thrown one single punch. In fact, she was laying there covering her face with her hands.

A minute later, two teachers pulled the girls apart.

Daneisha grabbed hold of Brontae's shirt and it ripped in the front, showing her flat chest.

"Ooooh, Brontae ain't got no titties!"

The crowd roared in laughter.

It was Daneisha's first trip to the principal's office. She was so scared, wondering what would happen. As soon as her mother found out, she was going to beat the hell out of her.

"Don't worry about anything," Donny said as he followed her to the office. He volunteered to tell Principal Bell what happened.

Daneisha and Brontae sat in opposite corners in the office.

"This ain't over," Brontae whispered.

Daneisha held up her fist like she was ready to serve a knuckle sandwich. "You better shut up before I beat you up again."

"You ain't beat me up." Brontae stuck out her tongue. "And your mama and your grandma still a ho, so there."

It amazed Daneisha how she just kicked this girl's butt in front of the whole school, but she still felt bold enough to insult her mother and now her grandmother.

Oh, it was on!

Daneisha stood from her seat, but sat down quickly when Principal Bell's door opened.

"Thank you, Donny, for being a witness." Principal Bell handed Donny a piece of candy. He sat down in the chair beside his sister.

Principal Bell strutted over to the secretary's desk in her apple green heels that matched the blouse underneath her tan skirt suit.

"Ms. Shears, did you contact the girls' parents?" Principal Bell asked.

"Excuse me, they don't have parents." Ms. Shears wrinkled up her face. Her evil eyes peered over her tiny glasses. "Both of those girls' mothers are single."

"Well, what does their marital status have to do with anything?" Principal Bell sounded irritated.

"They're in the office, aren't they?" Ms. Shears replied. Her voice was scratchy.

Daneisha, Donny, and Brontae were all up in their conversation as Principal Bell put Ms. Shears back in her rightful place. Daneisha couldn't stand that woman. Every time her teacher sent her to deliver the morning attendance, Ms. Shears always stared at her like a hawk eyeing its prey.

It was rumored Ms. Shears was a black widow, since all three of her husbands were dead and she had enough money from their insurance policies that she didn't have to work. Ms. Shears was a dried-up old witch that didn't have any children of her own, so she kept working just so she could torture the kids at Garner Elementary.

When Principal Bell was through with Ms. Shears, she was apologizing for her rude comments. Even at her young age, Daneisha wasn't stupid. She knew it was just an act so she could keep her job.

Principal Bell called Daneisha and Brontae into the office. Brontae continued to lie about what really happened. It helped that Daneisha had a witness to back up her version of the incident. Since her brother was known as the "golden child" at the school for his good behavior and grades, the principal believed Daneisha. And only Brontae was written up on a referral and suspended for two days.

Daneisha zapped back into reality, where LeQuisha's lecture was nearing an end. With her mother's popular form of amnesia, Daneisha would be wasting her time trying to convince her mother she was wrong about Lamium. Instead, Daneisha let her mother continue to rant on about how she disapproved of their relationship from the very beginning.

"Lamium has been nothing but trouble from day one. Did you forget how the boy beat you up, and I had to come rescue you? The whole right side of your face was black and blue."

There she goes talking about shit she don't know nothing about. Leroy was the one that beat me up. I wish I could tell her the truth and see that stupid-ass look on her face then.

Again, she decided not to say anything. Deep down, she was afraid her mother would end up in jail for attempted murder. Daneisha sighed as her mother continued. LeQuisha was on a roll and showed no signs of stopping anytime soon. It was a shame; her mother was wasting her time. Daneisha had her own ideas, and she wasn't about to let her mother change them.

"The next time you get some crazy call or someone

shows up at your door, you need to call the police. And I think you should change your phone numbers."

"I will probably do that." Daneisha thought about canceling her MySpace and website accounts too.

LJ peered from the hallway. "Grandma, can I stay with you?" He walked up to her and stared with sincere eyes.

"Sure, baby." LeQuisha placed him on her lap and kissed him on the forehead. "Daneisha, you sure you don't want to come too?"

"No, I'm-a stay here," Daneisha responded quickly. "I'll go get his stuff together." In his room, she packed his bag with enough clothes to last him a week. In her mind, she concocted a plan. She would need a few days to get to the bottom of all this craziness. Her first stop was to find Lamium. She decided to try the club, since she didn't have the slightest clue where he was living.

"Just let me know when you want me to bring LJ back," LeQuisha said as she stood in the doorway of LJ's bedroom.

"Thanks, Mama. I appreciate it," Daneisha responded.

LeQuisha grabbed her daughter's arm. "Just promise me you won't do anything stupid. One thing I will say about Lamium, he's a smart man. And I figure whatever is going on with him, I'm sure it has something to do with why he's no longer coming over here. He's probably trying to keep you out of it."

Daneisha's mind started to wander. What her mother was saying did make some sense. It was awfully sudden, the way he stopped answering her calls and coming home. No matter how many times Daneisha tried to wrap her brain around the notion that Lamium had another girlfriend, it did seem out of the blue even for him.

Daneisha thought back to the night when Lamium attacked her. He kept saying, "There's some shit going down." She worried the worst was about to happen and

Lamium had been tipped off about it. It would explain a lot. And the conversation she had with Myra at the club last night. It left her with even more unanswered questions.

Daneisha handed her mother LJ's bag and favorite SpongeBob doll. "I'll call you tonight."

She gave LJ a big hug and kiss before they left.

Daneisha decided to stop by Myra's house first. She wanted to finish the conversation they had at the club. Not wanting to make a wasted trip, she called first. The phone was disconnected.

Daneisha stared at her phone to make sure she called the right cell phone number. Then she called the house number. It was also disconnected. Pressing harder on the gas pedal, Daneisha sped the entire way, hoping she wouldn't get stopped by the police. She pulled up in the driveway, and eyed the "For Sale" sign in the yard. The house was completely empty.

Daneisha searched up and down the street for anyone outside on their lawn. There was no one in sight. She opened her car door and turned on the ignition. Just as she was about to drive away, she saw the next-door neighbor leaving her house to check her mailbox. The old lady with pink rollers in her hair and wearing a house coat walked with a limp.

Daneisha pulled up alongside her. "Hello, I'm friends with Myra."

She stared at Daneisha with a judgmental eye and frowned. "Yes, I've seen you a few times."

"Well, do you know when they moved out?"

"I really can't say the exact day." She pointed her wrinkled fingers in the direction of the house. "They've been gone for at least a week now."

Daneisha hugged the steering wheel. "Okay. Thank you." She drove away. In her rearview mirror, she caught a glimpse of the old woman limping back toward the house.

Daneisha was beginning to feel like an investigator. This was not the way she planned to spend her day. After her surgery, she was feeling so much better. She longed for the days of endless shopping sprees. She couldn't wait for all this to blow over so her life could return back to normal.

Daneisha called Kay from her cell phone.

"What's up, Princess?" Kay greeted.

"Where the hell have you been?" Daneisha snapped.

"Excuse me?"

"You're excused, bitch. You know I was calling your ass."

"Well, I was—"

"Fucking Rowan. I already know. Anyway, listen to this. Some crazy shit happened to me today. You're not going to believe it."

"For real?" Kay's voice went up an octave.

"Yes. Is Rowan there with you now?"

Kay hesitated for a moment. "Uh-huh."

"Can you get away for a minute?"

"Of course. Hold on."

Daneisha told Kay about Dirty Red coming to her house and the strange phone call a few minutes later. Then she told her about the conversation she had with Myra last night, and how the house was completely empty when she went there.

"So she hasn't even been living there? It seems very strange," Kay whispered. "Where are you?"

"I'm headed over to the club."

"Why are you going over there?" Kay asked, still trying to keep her voice down.

"Because I want to know what's going on."

"Why do you have to know every damn thang? Shit. You're going to mess around and get your head blown up. Curiosity killed the cat, you know."

"I'm just going to talk to the man. That's all."

"Yeah, right. I think you're trying to get your man back."

"Why does everybody keep saying that?"

"If everybody is saying it, it must be true."

"You know what? I'm not about to defend my actions to you or nobody else for that matter. Just answer your damn phone the next time I call you, heifer."

"Why I gotta be your heifer today?" Kay responded.

"I'm sorry about that. You know how I get sometimes when I'm stressed. Anyway, I'm almost there."

"Be careful. Don't hesitate to call if you need me."

"If I don't call you back in twenty minutes, call the cops."

"You're scaring me. Daneisha, don't go there. Just come over here instead. I'll help you figure this thing out."

"I'm already in the parking lot." Daneisha parked next to Lamium's Chrysler 300. "Twenty minutes. Okay?"

"All right."

Daneisha knocked on the door, where she'd entered less than twelve hours before. She waited patiently, but no one came. Just as she was turning around, the door slowly creaked open. A face appeared. It was Greg.

"What are you doing here?" he asked, his eyes scanning the parking lot.

"I need to talk to Lamium."

"What about?"

"Is he here or not?"

Greg hesitated for a moment. He opened the door wider and stepped aside. "Come on."

Daneisha entered the dark room.

"He's in the back."

She followed Greg to the back of the club. There were a few men inside sitting at the table playing cards. She recognized them from last night, only they were casually dressed this time.

Daneisha caught a glimpse of a man who looked like Dirty Red walking down the hall to the restrooms. She couldn't believe he had the nerve to be up there and wearing the same blue jacket from that morning when he was trying to kick her door in.

Daneisha hoped he wouldn't turn around and see her. When they got to Lamium's office Greg knocked twice, then waited.

"What are you doing? This ain't no damn club house." Daneisha shook her head back and forth. "Would you open the door?"

Greg held up his hand like he was about to slap her. "Would you just be quiet?"

"Come in!" Lamium shouted.

Greg opened the door.

"Hey, Boss. Got someone here to see you."

"Who the fuck is it?" Lamium asked.

"It's me. That's who the fuck it is." Without waiting for permission, Daneisha pushed past Greg to see Lamium sitting at his desk. The room smelled of marijuana. He was wearing the same clothes from last night, only the jacket was on the back of the chair. His face was unshaven.

Daneisha stood at the edge of the desk and leaned on one arm. "You look a mess. Have you been sleeping here?"

"I did last night. What are you doing here? Where's LJ?"

"He's with Mama. I'm here, because your boy Dirty Red came to my apartment this morning. He damn near broke the door down."

Lamium's eyebrows raised. "What?"

"Yes. Don't worry, I handled myself. Then I got a call a few minutes later. It sounded just like Dirty Red. He was telling me to stay away from you. That there was a hit on you."

Lamium got up from his chair. "Dirty Red was at your apartment this morning?" He stood inches from her face. "What? You fucking that nigga?"

Daneisha scrunched up her face. "No, I ain't fucking him."

"Then why would he do some shit like that?" Lamium raised his hand. "Daneisha, I know that muthafucka ain't do that shit. Tell the truth."

"I am." Daneisha cocked her head to the side. "What? You don't believe me?"

"No. I think you just trying to get me to feel sorry for your ass."

Daneisha took two steps back. "Look, I don't want you back. You've moved on. And so have I."

"With Evan, right?"

Evan?

Daneisha remembered she briefly spoke to him in the parking lot last night. She was starting to feel more paranoid than ever.

"Let's get back to the issue at hand. All you need to do is talk to your boy. Make sure he stays the hell away from me."

"All right." Lamium looked over in Greg's direction. "Tell Dirty Red to get in here."

"No problem." Greg left the room.

"Why are you calling him in here? I don't want to see him."

"What's wrong?" Lamium went back to his chair and sat down. "Are you ready to change your story?"

"Hell no. I just don't want to see him. His brother, Tony Red, was the one that shot my aunt all them years ago."

"Oh, this just gets better every second." Lamium laughed. "Just because the man uses Red at the end of his name doesn't mean he's related to no Tony Red."

"See, you think this is so funny, don't you? And you supposed to be so damned smart about the people you have working for you. That's why you in this shit right now."

"All I'm saying is . . . that man ain't related to no damn Tony Red." Lamium licked his full lips, like he was LL Cool J. "But, for real, you know I wouldn't do that to you."

Daneisha quivered for a second, remembering how soft his lips felt pressed to hers. She wanted to suck them dry. Quickly, she tried her best to dismiss the thought.

"What's wrong? Jillian not taking care of her man?"

Lamium waved his hand to dismiss her. "Just shut the fuck up."

"No, I will not. I'm not your woman anymore. You don't tell me what to do." Daneisha leaned on his desk and got close to his face. "I asked him flat out if he was related to Tony Red, and he told me that was his brother."

"You serious?"

"Yes. Why would I play about some shit like that!"

Another knock on the door. Greg entered. Then Dirty Red came in.

"What's up, Boss Man?" Dirty Red asked. His eyes grew wide when he saw Daneisha.

Lamium turned from side to side in his leather chair. "Where you was at this morning?"

Dirty Red gestured with his hands. "Just let me explain."

Daneisha crossed her arms.

"She tells me you showed up at her apartment. Is that shit true?"

Dirty Red stood with his legs spread wide, rocking from side to side. "No . . . see . . . it's not like that—"

"What? You got some kind of beef with my baby mama, because of your brother?"

"What does my brother have to do with this?"

Lamium leaned on the arm of his chair. He licked his lips again. "Oh, so you trying to play dumb. Just answer this question right here. Is Tony Red your brother?"

Dirty Red tried to force a smile. "Yes, everybody knows Tony is my brother."

"Well, if Tony Red is or was your brother, then you can't work for me no more. Sorry about that." Lamium waved his hand to dismiss him.

"What!" Dirty Red's eyes enlarged as big as the moon. "Come on, Boss Man."

"That's just the way it is."

"No disrespect, but, Boss Man, how you gon' do that to me? I got a family to take care of."

"I'll make sure I break you off some, you know, as a severance." Lamium scratched his chin. "With the way things are right now, I can't have you working for me when your background is questionable."

Dirty Red shook his head and marched toward Lamium. "This shit ain't right. One minute—"

Dirty Red stopped talking, once he realized Lamium had a gun pointed straight at him.

"Now, I know I'm not crazy. Was you about to disrespect me, right here in my office? In front of my baby's mother?" Lamium wiped his nose. "No, I know I must be losing my muthafucking mind up in here! See, I wasn't going to even kick your ass for showing up at my place of residence this morning, scaring the hell out of my wife and son."

Daneisha's jaw dropped.

Did he just call me his wife?

Dirty Red stepped back.

Lamium came from behind his desk and pointed the gun at Dirty Red's head. "See, for you, it's your lucky day. It's Sunday. And I don't make it a habit to kill muthafuckas on Sunday."

"I'm sorry, Boss Man." Sweat rolled down Dirty Red's face as he pleaded for his life.

"Wait a minute," Daneisha said. "Lamium, just let the man go. He said he was sorry."

Lamium cut his eyes in her direction, with a face Daneisha was all too familiar with. It was the same demonizing stare he gave her a few seconds before she was forced to cut him.

"I done told your ass before, Daneisha, stay the fuck out of my business."

"Okay. I'm out of it." Daneisha went toward the door. She wanted out of the office as quickly as possible.

"As far as Dirty Red is concerned . . . you won't have no more problems with him. Have a nice day." Lamium forced an evil grin.

Daneisha held her hands to her mouth as she left. Staring at the floor, her footsteps were heavy as she walked through the parking lot to her car. As she opened the door, she heard the sound of two gun shots. She screamed out of fear that she'd been shot in the back.

She felt all over her body, but realized she hadn't been shot. Suddenly, she thought about Dirty Red.

Oh, my God.

Not only was Lamium out of control, but she was the cause of an innocent man being killed. Whatever was going on with Lamium, it was obvious that he was taking desperate measures to protect himself.

The back door opened, and Greg appeared. He ran over to Daneisha's car. Even though she was frightened, she tried her best to seem calm. She let down the window.

"Hey, Lamium wants you to stay somewhere else for a few days. Can you do that?" Greg used a napkin to wipe blood from his forehead.

Daneisha watched in horror. "Sure . . . okay . . . I'll be at Mama's."

"All right. I'll let him know," he said as he walked away from the car.

"Greg!" she called out.

He turned around. "Yeah."

"Should I be concerned about anything? You know Lamium never tells me anything."

Greg shoved the bloody napkin inside his coat pocket. "I don't know what to tell you."

"You can tell me whether or not Angel has the flu. Then, I'll know how concerned I should be."

"No."

"I shouldn't be concerned?"

"No, my wife doesn't have the flu."

Daneisha took a deep breath. "Thank you."

Daneisha sped away from Club Sensations and raced like lightning to her mother's house. More frustrated than ever, she tried her best to put today's events together. Less than a month ago, her life was fabulous and she was the envy of many. Now, it seemed more like a nightmare than real life.

Daneisha realized, after driving over to see the one individual responsible for all of her problems, she still had no clarity. Lamium had a way of never letting her in, and she hated him for that. Daneisha and LJ could be in serious danger, and she would never know it. She resolved she would do whatever it took to keep her son safe.

Several scenarios went through her mind, to the point where she couldn't think clearly. Her emotions were all over the place. Stopped at the traffic light, Daneisha fished around in her purse for a bottle of painkillers as a migraine was surfacing. She hesitated for a moment, remembering her addiction to pain pills. Pushing the negative talk aside in her head, Daneisha swallowed four Vicodin. Then she drank from a hot water bottle that had been in her car for at least a few days. She washed down four more pills, knowing in less than an hour she would feel some relief.

Chapter Eight

A week had passed, and Daneisha was more confused than ever. She couldn't sleep. All she kept picturing was Dirty Red being shot right there in Lamium's office. The sight of him pleading for his life haunted her.

Sick of staying at her mother's house, it was like she was back in school again. With Dante back in his old room, Daneisha and LJ were hemmed up sharing the same bed. Before her mother left for work each morning, she left a list of things to do around the house. At first, Daneisha laughed when she saw the paper stuck on the refrigerator with a magnet. Meanwhile, Dante didn't bother to lift a finger. When LeQuisha came home and told Daneisha and Dante to leave her house, they knew she wasn't playing. The next day, the house was spotless.

With very little money and her website business on hold, Daneisha had no choice but to get rid of Valerie once and for all. At first, Valerie thought Daneisha was having another temper tantrum, but she finally convinced her it was no joke.

Even though Valerie took excellent care of Daneisha

while she recovered from her surgery, she despised the fact that LJ really thought of Valerie as his mother. Knowing his father wasn't going to be around, Daneisha figured LJ would latch onto Valerie. And she wasn't having that. Being a single mother was going to be hard. Daneisha knew she had a fight on her hands.

Secretly, Daneisha was hoping Lamium would come back to her and they would be a family again. She resolved in her mind that if it happened, she would insist on marriage. For some reason, Daneisha was beginning to realize that may not happen. In her heart, she knew it was time for her to grow up. Leaving Lamium behind in her past felt so very necessary.

Daneisha thought of how her mother never seemed to struggle when it came down to working two or three jobs, all while raising three children. Add in college classes to become a nurse, LeQuisha hardly ever had a day off. Whether or not Daneisha had the strength to endure motherhood on her own was another question; only time would reveal the answer.

With all things considered, Daneisha was ready to do what was needed to get LJ on the straight and narrow path.

LJ was doing so much better in school, and their relationship was showing some positive signs. Daneisha wasn't sure if it was safe to return to her apartment or send LJ back to school. For the past week, Daneisha drove to St. Augustine for them to have special outings at the park and just doing simple things like having ice cream.

She even took LJ to his play group, and it wasn't as bad as she expected. Fortunately, Angel didn't bother to show up. It was funny to hear the other moms comment on how snotty Angel acted, bragging incessantly about her daughter, Halle.

One morning, Daneisha treated LJ to breakfast at

IHOP. She was surprised that it didn't take much to make LJ happy. It was frustrating that Lamium wasn't answering his cell phone, which really made her question his devotion as a father to LJ. Daneisha wasn't sure if they were still in any sort of danger at all.

Even though it was close to noon, Daneisha and LJ enjoyed pancakes, sausage, and scrambled eggs that her mother cooked, before leaving for work. She sent LJ to get dressed while she finished washing the dishes.

The doorbell rang.

Daneisha was hoping it was Lamium there to beg for his family back.

She tried her best to mask her disappointment when she saw it was her best friend instead. Kay, sporting big sunglasses on her face, looked very stylish, like a black Paris Hilton. Daneisha cringed at the thought that Kay was trying so hard to be more like her, playing up her part of Rowan's girlfriend.

Daneisha leaned on the door, resting her other hand on her hip. "What a surprise!"

Kay kissed her cheek then walked inside. "I know it is. I tried to call, but your number is disconnected. And here's your jacket you left in my truck."

"Oh, thanks, girl." Daneisha put the denim jacket on the leather couch. "You know, I was wondering why I wasn't getting any calls. I forgot Mama changed all my numbers. I can't believe I can be so stupid."

"It's understandable, considering what's going on." Kay laid her purse on the end table. "I wanted to check on you. And I wanted to see my godson. Where's LJ?"

"He's in the room, putting on some clothes. I wanted to take him to the park or something. He hasn't been in school all week. And he's driving me crazy."

"You're taking LJ to the park?" Kay snickered. "In this cold weather?"

"Actually, we've been going every day." Daneisha poked out her chest proudly. "And it's not that cold once you start running around."

"Oh really?" Kay asked. "Okay, you're scaring me."

"Yes. And we've been getting along very well. Thank you very much."

"A minute ago, you said he was driving you crazy."

"Yeah, so what's your point? He's still LJ."

"Oh, okay. I get it. He's driving you crazy, but you're finding a way to have some fun with him in between the temper tantrums."

"Exactly."

"And then look at you." Kay took a step back to look Daneisha over. "You're not wearing any make-up, with your hair pulled back in a ponytail, and don't get me started on the clothes."

"What? You don't like my velvet pantsuit?" Daneisha twirled around in a circle.

"It's a leisure suit. One you obviously stole out of my closet."

Daneisha snickered. "I probably did. You know I wouldn't be caught dead wearing this get-up."

"Yeah, so where is my best friend?"

"It's the new me. Do you like it?"

"I won't go that far. You're supposed to be helping me out, remember? Not changing into me."

Daneisha tossed up her hand. "I could never get that bad. I ain't with no cotton blends or polyester."

Kay scowled. "Thanks for all the insults. And here I came to see about you. What was I thinking?"

"I'm sorry." Daneisha frowned. "This was a crazy week for me. And it actually felt good not to go through all the trouble to be all glammed up."

"Well, you go ahead, Miss Thang," Kay said. "And you still look good."

"Don't I?" Daneisha fanned herself. "I can rock the hell out of any outfit."

"You're a trip." Kay headed down the hallway. "Let me go see about my little man."

"You do that. Make sure he's dressed right and brushed his teeth."

Daneisha cleaned up the rest of the kitchen, while Kay was visiting with LJ. She went inside Dante's room, which had papers and clothes scattered all over the place. The only sign Dante was in the bed was his long dreadlocks draped across the pillow.

"You need to get your lazy ass out of the bed and get this work done before Mama gets home."

"Bitch, please!"

Daneisha put her hands on her hips. "I just know you didn't call me a bitch!"

Dante's head peered from his pillow. His beard and mustache was in need of a serious trimming. "Oops, my bad. I was talking in my sleep."

Daneisha jumped on top of his thin frame and punched him on his bare back. "No, you didn't."

"Stop it!" Dante turned over and tried to shield himself from another blow.

Daneisha hit him again, this time the jab landed in his stomach. "I'm not playing with you. You need to get up and help me clean up this house."

"Okay, okay. I'm getting up." Dante threw a pillow at Daneisha, hitting her in the head. "That's what you get!" He giggled.

Daneisha balled up her fist. "All right. Don't make me beat your porn-star ass now."

Dante cleared his throat. "It's independent film director."

"Excuse me. I stand corrected. I thought it was in bad need of a haircut and mouthwash."

"Aha! Very funny!" Dante held up his long index finger. "America, she's got jokes."

"Just get your behind up. You know Mama ain't playing with you about this house."

"Okay. I'll be there in a second or two."

Daneisha left his room, and sat on the couch in the family room. With her head buried in her hands, she silently cried to herself.

Oh my God. This is not my life! I'm so tired of this. Please help me.

Daneisha jumped when she felt a hand on her shoulder. Kay sat down beside her.

"I can't take this anymore."

"It's going to be all right." Kay opened her arms wide. Daneisha hugged her back.

"No, it's not. I've been trying to keep up a big front." Daneisha lifted her head up. "I don't have the strength to do this."

"You're very strong. Stronger than you even know. There is a lot of your mother in you."

"No, she's so much tougher than me." Daneisha leaned back. "She went through so much. I can't compete. I'm a terrible mother, daughter, and sister. I'm a bad friend. I don't even know why you're here."

"You need to stop talking about yourself that way."

"I'm all messed up. That's why Lamium doesn't want me anymore."

"Lamium is a jerk. Always has been, and you know it." Kay rubbed Daneisha's shoulder.

"He may be a jerk, but he sure could work it." Daneisha slouched down lower in the couch and crossed her legs. "He made a sista wanna holla."

Kay's eyes lingered for a moment. "I'm going to let that one go."

"Sorry." Daneisha puckered her lips. "I didn't mean to bring back any old memories."

"It's fine." Kay responded with a slight smile. "I have Rowan, so I don't care anymore. As for you, Princess, I need to get you out of this house."

"I don't know where I can go around here." Daneisha sighed with frustration. "I don't know if it's safe."

"I guess you haven't heard."

"What? Did something happen to Lamium?"

"Girl, that stuff with Lamium has blown over." Kay waved her hand in the air.

Daneisha sat up. "It has?"

"Yes, that's why I've been trying to call you."

"What happened?" Daneisha asked as she wiped her face. She used her shirt to blow her nose.

"Okay, that's nasty." Kay went in the bathroom and came back with tissue. "Here you go."

"Thank you." Daneisha blew her nose in the tissue.

"Anyway, Rowan said some New Orleans gang was trying to move in on Lamium's territory."

"Why would they try to do that?"

"They've been misplaced since Hurricane Katrina. With all the media attention, ain't nobody trying to move drugs through no New Orleans. Well, you know we felt sorry for the displaced victims and laid out the welcome mat for them. Some of the gangs are trying to set up shop here. Only way in is to take over someone else's territory. And Lamium was the target."

"Humph. I see. So, is that who Dirty Red was working for?"

"Now, that I don't know. The leader of the gang's name is G-Force. His real name is Gravity."

"What the fuck kind of name is that?"

Kay laughed. "I know. Well, that's his name."

"Is he still coming after Lamium?"

"No, they struck a deal. He's now working for Lamium. Greg took Jericho's place and left G-Force his old job."

"But what was the deal with Jericho and Myra all of a sudden moving like that?"

"Nothing. It was just like Myra said. She got the recording contract, and Lamium let Jericho go with no problems."

Daneisha leaned back on the leather couch. "You don't know how relieved I am to hear this. I was so scared. I was there when Lamium killed Dirty Red."

"What?"

"Yeah, and I've been messed up ever since. I feel kind of responsible."

"Well, it's not like you told Lamium to shoot the man."

"I know. But I made such a big deal about him being Tony Red's brother. Lamium was half-coked out his mind, and he just went off. It's like he's changed."

"Rowan noticed the same thing. Don't say anything, but I think Rowan wants out."

"Did he say that?"

"No, but I can tell."

"I don't blame him." Daneisha ran her hands through her ponytail. "I'm so glad this is over. I need to call Sebrina and get my weave done."

Kay turned up her nose. "Yes, and make it an emergency appointment."

Daneisha popped her best friend's arm. "Will you shut up? Don't get me started on you."

Kay stood up and jiggled her hips. "I'm drinking milk and working out." The tight jeans she was wearing showed that she'd lost some weight. Lavender sheepskin boots matched her Rocawear hooded jacket perfectly.

"Oh, I'm so jealous." Daneisha sucked her teeth. "Not!"

Daneisha and Kay took LJ to the Metro Park downtown.

Kay bored her to tears talking incessantly about Rowan. Daneisha only pretended to be interested, while her thoughts remained on Lamium. She knew her man, and with the way he was acting, there was no way it was over that quick. Plus, she remembered the conversation with Myra. She was sure there was more to the story than what Kay was telling her.

The next morning, Daneisha got up early to finish the laundry. She was planning to move back to her apartment, but didn't want to take a pile of dirty clothes with her. Daneisha no longer had Valerie to take care of the household duties. It would take some time to make the adjustment, but she was certain she could handle it.

Her mother was standing by the stove in a purple silk robe cooking breakfast. It was her day off. She worked a four days on, four days off schedule at the hospital.

The laundry room was adjacent, and Daneisha's stomach growled at the smell of sizzling bacon on the George Foreman grill.

"Well, I must say I enjoyed having you around. And my grandson is really behaving himself," LeQuisha said. She placed the cooked bacon on a paper towel, which lay on top of a plate.

Daneisha smiled. She liked the fact that they were getting along. The last time she lived in that house, she couldn't stand her mother. "I'm going to miss your cooking most of all."

"I'm going to miss coming home to a clean house."

"Ooohh." Daneisha pointed. "Then you need to kick Dante out."

"I can't do that to my baby."

"See, and you say I spoil LJ."

"Now, I know you're not trying to compare Dante to LJ. Because Dante got his butt tore up a few times."

"Yeah, right."

Mike came in, dressed in tan slacks, a blue shirt, and matching striped tie. "What are you so worked up about early in the morning?" he asked with his deep voice.

Daneisha tossed another pair of jeans in the washer. Sometimes, she wondered how Mike and her mother ended up together. Mike was always so prim and proper. Daneisha knew she was the one that convinced her mother to even consider going out on a date with Mike in the first place. Back then, LeQuisha was hurt over the loss of her boyfriend Tate leaving her for a girl he got pregnant.

For months, Daneisha watched her mother work at the hospital all day, go to school at night, and still manage to take care of three children. She got used to seeing that exhausted look on her mother's face—the one where her eyes held permanent bags underneath. When LeQuisha and Mike started dating, things took off very quickly. And in less than a year, they were married.

Standing six inches taller, Mike lowered his head to greet his wife with a kiss.

"Oh, we're just talking about Dante, sweetie."

Mike rubbed LeQuisha's back. "What about?"

"Mama says Dante used to get whoopings," Daneisha responded as she emptied the pockets of her denim jeans. "And I said I don't remember Dante getting any. He always wriggled his way out of getting one."

"Ah, I see." Mike poured coffee in his mug. "So, you don't concur?"

Daneisha shook her head. "That is right."

"I'm with Daneisha on this one."

LeQuisha put her hands on her hips. "Mike, now you know I have beat his behind when he acted up."

Mike poured cream in his mug. Then he took a sip. "You've threatened, but I don't remember it happening. You know I don't agree with spankings."

LeQuisha placed a plate in front of her husband.

"It's not spankings, it's a beating," Daneisha corrected.

Dante entered the kitchen. "What's going on in here? It sounds like a party." He picked up a piece of bacon and took a bite.

"Did we disturb you while you were sleeping, Prince Dante?" Daneisha asked. "Since we all know you just came home two hours ago."

Dante put his hand by his face and shot Daneisha his bird finger. "You're foul."

"Whatever!" Daneisha stuck out her tongue.

"Oh, you're so mature, Daneisha," Dante responded. He fixed a plate of eggs, bacon, and grits.

LeQuisha raised her hand. "I know you didn't walk in this house at no five in the morning."

"Yes, he did," Daneisha chimed in.

"Would you shut up, Daneisha, and see about your own nappy-head son in the room slobbering down the pillows?"

Dante sucked his teeth. He caught a glimpse of his mother giving him the staredown. "Mama, you know I wouldn't do that."

"Yes, he did it," Daneisha said.

LeQuisha crossed her arms. "All I have to say is, don't let me catch you."

"Anyway, let's move on and clear this argument up once and for all." Daneisha cleared her throat. "Dante, how many beatings have you had in your entire life?"

Dante made a "0" with his fingers. "Zero."

Mike and Daneisha laughed out loud.

LeQuisha's jaw dropped. "Why are you telling that lie? I know I spanked your behind at least once."

"No, you didn't." Dante's smile revealed his dimples. "You always would say you were going to do it, but you never did."

"Well, that's where I went wrong. Mike, take off your belt."

Without hesitation, Mike removed his leather belt from his slacks.

"No, the man of the house should do the spanking," Daneisha ordered.

Mike seemed bewildered by her comment. "Now, we were on the same side, until you said that." He stuck out his hand. "Give me my belt back. I don't have time for this foolishness."

"No, I gotta do this, for my own sake." LeQuisha walked toward Dante with the belt held up in the air.

When Dante realized his mother was serious, he grabbed his plate and ran toward the living room. LeQuisha sprinted like a track star after him.

"They're a trip." Daneisha chuckled.

"Yes. Your mother is funny." Mike placed his empty dishes in the sink. "Well, I'm off to work, as soon as I find another belt for my pants."

"Okay." Daneisha smiled. "Me and LJ are going home today. Thanks for letting us stay at the house."

"You don't have to thank me." Mike raised his thick eyebrows. "Daneisha, this is just as much your home as it is ours. And don't you forget it."

Thinking back to their history, Daneisha felt touched by his comment. "I appreciate that."

Mike came closer, and Daneisha grew nervous. He stretched out his arms to embrace her like a father would his own daughter. Slowly, she hugged him back.

"I love you, Daneisha."

"I love you, too."

Mike placed a wad of money in her hand. "Have an awesome day in the name of Jesus."

"You too."

When Mike left the kitchen, Daneisha wiped a tear

from her eye. She counted out two hundred dollars. She figured Mike was waiting for the right time to give her the money, because he was never the type to carry cash. There were many times Daneisha was embarrassed that Mike had to use his check card for purchases that totaled less than five dollars.

Even though the circumstances were all wrong, Daneisha thanked God for the opportunity to spend time with her family. It turned out to be healing for Daneisha's relationship with her mother, Mike, and LJ. It was amazing how God gave her exactly what she needed at the right time.

Daneisha finished her prayer and tossed her denim jacket in the washing machine. She forgot to empty out the top pockets. Fishing it out of the soapy water, she pulled out a receipt and card. It was Evan's business card from that night at the club.

Daneisha decided to call him. After four rings, his line went to voice mail. Daneisha left him a short message.

LJ walked in rubbing his eyes. "Are you calling Daddy?"

Daneisha rested her cell phone on the counter. "No. But I will. Do you miss him?"

LJ nodded. "A little bit."

Daneisha frowned. LJ used to be so crazy about his dad. He worshipped the ground he walked on.

"Are you still mad at your daddy?"

"Yeah. I didn't like it when he hurt you."

"Oh, baby. Your daddy was very sick then. He didn't mean to do it. I've forgiven him, and I think you should too."

LJ shrugged. "But he doesn't live with us anymore."

"That's true. Lamium will always be your father, whether we live together or not, and I know he misses you so much."

LJ's eyes grew wide. "He does?"

"Of course."

Daneisha scooped him up and placed him in a chair at

the table. "After you finish your breakfast, I'll let you call Daddy. Deal?" She held out her hand.

LJ smacked her hand as hard as he could. "Deal."

While Daneisha sat down and ate breakfast with her son, they watched cartoons. "You know, when I was your age, we didn't have so many cartoon channels."

LJ leaned forward. "Really?"

"Yes, cartoons only came on for a few hours a day. And that was it."

"If I couldn't watch cartoons all day, I would be sad."

Daneisha laughed. "You're too cute."

Her cell phone rang. It was Evan. She took a deep breath before she answered.

"Hello." Her attempt to sound sexy didn't work. She actually sounded hoarse like T-Boz from TLC.

"Daneisha, it's Evan. Sorry I missed your call. I was in a meeting."

"It's all right."

"I have a bone to pick with you."

"With me?"

"Yes, I don't like getting the runaround."

"I don't know what you're talking about. I called you, didn't I?"

"Imagine my surprise to hear your voice after you gave me a fake number."

"What?"

"For giving me the wrong number, I called the number you gave me and it was disconnected."

Daneisha covered her mouth as she laughed. "Oh no."

"It's not funny. You did a brother wrong."

"No, I'm not laughing at you. My mother had my number changed."

"Daneisha, I know you can come up with a better story than that."

"It's the truth. I don't have a reason to lie."

LJ interrupted. "Is that Daddy?"

"Can you hold on for a second?" Daneisha pressed the mute button. "No, this isn't him. Finish your eggs, and we'll call him when you get dressed."

"Okay." LJ rammed a mouthful of eggs in his small mouth.

Daneisha used a napkin to wipe grease from his pink lips then released the mute on her cell.

"I'm back."

"You're a single woman now."

"Yes, but even if I wasn't, I wouldn't do that to you. Honestly." Daneisha left the table and placed her plate in the sink.

"Well, there's only way you can make it up to me."

"How's that?" Daneisha leaned up against the counter.

"Meet me tonight. I'm attending a party for a client of mine. And I need a date."

"I don't know. I need to check on that. Nope. Can't do it."

LJ got up from his seat and walked away from the table. Daneisha snapped her fingers at him and pointed at his empty plate. LJ smiled as he went back to get it. He placed it in the sink and left the kitchen.

"Oh, what's more important than hooking up with an old friend?"

"Well, I would have to . . . let's see . . . get my hair and nails done, find something to wear, and I just don't have the funds to do all that."

"Oh, I see. You haven't changed one bit."

Daneisha filled the sink with dishwater. "Not when it comes to my money. No, I haven't."

"That's what I like about you."

"Is that all you like about me?" Daneisha teased.

"There are things that I like, and things that I love. But we won't get into that right now."

"Okay." Daneisha rested the phone on her shoulder as she washed the dishes in the sink.

"I'll reimburse you for all your expenses when I pick you up. What's your address?"

"You really want me to go that bad? I mean, there's always tomorrow, you know."

"No, I want to spend some time with you tonight. We need to catch up. No. Scratch that shit, I want to see you today. Is Sebrina still doing your hair?"

"Yes. I can't believe you remember."

"There are very few details I forget."

"I see that."

"Why don't you call up your girl, and find out if she can fit you in? Then I'll make a quick stop in between meetings to check in on you. And, of course, take care of the bill."

"Okay. I can do that."

Daneisha talked with Evan for a few more minutes. Then she called up Sebrina and scheduled an appointment. It was just her luck that she had a cancellation.

Daneisha went in Dante's room, where he and LJ were playing the *Matrix* on PlayStation 3. She hung in the background for a few minutes, observing all the special effects.

LJ bit down hard on his lip. "Take that." He fired shots from a double-barreled shotgun.

"This is just like the movie," Daneisha commented.

"Uh-huh, that's why I'm about to pull my acrobatics on ya li'l boy." Daneisha watched intently while Neo bent completely backward to avoid the bullets.

Daneisha scrunched up her nose. "This game is violent."

"Just like the movie," Dante responded.

Daneisha shook her head. "LJ, I don't know if I want you playing this game. I think you're too young for this."

"Mommy, I like this game," LJ whined.

"He's playing it with his uncle," Dante defended and waved his hand. "Now watch this." He gripped the controller harder as Neo ran alongside a wall. "Stop your worrying."

Daneisha stretched her arms and yawned. "I don't want you playing this game by yourself, LJ. Oh, and I'm going out tonight. I'm going to see if Grandma can watch you."

"Where are you going, Mommy?" LJ asked.

"Out with a friend. His name is Evan."

"Mama is going to Bible study tonight," Dante replied.

Daneisha popped herself on the forehead. "Oh, I forgot."

"Dante, you want to earn some extra cash?"

"No, I have plans."

Daneisha frowned. "Hanging out with those computer geeks hardly qualifies as a plan."

"Hey, quit insulting my friends."

"Who is Evan?" LJ inquired. He stared up at her with his big brown eyes.

"He's someone I used to know a long time ago."

LJ poked out his lips. "Oh."

Daneisha rubbed LJ's curly hair. "Did you want to ask me anything else?"

"I thought I was going to call Daddy."

"You can, but . . ." Daneisha pulled his head back and stared him directly in the eyes. "I don't want you saying anything about Evan, okay?"

LJ seemed perplexed for a four-year-old. "Is Daddy going to be mad?"

"No, but it's none of his business what I do anymore. Do you understand?"

LJ nodded. "I won't say anything."

"Good boy. I'll be right back." Daneisha left the room to get her cell phone.

Lamium was cordial, trying to figure out where she was

staying. She told him she was still at her mother's house. Lamium was anxious to see LJ, so she agreed to let him stop by the house later. Her mother agreed to take LJ with her to Bible study. Daneisha knew her mother was happy she was going on a date with someone other than Lamium. It seemed like everything was working out perfectly.

Daneisha was sitting under the dryer at the hair salon when Evan showed up. The women were taking notice of her soon-to-be man, because he was looking ever so handsome in his three-button-down window pane suit. He only stayed long enough to say hello and flash his gorgeous smile. Daneisha watched him hand Sebrina his credit card.

Evan sat in the empty chair next to her, and Daneisha lifted the dryer from her head.

She ran her hands along his arm. "Nice suit."

"Thank you. It's Sean John."

"I know."

Evan chewed on his toothpick. "A woman who knows her labels. I'm impressed."

"Not all the labels, just the important ones."

"I see."

"Well, I wanted to give you this." Evan slid his credit card in her hand.

Daneisha stared at it in disbelief. "This card has my name on it."

"Well, I took the liberty of adding your name to my account."

Daneisha raised her arched eyebrows. "You can't get no credit card that fast."

"When I saw you at Club Sensations that night, I couldn't think of anything else. I knew I wanted to take care of you for the rest of my life. I know it was presumptuous of me, but I actually ordered it the very next day." Evan's eyes remained fixed on her.

Daneisha's smile widened. "Evan, I don't know if should slap you or hug you."

"I'll take that hug," he said and rose from the chair.

Daneisha felt somewhat embarrassed from the attention of others in the shop. She could sense they thought a proposal was about to take place.

When she stood up, she adjusted her blouse. She closed her eyes as she hugged him back, completely entranced by the sweetness of his cologne.

He smells so good.

Daneisha opened her eyes slowly, wanting to etch it in her memory forever.

"Well, I hate to run, but I have to meet a client in less than an hour." Evan kissed her on the cheek. "Bye, beautiful."

Daneisha grinned. "Bye."

"Call me with your address, so I can pick you up around seven."

"I will do that."

Daneisha waved as he turned around once more.

Evan winked.

Daneisha almost melted in the chair.

"Girl, is that your man?" one girl asked with a head full of pink and yellow rollers.

"I guess he is. Nothing's official though," Daneisha responded.

"You better claim that man!" an older lady shouted.

"I know," Shirley Ann added. She was one of the newer stylists at the salon. "Because he is so fine. Now, I love me a clean brother."

Daneisha laughed and went back to flipping through an old *Vogue* magazine she'd picked up from the front table.

Those women had no clue Daneisha was still fienin' for her baby daddy. She was nowhere near over the pain of her breakup with Lamium. It would take time, but she needed to move on. She knew they were right. Good men didn't come along very often.

She thought about the credit card and decided to call Kay and ask her opinion.

"What's up, Princess?"

"Girl, you're not going to believe what Evan just put in my hand today."

"I know I'm going to regret it, but what?"

"A credit card, with my name on it." Daneisha suppressed a grin. "I couldn't believe it."

"See, that's why I can't stand you."

"You know I'm getting tired of you hating on me."

"I'm not hating. Well, maybe just a teeny, tiny bit."

"I knew it. I promise I'll take you shopping next time we get together."

"How much is the limit?"

"He didn't say."

"Oh, hell no! I wouldn't trust that shit. That card is probably stolen."

Daneisha shook her head. "I don't think so. He's a big-time business man. Evan wouldn't do that."

"Well, if I was you, I would call the number on the back. Just to make sure it's on the up and up."

"See, that's why I'm glad I called you. I'm going to do that."

"Good."

"Where is he taking you tonight?" Kay asked.

"I don't know. I have to call and give him Mama's address."

"Wait, Evan is going to pick you up from your mom's house?"

"Yeah."

"I thought Lamium was coming by to get LJ."

"Oh shit! I don't want Lamium and Evan showing up at my mother's house at the same time. I'm so glad you picked up on that. Kay, what would I do without you?"

"Hopefully, you'll never have to find out."

"All right. Let me go. I'll call you later."

Sebrina waved Daneisha to come back to the chair. "I'm ready for you."

"Hold on. I need to make this call first. Just take the next person."

Sebrina nodded. "Come on, Ms. Jacobs."

Daneisha dialed Lamium's number. He answered on the first ring.

"I can't believe you answered the phone two times in one day."

"I do that every now and then. I'm in the middle of something, so make it quick."

"Where are you?"

"What you need to know that for?"

Daneisha frowned. "I was going to drop LJ off where you was at."

"Can you bring him by the club?"

"Can you say *hell-to-the-no*?"

Lamium laughed. "What's wrong with my club?"

"Don't try me, Lamium. You know I don't want my son within a hundred feet of that place."

"I understand."

"So, I don't want you coming round to my ol' lady's house. Let's meet somewhere."

"Fine. I'll meet you at the Metro Park at three o'clock."

"Bet."

"Don't be late picking him up or bringing him home either. Mama's taking him to Bible study tonight."

"I won't."

"And, Lamium, I swear to God, you better not have my

baby anywhere near no drugs." Daneisha twisted her lips. "If LJ tells me something I don't want to hear, you can forget about seeing him again."

"How you gon' keep me away from my own son?" Lamium asked.

"Lamium, don't you even fucking try me. One mention of you even so much as smoking a cigarette—"

"I'm-a cut you off right there," Lamium interrupted. "Daneisha, I'm clean now. Stop all your worrying. I must admit I like the way you acted like a real mother for once."

"I am a mother." Daneisha closed her eyes as she uttered those words.

"Well, Daneisha, I promised you I would always be there for you and my son. Did I not make that promise to you?"

"Yes, you did." Daneisha's body tingled. He would always possess some kind of power over her emotions. She cleared her throat. "I hope you stay true to your word."

Lamium chuckled. "My word is bond, baby. Believe it."

Daneisha hung up.

If things progressed between her and Evan, she knew Lamium wouldn't like it. However, he would be left with no choice but to accept it. Whether things would go further was yet to be determined. Evan still had a lot to prove. While it was fresh on her mind, Daneisha called to make sure the credit card was legitimate. She was relieved the card wasn't stolen. For Evan, it was definitely a step in the right direction.

Chapter Nine

Daneisha arrived at Kay's new apartment. Kay wanted her best friend to be the first one to see it. It was a nice place, quite small for Daneisha's taste. She couldn't understand why Kay would rent a one-bedroom when she could afford a larger place.

The only furniture was in the bedroom. Daneisha volunteered to help her decorate. She brought over a few catalogues to share some ideas. Within an hour, Daneisha had the living room and a small dinette picked out for the kitchen. She tried to get Kay to splurge on two bar stools, but she refused to go over her tiny budget.

When they finished with the furniture selections, Daneisha showed off the pictures from the party she attended with Evan, where she dawned a navy Gucci suit with a beaded embroidered top underneath.

"Check this out." Daneisha pulled up a picture of Evan. "We're both in navy suits, and it wasn't planned that way. Girl, we turned it out!"

"As always," Kay said wryly. She handed Daneisha back her cell phone.

"And, you have to see a full shot of me." Daneisha giggled. "The pants were flared, but check out my silver Claudia Ciuti sandals."

"Who is that?"

"A well-known designer." Daneisha waved her hand. "Forget about it, you wouldn't know anyway."

"The temperature was in the forties. I know your toes had to be freezing."

"Who cares! Listen, if you want to dress fashionable, some sacrifices have to be made."

"I love my man, but I have to be comfortable."

"You just get used to it." Daneisha couldn't understand why Kay's attitude was so sour. Kay finally had her own place, and Daneisha felt she should be happy to be away from her mother's constant criticism. Daneisha loved Reesy and thought of her as a second mother. Whenever Reesy opened her mouth to speak, there was no telling what she was going to say. Many times, she was brutally harsh, and she never hesitated to share exactly what was on her mind. When it came to Lamium, she never bit her tongue in saying how disappointed she was in Daneisha for having a drug dealer for a baby daddy.

Kay stood up from the bed to use the bathroom. When she came out, she went in her closet. "Anyway, did you have a good time?"

"Yes, I did. Evan is so sweet and romantic, just how I remembered him." Daneisha leaned on her side across the bed. "I can appreciate a man like that now at this point in my life."

Kay laid brown pants and a gold silk blouse across the bed. "This is true. Does that mean you're giving up on all your side hustles?"

"As long as Lamium keeps up his end and I have Evan to buy me everything else, then I won't have to run my businesses." Daneisha clasped her hands together with excitement. "My life is coming together, and it feels so damn good."

"Good." Kay removed her robe to put on her blouse. "If you ask me, I think you need to let it all go. It's like you're always depending on men to take care of you. When are you going to get a job like the rest of the working women in America?"

"I'm sorry I don't think that way." Daneisha sat straight up. "I don't want a nine-to-five-then-come-home-all-tired-and-stressed-out life like yours. I'm-a just keep working to find me a man that understands that."

Kay zipped up her pants then slid a gold belt through the belt loops. "You can probably make it another ten years with your looks. What about when that man drops you for a younger version? Hell, Lamium left you for an older woman."

Kay held up two shoes for Daneisha to choose from. One was a gold heel, the other a brown pump. Daneisha pointed at the leather brown. "I already told you, Lamium will be asking me to take him back."

Kay sat in an old chair to put on her shoes. "What if he doesn't?"

"If he doesn't, then someone else will take care of me. I'm-a do like Anna Nicole and marry me a rich old man. Then when he leaves me his millions, then I'll be living large and doing what I want to do." Daneisha laughed at her own sense of humor, even though she was somewhat serious.

Kay leaned back in the rocking chair and crossed her legs. "I wonder if you're setting a good example for LJ."

"I'm raising a young man. LJ will learn that he needs to get a good job and take care of his woman someday." Daneisha cocked her head to the side. "What's your problem anyway? You asked me to come over here, and you've given me nothing but your stank attitude."

"You're my best friend, and I love you. I'm trying to earn a law degree and you want to earn your ho degree. I don't see how this is going to work."

"Excuse me?" Daneisha cleared her throat. "You're starting to sound all high and mighty to me. First of all, I would hardly call a paralegal certificate anything close to a law degree. It still doesn't take away from the fact that your boyfriend is a drug dealer. And don't forget you used to live the same life as me."

Kay pointed. "There you go. I *used* to do it. Sleeping with men for money got old for me."

"Well, I don't see it that way."

Kay glanced down at her watch. "Well, I would love to keep this going, but my boyfriend is on his way here, and I need to get ready."

Daneisha got within inches from Kay's face. "You're just jealous. I don't know why I didn't see it before. Kay, you're no different than all the other trifling females in this ignorant-ass town."

"Jealous of you?" Kay scoffed. "Not hardly." She flipped her bone-straight hair.

"Check yourself out in the mirror, honey. You know you want to be just like me." Daneisha grabbed her Dooney. "It's too bad I don't have enough time to go into why that won't ever happen." Daneisha snapped her fingers and sashayed out the door.

Daneisha's heels clicked as she walked along the brick walkway. She was so upset, her vision went blurry. Fumbling with her car keys, she blinked several times until her sight returned.

As she sped off in her Lexus, she heard the small siren from her cell phone. She checked her text message. It was from Kay.

Daneisha read the message aloud. "Sorry for the way I acted. I was a little jealous."

She dialed Kay's number. "I'm sorry, too."

"Sometimes, it's hard to be friends with you."

"What?" Daneisha asked in a sharp tone.

"When I came to your mom's house to see you two weeks ago, it seemed like you were changing."

"I have changed. Kay, you're supposed to be my best friend. How can you say it's hard to be friends with me?"

"It's because I work hard every day. I go to my job and deal with these lawyers and their attitudes. Then, I'm in class at night. Not to mention the time I spend studying and writing papers. And you just sit around on your ass all day, while men give you handouts. Then you're burning up my cell phone talking about stuff I really don't want to hear about."

"Like what stuff? You need to explain this shit."

"You want to tell me about how you spent five hundred dollars at the mall. At the mall? When you already have a closet full of clothes you don't wear because you have nowhere to go. Do you know that would cover tuition for one of my classes? And you spend that kind of money with no regards to your future, or even LJ's future."

"I can't help it if I want to look good."

"But for who? Daneisha, I was hoping you would realize that your life is really about you. And you don't leave any room for anyone else, not even your own son. It's a shame."

Daneisha held a pissed-off look on her face. "You don't know how badly I want to be mad at you right now."

"Be mad. Somebody needs to tell you the truth. And for once in your life, you need to listen. You know I'm not saying these things to hurt you. I love you, Princess."

Daneisha adjusted her Bluetooth in her ear. "I know you do."

"And you're probably right, too." Kay cleared her throat. "I am a little jealous of you."

"I was just saying that out of spite. I know you're not like that."

"In some ways, I wish I could have your life. But I don't."

"Please." Daneisha sighed with frustration. "I wish I could be more like you. You're such a free spirit, patient, and so generous. I'm none of those things, which is why you will be a better mother than I will ever be. And the reason why I don't have a job is because you know how I am. I wouldn't be able to handle someone telling me what to do."

"I see what you're saying. Well, I haven't been completely honest either. Part of the reason why I went off is because I didn't tell you that my mom put me out."

"I know you're lying on Ms. Reesy. She wouldn't do that to you."

"Mama started asking around about Rowan. When she found out he's working for Lamium, she told me either to break up with him or move in with him."

"What! I can't believe it. I thought you said she liked Rowan."

"She did. But you know how my mama is. She's a private eye when it comes to her daughter."

"I wish you would've told me, instead of keeping it to yourself. I'm supposed to be your best friend."

"Well, I hinted at it once, when I volunteered to be your roommate."

"I remember. The day you came to visit me after my surgery."

"Yeah. I was so scared. But you had bigger problems than mine. I didn't want to burden you with my issues."

Daneisha sighed with relief. "Now, it all makes sense."

"I'm sorry. I took my frustration out on you, and that's not right."

"I understand. That's what friends are for."

"True. Well, Rowan is at the door. I'll call you in the morning."

"You can be my wake-up call. I told Mama I would go to church with her."

"I could use some inspiration myself. I'm-a go with you."

"Even better. Then I will see you tomorrow."

Daneisha felt so stupid for not realizing Kay was going through a tough time. Focused on her own problems, Daneisha never noticed any signs that Kay was stressed out. Then again, she never paid much attention to anyone other than herself. Many times her mother told her that she was selfish. Now, she had the perfect example.

On her way back to her apartment, Daneisha did something she rarely did. She prayed for LJ, her mother, brothers, dad, stepdad, and the list went on and on. Most importantly, she ended her prayer asking God to bless her best friend.

Daneisha went to Bethel Baptist that Sunday with her mother. Kay also attended the service. Pastor McKissick, Sr. preached on God's grace and favor. With all that she was going through, the message was right on. For the next three Sundays, Daneisha made sure she was not only there, but on time. Daneisha enjoyed each service, and connected most with Co-Pastor McKissick, Jr.

Rudolph McKissick, Jr., called Rudy by his parents and closest friends, stood at five foot eight inches tall and was in his early forties, resembling a lighter-skinned version of Cedric the Entertainer. With his deep voice, he carried a presence of someone much older and taller, his three-piece Armani suits with the vest, showing preachers had come a long way in their fashion taste. She often heard her mama rant about his gorgeous hazel eyes and his soft hands. LeQuisha loved herself some Pastor Jr. and would beat anybody down that had anything negative to say about him being arrogant or cocky.

His delivery was smooth and direct. He was also on point with what people were facing, giving explicit examples of how people tend to mess up their lives. Now, she loved the way Pastor Jr. would go off on the congregation, like he was getting all up in their business. It was quite entertaining for her to watch him strut, dance, and shout across the pulpit. What really touched her was how he not only tore each person down, but explained what was needed to be restored.

As a teenager, LeQuisha got saved and attended regularly. Daneisha and her brothers went to children's ministry, and she loved going. Once Daneisha became rebellious and thought she was already grown, she lost the desire to attend.

It was November, four days before Thanksgiving. Daneisha and Kay entered the sanctuary together and walked the steps to the upper level. The pews were filling up quickly. While Kay searched for seats, Daneisha checked her outfit to make sure she looked perfect. Although it was church, that didn't stop the members from strutting across the red carpet like they were at a Hollywood premiere.

And Daneisha was not one to let any of the haters be disappointed. Since she'd been seeing Evan, her taste in clothing went to a whole 'nother level. After her blow-up with Kay, she realized she needed to project a more professional appearance if she was to be on the arm of a successful mortgage broker who owned his own business.

Just last week, Evan invited Daneisha to Orlando while he was there attending a conference at the Convention Center. During the day when Evan was gone, Daneisha treated herself to shopping at the outlet stores and fell in love with the Mall at Millennia. She shopped her heart out at Bloomingdale's.

On this Sunday, she was wearing one of the outfits she'd

purchased in Orlando, a Donna Karan fuchsia tweed jacket with an oversized collar. To complement her bold jacket and slim figure, a black pencil skirt formed the touch of elegance she was aiming for.

Under her breath, Kay mumbled, "To your right, on the front row is your girl."

"Who?" Daneisha asked nervously. She was hoping it wasn't Jillian. No matter how well she put together the outfit, she definitely didn't have the courage to face that diva.

"Brontae Dixon. Well, it's Williams now."

"Someone married that fat . . . see I almost cursed in the sanctuary."

"She married Reggie."

"No!" Daneisha stared down at the ground to hide her expression. "All I can say is there are some desperate men out there."

"Ain't that the truth?" Kay responded. "Are you ready to do this, Princess?"

"Yes."

Daneisha and Kay hit the red carpet just as the choir sang the first note of "The Blood." Their steps were perfectly synchronized as if it was choreographed in a gospel play. Daneisha dug deep in her tall Cole Haan boots, careful to sashay her petite hips gracefully.

From the corner of her eye, she snuck a glance in Brontae's direction. She saw her whisper in the ear of her sidekick from elementary school, Stephanie. Daneisha thought it was nice to see that both of those heifers were trifling as ever, while she could easily grace the cover of *Vanity Fair* magazine.

Daneisha knew they recognized her and were hating on her just like all the other females. It felt good knowing the men—married, single, and gay—all wanted her too.

Once seated, Daneisha laughed to herself.

"What are you laughing at?" Kay asked.

"At Brontae and Stephanie . . . all I can say is success is the best revenge."

Kay sucked her teeth. "I don't want to hurt your feelings, but I would hardly call parading around in nice suits being successful. Especially when Brontae is a school principal and Stephanie is a pharmacist."

Daneisha playfully punched Kay in the shoulder. "Thanks a lot. You really know how to kick a girl down, just when I was starting to feel good about myself."

Kay smirked. "Hey, I'm just trying to keep it real."

Daneisha clenched her teeth. "Yeah, that's exactly what I needed. A dose of reality."

"Anytime." Kay held up the peace sign.

Daneisha ignored her and clapped her hands to the music. She watched her mother on the lower level standing next to Mike clapping too. She hoped her mother wouldn't embarrass herself by shouting down the aisle again. That was exactly the reason why Daneisha refused to sit with them.

It wouldn't be so bad if her mother's shouting resembled what the other women were doing, but, no, her shout was more like the latest moves at the club. Daneisha knew her mom wasn't trying to dance like that on purpose. LeQuisha was shaped like a Coca-Cola bottle, and with a figure like that, simple steps from side to side resembled dance moves.

The message was titled *Second to Number One Is Still Second Place.* It was for women who ignorantly chose to be involved with men who were married.

"And to the young women who are willing to put yourself in a number two position to the woman that is married to that man, raising his children, doing all the cooking and cleaning, shame on you!"

All the married women stood to their feet and clapped

loudly. Of course, her mother was standing and yelling out as well.

What a hypocrite! Knowing full well she done slept with a few married men herself. See, these church folk ain't right.

"And to the men. Y'all know I'm an equal opportunity preacher. Double shame on you for taking advantage of these young girls, when you know you got a good Christian woman at home."

Daneisha had to jump up at that one. Pastor Jr., as he was nicknamed, was turning it out. There wasn't a single person sitting down at this point. By the end of the sermon, Daneisha was in tears. She grabbed her last Kleenex to wipe her face, before she realized Kay needed it worse than she did. She handed it to Kay, who was crying uncontrollably.

When Pastor Jr. held the altar call, Daneisha was shocked when Kay stood up.

"What are you doing?" Daneisha asked in a whisper.

"I'm going down there," Kay responded.

"Do you know what that means?"

"Of course. I'm going to walk into my blessings." Kay tossed her purse on Daneisha's lap. "You need to come with me."

Daneisha twisted her lips. "I don't think so."

"It's your loss." Kay walked the aisle, down the steps toward the stage.

"From the upper level, I see you coming." Pastor Jr. waved the group of people in his direction. Each week, at least fifteen to twenty people got saved.

Daneisha crossed her legs and leaned back in the pew. She couldn't believe she was watching her best friend follow one of the ministers to the side door. Her heart ached some, but not enough for her to march boldly in front of the congregation. Silently, she asked God to forgive her for being such a coward. It was only a matter of time before she would do the same and give her life over to the Lord.

Besides, she couldn't take the chance that someone might recognize her, and she didn't want the word to get back to Lamium. If Lamium knew Daneisha had turned her life over to the Lord, he would exploit her emotions every chance he got. Not to mention, she still held out hope that he would come back to her. Even Lamium regarded a Christian woman as being sacred, and with the life he led, he wouldn't dare go there. The way she figured, she was still young. As a mother, it was more important for Daneisha to keep her family together. She knew God understood that.

It was obvious that Daneisha loved the time she spent with Evan. But if Daneisha were to be completely honest, she wasn't completely over Lamium. While she adored Evan, she loved Lamium. Although she hated to face the truth, she knew it'd be years before she was completely over him.

When Pastor Jr. dismissed the congregation, Daneisha caught up to LeQuisha and Mike in the front area of the church.

"Pastor tore it up, didn't he?" LeQuisha asked.

Mike nodded his head.

"Yes, Mama. It was good."

"Please . . . it was excellent." LeQuisha waved her hands.

Daneisha scratched the back of her neck shamefully. She wished her mother would lower her voice, though she wouldn't dare suggest it.

"I have to get in line to get my tape." LeQuisha grabbed Mike's arm. "Come on, honey. You want me to get you a copy?"

Daneisha turned up her nose. "No, I don't listen to tapes."

"Oh, excuse me, Ms. High Society." LeQuisha stuck out her hand. "Where's your money for a CD then?"

Daneisha reached in her purse and pulled out a twenty. "And get me last week's too."

Daneisha felt a tap on her shoulder. She turned around to see it was Kay.

LeQuisha pushed past her daughter and wrapped her arms around Kay, almost dragging her to the ground. "Welcome to the family, Kay. I'm so proud of you."

"Thank you," Kay said through a muffled voice. Her face was buried in LeQuisha's chest.

"I wish Reesy had made it to service to see her daughter get saved. Where is she today? She never misses a service."

"She didn't miss it. Mama got up early and came to the first service. She's getting the house ready for the holiday."

"Is your Uncle Buck coming down with his family?"

"Yes, ma'am." Kay glanced at her watch. "That's where I'm headed now, to pick up some neckbones and all the stuff she needs to make macaroni at the grocery store."

"So, you want me to ride with Mama and Mike then?" Daneisha asked.

"Well, LJ's booster seat is in my car. I can take him with me if you don't mind."

"Sure. Take the little rug rat."

Kay kissed LeQuisha on the cheek and hugged Mike before she scurried off.

Back at her mother's house, Daneisha enjoyed Sunday dinner. Dante pigged out as usual, and Donny stopped by to show off his new girlfriend.

While she and her mother cleaned up the kitchen, Daneisha giggled.

"Donny should have been in church today."

"I know," LeQuisha said as she wiped her hands with a

dish towel. "He got some nerve bringing that married woman to my house."

Daneisha tried to lower her voice, so they wouldn't hear her. "Mama, the woman looks older than you."

"Well, that's because your mama is fine." LeQuisha shook her booty from side to side.

"Mama, you're crazy."

LeQuisha stopped and leaned on the counter. "You know I'm going to talk to him about this when I see him tomorrow."

"Try to keep your lecturing down to less than an hour. It never worked with me."

LeQuisha frowned. "Unlike my hard-headed daughter, my boys actually listen to their mama."

"Mama, please. Everybody knows the boys have you wrapped around their fingers."

LeQuisha leaned back and rested her hands on her hips. "No, they don't either."

"Whatever." Daneisha waved her hand. "Save it for Mike. Now, he's the one that listens to you."

LeQuisha grinned from ear to ear. "That's my honey."

"You guys get on my nerves," Daneisha said as she placed the last plate in the dishwasher. She looked up at the wall clock. "It's almost eight o'clock. I wonder where Kay is."

Daneisha called her best friend for the fifth time with no answer. "She's still not answering her phone."

"You know how Reesy gets when it comes to her Thanksgiving dinner," LeQuisha chimed in. "She proba-bly has that girl running all over town."

"It doesn't make sense that she wouldn't at least answer her cell phone."

"Her battery might be dead."

"Could be." Trying not to sound too concerned, she de-cided to call Kay's mother.

"Hello, Ms. Reesy. I'm sorry to call your house this late, but I wanted to know if Kay was over there."

"No, she left here hours ago." Ms. Reesy's loud voice blared through the receiver. "Have you tried her cell phone?"

"Yes, ma'am. I've called about five times so far."

"Well, that's not like Kay not to answer. She keeps it glued to her body. I tell you, you young people—"

"I'm sorry, but I can't hear you. I think I'm losing reception," Daneisha lied.

"That's all right, baby. Well, when you hear something, you let me know."

"I will."

"Where's LeQuisha at?"

Damn, didn't I just tell her my phone was losing reception?

"She's right here. You want to speak to her?"

"No, I'll call her later. I got so much cooking to do."

"I understand. I'll tell Mama you asked about her." Daneisha wriggled back and forth; she really needed to use the bathroom.

"All right, sugar. I'll be waiting on your call. And if I hear from Kay, I'll have her call you."

"Okay."

"Yeah, I don't know how that girl can be out with LJ this late like that. It's just not like her."

Daneisha took a deep breath. Ms. Reesy had the gift of gab. "Bye, Ms. Reesy."

Daneisha finally got in touch with Rowan. To her alarm, he hadn't heard from Kay either. He told Daneisha he would keep calling and drive over to her apartment to see if she was there.

When the house phone rang, LeQuisha checked the caller ID first. "That's Reesy now."

"Oh yeah, she said she was going to try to reach you."

Daneisha finally made it to the bathroom. She closed

her eyes as she felt a flooding of relief. It almost felt like an orgasm.

"Oh my Lord!" LeQuisha shouted. "Jesus! No!"

Daneisha almost fell in the toilet when she heard her mother's cries. She pulled up her skirt and ran down the hall. When she reached the kitchen, Mike was holding her mother in his arms. She had fainted. Her eyes were glossed over.

Being a doctor, Mike immediately checked his wife's vitals.

Donny snatched the phone from LeQuisha's hands.

"Mama, what's wrong?" Daneisha asked.

Her mother was unable to respond.

She overheard Donny ask, "Which hospital?" Then he jotted some notes on a pad before he hung up.

"What happened?" Daneisha ran over to Donny. "Is it LJ?"

"Kay was in a car accident."

Daneisha grabbed Donny's shirt, ripping a few buttons apart. "What happened to my baby?"

"He's been injured." Donny held onto Daneisha's shoulders. He locked eyes with her.

Daneisha knew it had to be bad. "What do you mean?"

"He's—"

"He's what? What's wrong with my baby? Oh my God, Donny."

Donny wrapped his arms around her. "He's being treated right now."

"Would you stop sounding like a doctor! Tell me what's wrong with my baby!" Daneisha spat out.

"LJ suffered some injuries, but he's going to be fine."

Daneisha squeezed her eyes shut, praying for twice the good news. "And Kay?"

Donny took a deep breath. "She didn't make it." His

voice went low. "They pronounced her dead before she reached the hospital."

Daneisha hollered, "Lord, please no! I can't take it! I can't take it, Lord!" She began to hyperventilate. "No . . . ahhh . . . ahhh . . . no . . . ahhh . . . no . . ."

Chapter Ten

The car accident happened when Kay was attempting to make a left turn at the light. It was the busy intersection of Beach and Atlantic. An oncoming car trying to run a red light clipped her SUV from the passenger side, flipping her truck completely over on its driver side.

Several people approached the accident to provide assistance. Two men tried to pull Kay from the front window, but her legs were stuck under the engine. When the engine caught fire, the men backed off. While her legs were burning, she yelled for them to help LJ. Somehow, she struggled to free LJ from his booster seat.

One man broke out the window and lifted LJ out to safety. When he and his wife attempted to climb inside to rescue Kay, the fire grew larger, making it impossible to enter. Kay's screams could be heard a mile away, and many cried as they witnessed her suffering.

A fire truck arrived and put out the fire. Although, ninety percent of Kay's body was burned, she was barely conscious. She died in the ambulance. It broke Daneisha's heart to know her best friend suffered and her son had witnessed it.

Daneisha was dressed in the leisure suit she stole from Kay's closet. Her hair was pulled back in a ponytail. This morning was the first time she'd managed to shower.

Carefully, Daneisha listened out for LJ to wake up while she rested on a pillow on the couch. He required some medical tending to, as he was very much shaken up from the accident. She hadn't slept for at least forty-eight hours, only catching a nap here and there.

Thanksgiving was the next day, and while she should've been preparing to eat to her heart's delight, Daneisha was nursing her son at home. LJ was released from the hospital Monday morning with a broken arm. He suffered from smoke inhalation and bruising on his neck and back. It was going to take a few weeks to heal.

Most of Kay's family were already scheduled for flights into town because of the holiday, but now they were coming to paying Kay's mother their respect. Kay was her only child. Daneisha was waiting for Dante to come over to babysit LJ so she could drive over to Reesy's house. To her surprise, LeQuisha and Dante entered, using the key Daneisha gave her mother a month ago.

"How are you doing?" LeQuisha asked as she hugged her daughter. "Did you get any sleep?"

"Not yet." Tears rolled down Daneisha's face. "I guess I'm still in shock."

"I understand. That's why I'm taking you over to Reesy's. I don't need you out there on the road when you haven't slept."

"Is LJ in the bed?" Dante asked as he placed his backpack on the couch.

"Yes, he's still sleeping."

Dante plopped down on the couch and turned to

TODAY. "I'll go check on him in a little while." He kicked his feet on the table.

LeQuisha pushed his feet to the floor. "Get your feet off this table. Where do you think you're at, the Holiday Inn or something?" LeQuisha grabbed his arm. "Get your behind back there and check on my grandson."

"Okay, Mama." Dante yanked free from his mother's tight grip. "You ain't got to snatch on me like that."

"Boy, you watch your mouth." LeQuisha pointed down the hall. "As much painkillers as Dr. Allen prescribed for LJ, someone has to be watching him around the clock."

"All right. I'm going." Dante held up his hands. "Daneisha, will you get your mama out of here, please?"

Daneisha picked up her jacket and purse. "I'm ready."

"Good." Dante sighed with relief.

LeQuisha balled up a fist. "Don't give me a reason to knock you out, Dante."

"Mama, please. Just go. You're taking all your frustration out on me. And I'm tired of it."

"Oh, I didn't realize . . ." LeQuisha stared up at the ceiling and fought back the tears. "Maybe I am. I'm sorry, baby."

"It's okay," Dante replied. He rubbed her back as she took a moment to calm her nerves.

"I'm not playing about LJ, though." She held up her finger.

"I know." Dante held the door open for them to exit. "Bye."

In her mother's car, Daneisha leaned against the window and dozed off to sleep. When she woke up they were at Reesy's house. It was early, but that didn't stop the people from coming. The cars were lined up and down the street.

Once inside, the first person Daneisha spotted was

Kay's boss, Vicki, sitting in a small kitchen chair stuck in a corner by a dusty plastic tree.

"Mama, look." She pointed in Vicki's direction.

"Lord, don't they know this woman is a millionaire?" LeQuisha shook her head in disappointment. "They got her perched up in here like a ghetto queen."

LeQuisha went over and greeted Vicki. She told two teenaged boys that were hogging up space on the couch to get up. Then she ran in the kitchen and came back with a handful of bottled water. She handed one to Vicki and passed three more to Kay's relatives.

Daneisha followed her mother back to the kitchen.

LeQuisha wiped her sweaty upper lip as she fanned her face. "I'm going to adjust the AC in this house. I need you to call up KFC and order about forty-eight pieces of chicken, and order some side items too."

"I think I should call up Hector instead. As much as he loved Kay, I know he won't mind cooking up some dishes at the last minute."

"Good thinking." LeQuisha leaned on Daneisha's shoulder for support. It was apparent the sadness in the house was starting to affect her. "I need to check on Reesy. You stay out here and make sure these children go out to the backyard to play. And the grown folks are taken care of. I'm going to call Mike and have him drop off a cooler full of sodas."

"Don't worry about anything," Daneisha said, pulling her mother's hair back off her shoulders. "I got it under control."

LeQuisha hugged her daughter then disappeared down the hall.

Less than two hours later, Hector arrived with a full crew and set up shop on the counter in the tiny kitchen. Daneisha directed his staff to set up tables and chairs in the backyard. The skies were blue, sun shone brightly, and the weather warmed up like typical Florida weather.

They served Cajun chicken, rice and beans, corn, and buttery biscuits to the guests as they arrived. His wife stopped by later to deliver three dessert dishes. Reesy's small home and backyard miraculously held close to fifty guests at a time, including members of the women's ministry.

Daneisha hugged Hector around the neck. "Thank you for doing this. Mama wanted me to call Kentucky Fried Chicken, and I thought of you instead."

Hector wiped his hands with a towel. "It was no problem. Kay was like a daughter to me."

Daneisha smiled warmly. "I know Kay is looking down at us right now with that silly grin on her face."

"I bet you're right."

"When I first got here, everybody was so sad. You see what your food does for people?" Daneisha waved her hand then placed it on her hip. "They're all laughing and talking, like a party is going on."

"That's exactly how it should be. It's about the celebration of someone's life, and Kay passing over to other side."

"You're right."

Daneisha recognized most of Kay's family, especially her cousins. She chit-chatted with them for a bit then went to Reesy's bedroom to check on her. There was several people inside, including Reesy's brother, Buck. Le-Quisha was sitting in the bed, holding Reesy in her arms. Daneisha almost didn't recognize her without her wig on. Her face was pale white like snow. Her eyes held that glossed-over daze that Daneisha saw on her mother's face.

Seeing her like that made all Daneisha's raw emotions surface. She left the room and went to the bathroom. There, she cried harder than she willed herself to. Just when Daneisha felt like she'd gained her composure, she wiped her nose once more.

As she opened the door, she felt another cry coming on. She closed it and sat down on the toilet. She bent over, rested her head on her knees, and let all of her emotions flow.

Daneisha screamed.

She yelled.

She kicked the wall.

She tore down the shower curtain.

Anything to make the pain leave, but nothing worked.

A few minutes later, she heard a tap on the door.

"I need to use the bathroom," a young voice said.

"Okay." Daneisha checked herself in the mirror. She was a mess, and there was no way she could fix herself up. She would need a brush, comb, and a flat iron to work that weave back into shape.

Daneisha opened the door and peered out. A very young girl was standing there. "I'm sorry," she said to the girl's mother who was behind her.

Daneisha finger combed her hair, straightened her leather jacket, and headed back to the den. Her heart stopped when she saw Rowan sitting on the couch, with Lamium next to him. Quickly, she turned around and snuck into Kay's bedroom. She locked the door behind her.

Even though Kay had moved out, her room was exactly the same. Daneisha picked up a few of Kay's stuffed animals. She held onto her Raggedy Ann doll and laid down on her bed. She envisioned Kay entering the room and laying down beside her, just as they had as teenagers.

Kay was humming one of her favorite tunes. Daneisha pictured her bopping her head back and forth like a white girl.

Though tears were in her eyes, Daneisha laughed out loud.

Kay smiled. "What are you laughing at?"

"You, silly," Daneisha answered.

"Who me?" Kay pointed at her chest, her eyes wide. "See, I'm Supa Fly, Supa Dupa Fly."

Daneisha closed her eyes, singing along with her best friend. "I can't stand the rain."

She grabbed Kay's pillow and inhaled her scent. She made a mental note to take it home with her, right before she drifted off to sleep. The sound of a ringing phone woke her up. When she opened her eyes, it was pitch black in the room.

Daneisha answered. "Hello." She wiped the crust from her eyes.

"Is this Daneisha?"

Daneisha cleared her throat. "Yes, it is." Her voice sounded hoarse.

"I've been calling everyone I know today. I tried to reach you on the cell phone, but it was no longer in service. I searched through all my numbers and finally came across Kay's home number."

Daneisha was puzzled. She sat straight up and finger combed her frizzy curls. "I'm sorry, who is this?"

"Myra."

Daneisha put her hand to her mouth. "Myra, what's up, girl? Do you know I've been trying to get in touch with you? Where are you?"

"Well, today I'm in New York recording in the studio. But Jericho and the boys are back home."

"It's so good to hear from you. I've been so worried about you, girl, I—"

"I don't mean to cut you off, but I'm calling from my cell phone while I'm riding in a cab. I don't want this call

to end. Like I said before, I've been trying to reach someone all day, ever since I heard the news about Kay."

Daneisha checked the caller ID to jot down Myra's
number, but it read UNKNOWN CALLER. "You heard about
Kay being killed?"

"Yes, I caught the story on CNN a few hours ago. I
couldn't believe it was our Kay they were talking about. It
took me a minute to put it all together, when they said
Kendall Harms, but then her picture popped up on the
screen. I completely lost it."

Daneisha could tell Myra was crying because her voice
was breaking up. "I just can't believe it. Kay was so sweet."

"I know." Daneisha felt a knot in her throat.

The phone went dead.

"Hello."

There was nothing but a dial tone.

Daneisha waited a few minutes for Myra to call back.

Oh no. I have to check on LJ.

Daneisha sat straight up. She unlocked the door and listened for voices. It was completely silent throughout the
house.

"Mama," Daneisha called out.

LeQuisha appeared at the end of the hallway. "There's
my sleepyhead. You want something to eat?"

Daneisha rubbed her stomach. She was hungry. "I have
to check up on LJ."

"I've been calling Dante every hour. He's fine. Now
come and get something to eat."

Not sure if food would satisfy her depression, she was
up for some company. She sat down at the table and
munched on the chicken dinner.

With it being a holiday, the funeral had to be pushed
back another week for Reesy to get all the arrangements

together. The funeral took place on Saturday. A cherry wood casket sat in front of the church. It was closed. There would be no viewing of Kay's severely burned body.

Saying good-bye to her best friend was the hardest thing she had to do. Evan was at her side the entire time, holding her and LJ's hand. There were times when Daneisha felt her legs buckle, and she was glad Evan was there to hold her up. All of Daneisha's family sat on the same row, including her grandmother Gayle and Leroy. For Daneisha, it seemed like cruel and unusual punishment. She tried her best not to even look in his direction, wishing it was his dead body they were there to pay their final respects to. Daneisha knew there was a special place reserved in hell for him.

It was time for Kay's closest family and friends to make personal statements. Many who disapproved of their relationship gasped out loud when Rowan marched up to the podium. In his black suit, Daneisha thought he was strikingly handsome.

Rowan straightened his jacket and grabbed the microphone. He cleared his throat as if he was trying to swallow a frog that was lodged there. "For those of you who don't know me, I was Kay's, Kendall's boyfriend." Rowan tried to swallow harder this time. "I loved her . . . and I . . . I'm sorry." Rowan put the microphone back on the stand. He gripped his stomach as if he wanted to vomit. "I know everyone didn't approve of our relationship. I respect that. I just want everyone here to know I loved that woman. I tried so hard to make her happy."

Rowan fought back the tears. "Kay was everything to me. And now, I don't know what I'm going to do without her." His voice trembled.

Rowan stopped in front of the casket. An older woman walked up to him and handed him a large bouquet of flowers, and he placed them on top of the casket. Then she handed him a smaller bouquet, which he handed to Reesy before he took his seat.

Daneisha turned to watch him use a handkerchief to dry his eyes. He was sitting beside Lamium and Greg. She was relieved Lamium didn't cause a scene about her being at the funeral with Evan. Daneisha figured Greg's pitiful face was more about him losing his family than Kay's death.

When Myra finally called Daneisha back the next day she inquired about where to send flowers, even though she wasn't able to make the funeral. Daneisha wanted to press Myra about her whereabouts, but she felt it wasn't the right time. She did ask about Angel, since she seemed to have disappeared from the radar too. Apparently, Angel moved back to the DC area with her daughter and filed for a divorce.

She lifted her classic aviator sunglasses long enough to wipe the tears from her eyes. They were so swollen, and each brush with the Kleenex stung.

When Daneisha walked to the front of the church to speak to the congregation, she held her head high, knowing Kay was watching her from heaven. She wanted to make her proud.

"Kay was already an angel before the Lord called her back to heaven. I remember the first time we met. I was seven in the second grade. We were in the same class. Mrs. Burke was our teacher. I remember that was my first black teacher. She was pretty, and looked like Claire Huxtable."

The crowd laughed.

"Kay was this skinny, snaggle-tooth girl with two curly ponytails. Those ponytails were so thick, they looked more like pom-poms. She smiled at me and we were instantly the best of friends. She was there for me, through the good times and the bad. She sat at my bedside as I gave birth to my son. She was his godmother, and now I know, without a shadow of a doubt, she will be watching over my baby. She saved his life, and I'll never live another day without remembering how she sacrificed her own life for his."

Daneisha's brothers, Rowan, and three other men served as the pallbearers and carried the casket to the car. In the limousine, as Daneisha stared up at the clear blue sky, she felt the warmth from the glass window. The weather was perfect. When they arrived at the cemetery, LeQuisha and Reesy's brother, Buck helped her to her metal chair. Reesy leaned onto LeQuisha's shoulder for support as the casket was lowered into the ground.

"She was my baby girl," Reesy whispered in a faint voice. "I don't want to let her go."

Hearing Reesy's cries made Daneisha want to end her pain. She wished to God she had the power to go back and erase all of it.

I want my best friend back. I want Kay to be here with me. God, why did you do this? She didn't deserve to leave like this.

She leaned on her mother's other shoulder, feeling as if she was on the verge of vomiting. Inside, her heart was broken and a piece of her went down in that hole and laid to rest beside her best friend.

Against her better wishes, Evan convinced Daneisha that going to church the next day would help her feel better. It was strange sitting in the pew on the upper level as she had with Kay. She wasn't sure if she wanted to keep coming, because it hurt too much. Daneisha wondered if going to church was even right for her. She remembered how Kay walked down those steps and gave her life over to the Lord. The last thing she said was, "I'm going to get my blessings."

Daneisha said to herself, *How cruel was God to take her life on that very same day?*

* * *

On Monday, she planned to take LJ to meet with Pastor McKissick, Jr. for his initial counseling session. She hoped to get the chance to ask him about that. Daneisha flipped through the pages of *Vogue* magazine while she waited outside the pastor's office.

When LJ walked out, Pastor Jr. patted him on the head. Pastor's crisp white shirt was tucked inside his finely pressed slacks. He smiled in Daneisha's direction. "You have a good boy there. He reminds me of my son, Joshua."

Daneisha blushed. "Thank you. I'm very proud of him."

Pastor Jr. pointed toward his door. "I told LJ to walk down to Stella's office, she has a little something for him. That way, I can talk to you for a minute."

Daneisha twisted her lips as she glanced down at her watch. "What about? I need to get LJ home. It's getting late."

"Oh, I won't take up too much of your time. Kim is waiting for me to get home too. I know how it is. These kids have so much homework and projects to work on. The girls are up as late as I am sometimes."

"Okay." Daneisha watched LJ go in the next office before she went inside with the pastor.

Once Daneisha was seated, Pastor Jr. sat down in his chair behind his desk. As promised, he was brief, alerting her of certain behaviors to be on the lookout for. Also, he made a few suggestions on what she could say to help LJ through this process.

"And as far as what you're going through, don't be afraid to express your grief or anger either."

When the conversation shifted to her, Daneisha grew more uncomfortable. She began to fidget with her hands.

Pastor McKissick continued, "Your emotions are very real. Anytime you feel the need to talk, I'm here to listen."

"I appreciate that, Pastor Jr."

"Now, I have one more question I'd like to ask you."

Daneisha shifted lower in her seat. She had an idea what he was going to ask. "Yes, uh-huh?"

Pastor McKissick laughed. "You seem like you already know what I'm about to say."

"I might have a clue."

Pastor McKissick clasped his hands together. "What is it then?"

"No, you go ahead. I could be wrong and get myself in more trouble."

"Okay. Have you given your life over to the Lord?"

Daneisha took a deep breath. "No."

"Why not?"

"Well, I used to say it was because I'm too young to be tied down to church. I have a young child to take care of."

Pastor McKissick leaned forward. "If you notice, I didn't say anything about going to church."

"True."

"Let me explain something to you. Do you have the time?"

Daneisha nodded. "Yes, I do."

"The Lord I serve is already working in your life, whether you care to admit it or not. Having said that, I want you to think back on all the times God has helped you survive so many things that could've killed you."

Daneisha stared at the picture of Jesus on the wall, as she concentrated on what he said. "Yes, He has."

His hazel eyes stared intently at her. "I'm glad you can agree to that. While I know this is a very painful time for you, I want you to see how God has blessed you. While you're going through this ordeal, you may be hurt, you may be angry. What I want you to understand is that while God does not always provide the answers we want, He always provides comfort."

Daneisha slightly tilted her head. She wasn't prepared

to deal with her own pain, only what LJ was going through.

"LJ told me his father was out of the picture. Now, I don't mean to pry, but—"

"No, it's okay. Me and his father are no longer together."

"With that said, I need to challenge you by asking you this question." Pastor McKissick jerked his arms forward. He was getting all worked up, like he was preaching from the pulpit.

"Go ahead."

"What more do you need to lose before you realize that maybe God is trying to shake you to change?"

Daneisha gripped both hands on the ends of the chair to steady herself.

"Daneisha, I know you attended Bethel with your mother. You see how your mother's life has changed."

Daneisha tried to picture in her mind the way her mother used to be. "Yes."

"So you see, Daneisha, Jesus is the way to finding that wholeness and peace in your life. There is no other way around it. I think you know that. Otherwise you wouldn't be sitting in that chair right now."

Daneisha pursed her lips. What Pastor Jr. was saying made complete sense to her. She didn't know why she was fighting what her heart was telling her to do.

"Yes, I do want it. I just don't know how to get there."

"It's funny you should say that." Pastor McKissick grinned. "What if I were to tell you there is one simple thing you can do to get there? And, it will only take one minute of your time."

Daneisha shot him a dumbfounded look. "That's it?"

"Yes. It's called the Sinner's Prayer. Are you familiar with it?"

"Yeah. So, that's all I have to do?"

"That's it, for now. We have a number of support groups in place for you after you take the first step. You would go to membership classes, and there are a few young adult groups you might be interested in joining."

Daneisha nodded. "Okay, I might be able to do that."

"So, you see, Daneisha . . . forming a relationship has nothing to with your age. But I know how it is for you young people. You want to be around people your own age and discuss the issues that are important to you. That's why Bethel offers a variety of things that I know you will enjoy. And then LJ can hook up with the children's ministry."

Pastor McKissick went on to explain the services at Bethel before he handed her some literature. He advised her to think about it. Daneisha didn't need more time. Tomorrow wasn't promised to anyone. She was ready to make the commitment. Even though she was angry with God about what happened to her best friend, Daneisha knew she wanted to accept Jesus Christ into life.

As the pastor so eloquently stated, "God can help you get through anything."

During the drive home, Daneisha replayed the moment when Pastor McKissick prayed with her over in her mind. She went through a life-changing event, and felt all jittery, barely able to keep her hands calm on the wheel.

LJ interrupted her thoughts. "Mommy, you were in there for a long time."

"Well, we had a lot to talk about." Daneisha tightened her hands on the steering wheel. It was getting harder for her eyes to stay fixed on the road.

"Did you talk about me?" LJ asked.

Daneisha glanced back at her son, sitting in his booster seat, kicking his feet up and down. "Yes, we talked about you. Also, about Mommy, too."

"Mommy?"

"Yes, LJ."

"What does *saved* mean?"

"Oh, you're a smart boy. What do you think it means?"

"I think it means when you die, your body goes up to heaven with God and all the angels."

"Yes, you're right. But I think it means a whole lot more than that."

Daneisha stopped by McDonald's to pick up a happy meal for LJ and a Big Mac combo for herself. When they arrived home, they sat at the table and ate dinner silently. Daneisha had a lot on her mind.

"Mommy, I'm done," LJ said.

"It's time for your bath."

"Okay."

LJ skipped down the hall.

Daneisha finished her food then tossed the remaining contents in the trash. She wanted to call her best friend so bad. She longed to hear her say, "What's up, Princess?"

Daneisha gave LJ his bath. Then they sat in front of the TV watching cartoons.

There was a knock at the front door.

She knew it was Evan.

Daneisha leaned against the door and checked him out from head to toe.

Sporting a gray blazer, striped shirt, and blue jeans, his casual style of dress was just as appealing to Daneisha and turned her on.

"Why do I always feel like I need to pose for you or something?"

Daneisha shot him a mischievous grin. "I'm uh . . . just . . . hmmm . . . admiring what I see.

"So you like that?

Daneisha nodded. "Oh, hell yeah."

Slowly, he leaned forward and kissed her on the lips.

"And before I forget"—He held up a handful of beautiful calla lilies. "I thought you would like these.

Daneisha smiled widely. "Thank you. I love them."

"I know they're your favorite."

"Let me put them in water." Daneisha went in the kitchen and pulled out a brown vase from underneath the sink.

Evan removed his blazer and placed it on the arm of the couch. "Hey, LJ. How ya doing?"

LJ giggled as Evan tickled him in the stomach. "Good."

"Are you sure?" Evan tickled him harder.

"Yes."

"I couldn't hear you."

"Yes!" LJ shouted, almost out of air.

"Okay. I believe you."

Evan picked him up and carried him to his bedroom. "Are you ready for bed?"

"No."

"I know you want to hear the rest of my story, don't you?"

"Uh-huh."

"It's the Adventures of Captain Negro!" Evan and LJ shouted together.

Daneisha shook her head as she overheard Evan making up his crazy story of the young black captain that was destined to save the planet. It resembled the story of Moses, only the baby had a short afro, and his mother's name was Dashiki.

Daneisha flipped the remote to watch *Grey's Anatomy*. She couldn't believe she looked forward to watching it every Thursday night. It was her mother's favorite show, and Daneisha became addicted while she stayed there. Although her mother didn't want to admit it, she was in love with Dr. Preston Burke, a black male doctor on the show.

It was interesting how Dr. Burke was in love with

Christina, even though they were so different. He loved
her in spite of her flaws, just like Mike loved her mother.

During the last half of the show, Evan sat down beside
her.

"Is he 'sleep?" Daneisha asked.

"Fast asleep."

"What time is your appointment tomorrow?" Evan inquired.

"It's at nine."

Dr. Baldwin was going over her latest test results.
Daneisha's cramping had returned. It started off as a
swelling in her inner hip with short bouts of pain shooting
down her leg. The morning of Kay's funeral, she felt
cramping. Not sure if it was stress related or the endometriosis returning, she called Dr. Baldwin's office and
was immediately scheduled for an ultrasound.

"Are you nervous? Do you want me to go with you?"

Daneisha turned to face him. "You would do that?"

Evan grabbed her hand. "Yeah. I have to show a house
around noon, but I'm sure you'll be finished by then."

"You don't have to. Mama is going. She's taking the day
off."

"I wish I had a mother like yours." Evan played with
Daneisha's hair. "How did LJ's counseling go?"

"Quite interesting. LJ wasn't the only one to get some
counseling today."

"Oh really? You got some too?"

"Yes, I did. And guess what?"

Evan turned to face her. "I'm afraid to ask."

"Don't be."

Evan smiled. "What happened?"

Daneisha laughed nervously. "I got saved."

Evan raised his eyebrows and chewed harder on his
toothpick. "Whoa!"

"I guess you're surprised."

"Yes. You know what?" Evan grabbed her hand and kissed it.

"The show's back on, be quick."

"I will. I was thinking it was time I became a member at Bethel. What do you think about that?" Evan asked as he pulled Daneisha into his arms.

Daneisha rested her head into his chest and kicked her feet up on the table. "I think it's a marvelous idea."

"Marvelous, huh? Did you read a dictionary today too?"

Daneisha slapped him on the chest. "Stop it."

"Okay, I'll stop with the jokes." Evan ran his hand along his goatee. "Let's get serious now."

"Can we wait until the show goes off first?" Daneisha hinted.

"No, we can't."

Daneisha held up her hands. "All right." She took a deep breath as she sat back on the end of the couch and folded her legs.

"I want us to get married."

Daneisha bit down on her bottom lip. "Oh." She cleared her throat. "I see."

"Is that all you're going to say?" Evan asked with a slight smile. He ran his hand over his lowly trimmed head.

"What did you expect?" Daneisha put her feet down.

His smile soon faded. "I expected you to act like any other woman who received a proposal."

"I'm sorry."

"Now I get an apology."

"I'm sorry, I can't be like every other woman," Daneisha said flatly. "I've been getting that my whole life. I gotta be me. I thought you knew that when you first met me."

"Daneisha, I don't know what to say about you." Evan reached for his blazer. "It's not about you being different. Just be real with me."

Daneisha shrugged. "You caught me off guard with all

this. I was telling you how I made this change in my life, and now you want to talk about marriage. Evan, we've only been messing around for a month."

"Is that how you see it?" Evan ran his hand along his head. "I am in love with you, woman. I don't care anything about no timeline you're keeping in your head."

This ain't happening right now.

Suddenly, Daneisha felt like she was Sandra Oh and Evan was Isaiah Washington. She couldn't quite understand why he was so upset that she wasn't taking his so-called spur-of-the-moment, corny-as-hell proposal seriously.

"The last time we were together, I was in love with you. And then Lamium fired me. I was okay with that, but I what I hated most was you didn't even deem it important enough to call. I thought my world was falling apart. It took me a long time to get over you."

"I cared about you, but I wasn't in love with you. Not then, and not now," Daneisha defended. "Evan, you're moving way too fast for me. Me and Lamium just broke up, my best friend is dead, and I'm still trying to help my son get back to normal and quit blaming himself for something he had nothing to do with."

By this time, she was in tears. "I'm not an emotional person. I usually don't cry this easy. That just goes to show how messed up I am right now."

Evan turned his head to the side. "And where does that leave me?"

"I don't know where you fit in right now."

"I'm glad we had this talk. Now, I know where I stand. I guess I was one delusional, stupid-ass muthafucka to think you ever cared about me." Evan grabbed the door. "You don't care about nobody but yourself. It's all about what everybody can do for you. You're full of shit!"

Evan slammed the door.

Daneisha chewed down on her bottom lip. She slouched

down on the couch and rested her head on the pillow. She wanted to be mad at Evan for cursing at her.

She wanted to let him know he had her messed up with the wrong one.

She wanted to call him a pussy.

A punk-ass bitch.

A sorry muthafucka.

Anything to make herself feel better, to replace the hurt she was feeling. To make matters worse, the cramping was back. It hit her body like a ton of rocks.

Is everybody out to get me?

She was starting to feel paranoid. Maybe she was being punished. She knew it was too good to be true. This was the same thing that happened to Kay. Just when she thought her life was going to get better, she died. And that was what God was planning for her too.

"I take it back!" she yelled. "I don't want you. I'm taking that shit back!"

Daneisha threw the cushions on the floor. Then she knocked over her vase, causing it to break into three large pieces when it hit the carpet. Enraged, she kicked the wall. Tossed her chaise to the floor.

She felt better.

Daneisha ran in her bedroom. Catching a glimpse of herself in the mirror, her hair was wild, her blouse hanging off one shoulder.

Daneisha opened the medicine cabinet and grabbed a bottle of Vicodin. She opened it and poured all of them in the palm of her hand.

"You see what you're making me do!" Daneisha shouted.

She wanted to swallow them all and disappear forever.

She heard footsteps coming down the hall. LJ appeared rubbing his eyes.

"Mommy, I had a bad dream." LJ was sobbing and held onto her leg.

In an instant, Daneisha dropped the pills to the floor. She hugged on her son to comfort him.

"It's okay."

"Mommy, I was so scared. He was coming to take me."

"No one is going to take you. I'm here to protect you. I won't let anything happen to you."

Daneisha thought of how stupid she was to think about taking her own life.

What if LJ would have found my dead body on the floor?

Daneisha realized it was selfish to make her son deal with his own mother's death after his godmother had died right in front of him two weeks ago. What child could survive something like that and still be in his right mind?

Daneisha pulled herself together and picked up LJ. She put him in her bed then climbed in beside him. A few minutes later, LJ fell asleep on her chest. His snores sounded more like heavy breathing. She loved that little boy so much.

Evan was heavy on her mind, and so was Lamium. The lines from the song "Torn" by LeToya sang in her head:

Torn in between the two.
Cuz I really wanna be with you.
But something's telling me I should leave you alone.

Chapter Eleven

It was Friday morning. Daneisha and her mother were returning from her visit to Dr. Baldwin's office. The news wasn't good, and she had an idea it would turn out that way.

It seemed like her life was spiraling out of control, and she had no idea of how to stop it.

Evan called a few times, but Daneisha let his calls go straight to voicemail. She knew it wasn't right, when he probably wanted to know how her doctor's visit went. However, she wasn't ready to speak with him.

"Mama, I didn't tell you how much I love your new hairdo."

"You do?" LeQuisha asked as she ran her fingers through her hair. It was a fresh cut bob with one side wavy.

"Yeah, that's the new style all the stars are rocking."

"Like who?"

"Mary J. and Rhianna."

LeQuisha clenched her teeth. "You don't think it makes me look like I'm trying to be young?"

"No, Mama. What did Mike say?"

LeQuisha puckered her lips. "He loves it."

Daneisha leaned back in her seat and crossed her arms.

For the rest of the ride home, they grooved to a burnt CD with old '80s slow jams. Daneisha entered her apartment and tossed her mahogany shawl on the couch, along with her Dooney and keys.

"I have to use the bathroom," Daneisha said as she went down the hall.

"Do you want me to fix you something to eat?" LeQuisha asked.

"That's okay. I'll take some tea," Daneisha answered. She went in the room and changed out of her DKNY jeans and turtleneck sweater into a pink sweatsuit.

When she came back to the living room, her mother stood over the sink, putting dirty dishes in the dishwasher.

Daneisha spotted a mug on the table. "Mama, I meant the cold tea in the refrigerator."

"The hot tea is better for your cramping."

Daneisha sat down on the couch and picked up the cup. She turned up her nose in disgust. "Oh no, I'm not drinking this green stuff."

"It's good." LeQuisha sat down next to her daughter.

"No, thank you."

"Just try it. You might surprise yourself."

Daneisha stared at the cup once more. Then she pinched her nose as she took a small sip.

LeQuisha frowned. "All that is not necessary."

"I have to be careful," Daneisha replied. "It's not bad."

"Exactly. Now finish it."

"Yes, ma'am." Daneisha took another sip. "So, what did you think about what the doctor said?"

"I agreed with what he was saying. Mike and I discussed that exact same course of treatment last night."

Daneisha rolled her eyes. She couldn't stand it when her mother told Mike every single detail about her life.

She wished her mother would keep some things to herself.

"At twenty-one, I get nervous when someone mentions menopause. That's what I don't like."

"The Depo-Lupron shot only starts a medically induced menopause; it's not the same as actually going through it. Trust me, I'm going through early menopause, and what you might experience is minor compared to what I'm going through."

"I know, but hot flashes."

"Hot flashes is nothing compared to the pain you could be feeling again. It's only for six months. It's possible you won't have to deal with this anymore after that."

"You're right. I just hate that I'm going through this."

"I don't like it any more than you do." LeQuisha took a deep breath. "As a mother, I want my children to have it far easier."

Daneisha finished the rest of her tea. Then she leaned back on the couch. "I guess if I have to get a hysterectomy, I'm-a be okay with it."

"So you don't want to have more kids?" LeQuisha rested one arm on the couch and leaned against it.

"LJ is enough to handle." Daneisha ran her hands across her thighs.

"What does Evan have to say about that?"

"Me and Evan are just friends."

"It didn't look that way at the funeral."

"I know, and he wants it to be more. I'm not ready for all that."

"All what?" LeQuisha asked emphatically.

"Marriage and stuff."

"Evan is a good man. He has his own business and everything. Please don't tell me you're still waiting around for Lamium."

"I know you don't want to hear it, but he is the father of

my child. It's only right that I would want to keep my family together."

LeQuisha pointed. "Let me tell you something. I know this might hurt you, but as your mother, I can't sit back and watch you do this to yourself."

Daneisha inspected her French manicure. Her index finger was chipped. She was going to have that fixed before she picked up LJ from school. "Mama, I've heard it all before. I have my mind made up."

"No, you haven't heard this. Now, you listen to me. And if you want to play stupid after I tell you this, that's your choice."

Daneisha sucked her teeth. "Go ahead."

"Okay. If Lamium wanted you to be his wife, he would've married you by now."

Daneisha pursed her lips.

LeQuisha tossed up her hands. "Let me finish. I went through this, and I know what I'm talking about. First, it was with your daddy. I had three kids from that man, and then he got locked up for two years. He used to write me all these letters, run up my phone bill with all them collect calls. When he got out that first time, I just knew he was going to straighten up his life and we was going to be a family." LeQuisha put up her hand as she belched silently. Then she continued. "Donny got out and hooked up with that schoolteacher. I kept asking myself what a teacher wanted with a convict. I thought she would leave him, then he would come running back to me. Now when I think about it, it seems so ridiculous for me to want somebody's sloppy seconds. But he was the father of my children."

"Your situation ain't like mine though."

LeQuisha held up her finger. "That's why you need to let me finish and quit interrupting me."

"Yeah, I remember Kenny. He was a trip."

"Yes, he was. And we were kicking it for a while. He helped me out a lot with the bills. Then he up and married that white woman. He was always complaining like he was going to leave her. It's funny, because he and that woman been married now for about ten years."

"I remember when Dante told us that he saw Kenny with this white woman and two little girls at the mall one time," Daneisha added. "I was so mad, because I liked him."

"Yeah, I've done my share of dirt over the years. And I'm not proud of it. I figure if I can help my children learn from my mistakes, then it wasn't in vain. Like when I had to talk with Donny the other day about messing with that married woman."

"What did he say? I noticed she wasn't at the funeral."

"Donny told her he couldn't see her no more, not until she at least filed for divorce."

Daneisha arched her eyebrows. "What? I can't believe it."

"I know. I was proud of him."

"So, is she going to do it?"

LeQuisha shrugged. "I'm not sure. Donny called me Wednesday night, saying he was through with her for good."

"Dang, that was quick."

LeQuisha stood and sashayed her way to the kitchen.

"It didn't have anything to do with her husband. Apparently, he was dropping her off at her house the other night. They went to see that Will Smith movie. And the woman dropped her purse and everything fell out of it. Well, Donny went to help put her things back, and he saw a bottle of pills."

"What kind of pills?" Daneisha felt a pinch in her stomach. She was hoping this conversation wasn't going to lead to another lecture about her taking pain pills. And if

Donny confessed to writing those prescriptions for her, she was going to kill him.

"Child, it was Valtrex." LeQuisha opened the refrigerator. She took out what she needed to make sandwiches for the two of them.

Daneisha put her hand to her mouth. "Shut up."

"Yes, but Donny politely placed the bottle back in her purse, and pretended like he didn't see it."

Daneisha rubbed her forehead. "So the woman has herpes? I hope he was using condoms."

"Yes, he was. And that ain't the worst of it. Donny said he done went down on her and she done went down on him."

Daneisha's eyes grew big. "That is so messed up."

LeQuisha put the plates on the table. "I know. You young people really need to pay attention. It's all kinds of stuff out there. I know. I work at the hospital every day. You wouldn't believe how many beautiful women, married and single, are walking around with HIV. It's bad. Even though I'm married to a good man, I still have to keep a watchful eye on Mike. I've been through too much myself."

Daneisha took a seat, across from her mother. "Since we're talking about your past love life, what about Tate?"

LeQuisha picked up her sandwich, and her long nails made an imprint in the bread. "What about him?"

"I mean, you kept telling us how you and him were going to get married. What happened with that?"

"Exactly what I'm trying to warn you about. He didn't want to marry me. I stuck around, put up with other women, hoping he would grow up and realize I was the best thing that ever happened to him. But he got this younger girl pregnant and felt obligated to marry her." She took a bite from her sandwich.

"I remember that night when you cursed him out. You

were crying so loud. We were scared something bad was going to happen."

"It was one of the hardest things I had to deal with. I made up my mind that I was no longer going to put my future in someone else's hands again."

Daneisha smiled. "And then you met Mike."

LeQuisha's face lit up. "Yes, I did."

"You wouldn't even be with Mike if I hadn't convinced you to talk to him. You were like, 'What does a doctor want with a single mother with three children?' "

"I still ask myself that sometimes."

"Mama, I know what you're getting at. It's not the same with Evan. He wants to get married, and eventually he's going to want to have a child. I probably won't be able to get pregnant."

"First of all, the doctor never said you couldn't have children. Secondly, have you and Evan even talked about children?"

Daneisha shrugged. "No, we haven't. That's why the marriage conversation threw me for a loop. I was like . . . where is all this coming from?

LeQuisha used a napkin to clean mustard lodged in between her fingers. "And that's the reason why you need to talk to the man. If I were you, I would give up on the notion that Lamium is coming back to you. Figure out what you want from your life, and then see if Evan fits in the picture."

"Mama, that's good advice. I appreciate you sharing some of your past experiences. You cleared up a lot of things." Daneisha picked up the empty plates and placed them in the sink.

"Mama knows a little something about life. It's not easy to admit all the mistakes I've made, but I learned. Through all my heartaches and pains, I learned. But I wanted you to know that it's not too late to turn your life around. You know I love you, right?"

"Yes."

LeQuisha wrapped her arms around her daughter.

"I love you too, Mama."

LeQuisha glanced down at her watch. "Well, I'm supposed to be meeting my honey. Call me later today."

"All right, I will."

Daneisha took a short nap then headed out to pick up LJ from school. She was dropping him off to spend the weekend with his dad. She planned to get her Christmas shopping done while he was away, hoping she would be able to use the credit card Evan gave her.

As she waited in the pick-up line at school, she dialed Lamium's number.

He picked up on the third ring.

"Where do you want to me to meet you?"

"Oh, I forgot li'l man was coming. I had so much to take care of. Just swing by the club."

"I told you I didn't want LJ up there."

"No, I'll meet you outside, I promise. I need to wait on my new recruits to get here first."

Daneisha took a deep breath. "Okay, but don't ask me to do this again. I want to make it crystal clear."

Against her better judgment, she gave in and drove LJ over to Club Sensations.

"What's this place, Mommy?" LJ asked as she parked her car next to Lamium's.

"Don't even ask." Daneisha searched for Lamium, but he was nowhere in sight. She dialed his cell number, but he didn't answer. She waited for another minute, growing impatient.

I should just take LJ home and forget all about this. But then again, LJ's been talking about this all week. I don't want to break his heart.

"I'll be right back. Lock the doors, and don't open this door for nobody but me," Daneisha instructed. She went up to club and knocked a few times.

Greg opened it.

"Hello, Daneisha. He's on his way."

"Okay." Daneisha peered inside and saw a few people at the table playing cards. Then she saw two teenaged boys leaning on the bar, holding beer cans in their hands. She shut the door.

A few seconds later, Lamium came out. "Sorry about that. I was tied up. LJ in the car?"

Daneisha crossed her arms. "What the hell are you doing with them young boys in your club, and drinking beer? Are you trying to lose your liquor license?"

Lamium held up his hands. "Don't worry about what I do with my business. Stick with that punk-ass nigga of yours, and let me tend to mine."

"I'm sorry, but I just don't agree with that."

"I told you to stay out of my shit."

"What if that was LJ in there? Would you want him to be doing what you do?"

Lamium chuckled. "Why do you think I'm working so hard to build this empire? Of course, I plan on having my own seed running it someday."

Daneisha cocked her head to the side. "Have you lost your mind? My son ain't gonna have shit to do with your business."

Lamium grabbed Daneisha by the arm. "Don't you fucking get loud with me. And you need to remember something, that's my muthafucking son too."

"You better get your hands off me!" Daneisha tried to snatch away, but Lamium pulled harder.

He whispered in her ear. "Don't make me have to kill your ass."

"Oh, like you did to Dirty Red? You're gonna blow my head off too?"

"Now, you know you wanted me to kill his ass. Don't try to act all innocent with me."

"I didn't tell you to do shit and you know it!" Daneisha cried out.

"Hey, Daddy!" LJ screamed from the car window. He held a huge smile on his face.

"Don't make a scene in front of your son. You know he's barely speaking to your ass now."

Lamium freed his grip from her arm.

Daneisha rubbed it and walked to the car. She wanted to drive off and get as far away from Jacksonville as she could. She regretted ever knowing Lamium and wished he were dead.

Lamium rubbed LJ's curly hair. "Let me help you with your stuff."

"Daddy, I can't wait to go with you." He hugged his father.

"Well, we're going to have a lot of fun, son."

Daneisha's face remained expressionless, trying not show any emotion. She watched Lamium put LJ in his booster seat.

Daneisha ran up to him. "Aren't you going to give me a kiss?"

"Yes," LJ responded and pecked her on the lips.

Lamium cooed, "Isn't that sweet? I should give your mama a kiss too."

Daneisha forced a fake smile.

Lamium pressed his lips on hers. Daneisha closed her eyes then turned away. She wiped a tear from her eye as she watched them drive off. Lamium thought he knew every damn thing. She wondered if now was the time to tell him he wasn't LJ's father. Leroy was, which explained why she had a hard time bonding with her son. At present, Daneisha learned to love him, despite the fact she wanted his biological father dead. The only reason he was still living was, she considered him a living organ donor to her son if needed.

Daneisha got in her Lexus and drove onto the street. Her cell phone rang. The caller ID showed an unknown caller.

"Hello."

"Daneisha Harris."

It was a woman's voice, and it sounded very familiar, although she couldn't recall it.

"Yes. Who is this?"

"We need to talk."

"Who is this?"

"I'm a federal agent, and I wish to discuss a matter concerning the murder of Milton Price."

"I don't know him. Please don't call this number again."

Daneisha hung up.

The phone rang again.

"Hello."

"I think you do know him, since you were one of the last people to see him alive. He's also known as Dirty Red. He was an FBI informant."

Daneisha gasped for air. "I don't know anything. Why are you bothering me?"

"You have been involved with a well-known notorious drug dealer, murderer, rapist, the rap sheet goes on. If you don't want to end up in handcuffs in the next few days, I think you should meet with me. We have a solid case, and we're about to close in on him and his entire organization within a matter of days. This is your only chance."

"I told you I don't know anything."

"You know more than you think you do. I'm offering

you a way out of spending the rest of your life in prison. I know you don't want your son to be without his mother and father, do you?"

"You can't do this to me. Please, just leave me alone."

"I'm trying to help you. The choice is yours. Meet me in half an hour, at the parking lot behind Ruth Chris. Do you know where it is?"

"Yes, but I really don't—"

"You should know you're being followed by another agent."

Daneisha almost lost control of the wheel. "Wait, I don't want to do this. I'm scared. I didn't do anything, I swear."

"I want to help you. You have to trust me."

Daneisha took two deep breaths. "Okay. I'll do it."

"Ruth Chris in thirty minutes. Park next to the black Envoy."

Daneisha drove downtown as she was instructed.

She was so scared, barely able to read the road signs along the way.

She pulled alongside the black SUV.

The door opened, and a black woman got out.

Daneisha's jaw dropped.

She knew she recognized the voice.

It was Jillian.

Jillian climbed in on the passenger side. A white man dressed in a navy polo shirt and gray pants sat in the back.

"Hello, Daneisha. We haven't formally met. I'm agent Roshanda Johnson, and this is my partner Steven Tolbert."

"I don't understand all of this. So your name is not Jillian?"

"No, it's not. Let me give you a brief history. The bureau has been investigating your boyfriend, or should I say ex-boyfriend, for quite some time now. I pretended to be a music producer, interested in Jericho Downs' wife, Myra."

Daneisha thought about Myra getting a recording contract shortly after she completed the demo. She wondered if Jillian had anything to do with that.

"Myra was providing us with the evidence we needed to build the case against him. One day I was at the studio, and Lamium came to hear her sing. He asked if I would be interested in taking a job as club manager."

"I'm very confused here. You're not Lamium's girlfriend then?"

Jillian tossed her head back. "No, I'm not."

"Does Lamium know that?"

"No, he doesn't. I don't want to get into that right now. We don't have the time."

Steven cleared his throat. "Yes, we should probably be wrapping this up." He was hinting that Roshanda was giving away too many details.

"To make the story short, we also had Milton Price, also known as Dirty Red as our informant. That is, until he was murdered."

Daneisha sighed. "I don't have anything to do with that."

Jillian raised her eyebrows. "Dirty Red was wearing a wire. We know you were in the office when the shooting took place."

"If he was wearing a wire, then you would know that I left before anything happened. I don't know anything, I swear."

Jillian clasped her hands together. "Lamium Jackson is going down in only a matter of weeks, and we got him on extortion, drug trafficking, tax evasion, and now first degree murder, which will put him away for a very long time."

Daneisha bit her bottom lip. "I still don't understand what that has to do with me. It seems like you're closer to Lamium than I am."

"I know you were there when Milton was killed."

"Your information is wrong. I wasn't there."

"Daneisha, you can either help us or hurt yourself. The choice is yours."

Roshanda handed Daneisha a business card.

"Either way, we have a case. I would hate for you to end up in prison."

"What Roshanda is saying is, we need you to cooperate with us. We would like to begin by searching your apartment."

Daneisha slung her hair off her shoulders. "Lamium didn't keep anything at my place. You need to contact the women he employed, like Keysha Turner and this white girl named Becky."

"I know for sure that you do have the information we're looking for at your apartment. I'm just trying to make this easy for you, but we can obtain a warrant if we need to. And you will risk the embarrassment and possibly being thrown out for harboring a notorious drug dealer."

Daneisha rubbed her sweaty hands along her thighs. It was her worst nightmare coming to reality. "I will look and see what I can find."

Roshanda touched the ring on her fourth finger. "Good."

Daneisha couldn't believe she had the nerve to have a husband at home, while she was fucking her man's brains out.

They got out of her car and returned to their own vehicle. Roshanda came back and tapped on the window. Daneisha rolled it down.

"There's one other thing. Once the arrests are made, we will need you to testify in court."

Roshanda got in her black Envoy and drove away. Daneisha buried her head in her hands. She felt a yank in her stomach and wanted to hurl. Adjusting her seat back, Daneisha stared up at the evening sky, wishing she could be like the birds flying away as the stormy rain clouds were moving in. That moment seemed to define everything that was happening in her life.

Back at her apartment, Daneisha paced back and forth in the bathroom. Wearing a black satin gown and her hair in a ponytail, she contemplated whether she should call her mother. Her rapid heartbeats made her feel she was on the verge of suffering a heart attack.

Lord, I need Your help.

With all the crying she was doing, she wondered if she was about to have a nervous breakdown.

This was all too much for her. Climbing into bed, Daneisha stared out the window. Her thoughts drifted back and forth, from her dreaded talk with Lamium and the discussion with Roshanda, AKA Jillian.

Daneisha felt paralyzed when Lamium told her he planned on LJ running his business one day. It certainly warranted him spending some time in prison. Unfortunately, she still loved him and didn't want him to end up there. That pissed her the hell off! It seemed so ironic that the woman he left her for was about to bring him and his entire organization down on its knees.

Daneisha wished there was some way she could get out of it. Glancing down at the notepad, the law firm Kay worked for stood out, Wotring and Associates, PA. Immediately, Daneisha called up Kay's old extension and was able to talk with the new receptionist. Fortunately, there were two attorneys still working late. Thanks to her hook-up from Kay, Vicki Wotring fit her in the schedule for Monday morning.

Kay, you're still looking out for me.

That Sunday, Daneisha went to church with her mother and Mike. After service, she went to their house for dinner. Once the family was there, including Dante and Donny, Daneisha decided to share with them what was happening with Lamium and the FBI agents.

"Can we all just sit in the family room for a minute?" Daneisha asked her mother.

LeQuisha scratched her chin. "Of course. Honey, tell the boys to come here."

"Sure, baby." Mike went down to Dante's room. A few minutes later, he reappeared with Donny and Dante.

Daneisha stood nervously as her family sat down.

She took a deep breath. "I'm just going to come out and say this. Lamium is being investigated by the FBI."

"What?" LeQuisha grabbed her chest. "How do you know about this?"

Daneisha shut her eyes tightly to fight back the tears. "I know, because they told me. They're trying to get me to testify against him and saying they're going to throw me in jail. And LJ isn't going to have anyone to look after him."

"Like hell they are!" LeQuisha announced boldy.

Mike put his hand on his wife's shoulders. "Baby, just calm down." He looked up at Daneisha. "Daneisha, don't you worry about a thing. These are just scare tactics."

"I kind of figured that out, so I called a lawyer just to be sure."

Donny rested his elbows on his knees. "When did you do this?"

"Friday," Daneisha responded.

"When did these agents first contact you?" Mike asked.

"It was the same day," Daneisha answered.

"Where were you? Did they come to your apartment?" LeQuisha asked emphatically.

Daneisha felt barraged by all the questions and tossed up her hands. "Okay, let me finish what I wanted to say. Then you can ask all the questions you want. I promise."

Mike shook his head in agreement. "Yes, let Daneisha just tell us what she wants us to know. Go ahead."

Daneisha scanned around the room. She hated seeing her mother so visibly upset. No matter how rebellious she'd been in the past, she didn't want to cause her mother any more pain. That was something she'd learned from Kay's death.

Having lost her only daughter, Reesy would never be the same person. It wasn't easy for Daneisha to watch someone suffer like that. She realized how blessed she was to be alive and enjoy her own mother. She promised herself she would make each day count with her own family and, more importantly, her son.

Daneisha explained how she contacted an attorney at the law firm where Kay worked. "I'm meeting with Vicki tomorrow."

"I'm going too," LeQuisha chimed in.

Mike turned to face her. "Are you sure Daneisha wants you to be there?"

LeQuisha cocked her head to one side as her eyes grew wide. "Excuse me?" She jabbed the air with her finger. "Oh, I'm-a be there, whether she wants me to or not."

"Mama, of course I want you to come."

"See, Mike? Why would you even ask me a question like that?" LeQuisha asked, her face getting hot. "You know how I am when it comes to my children."

"Woman, these are my children too," Mike defended.

Daneisha stared up at the ceiling and put her hands on her hips.

"You guys, please don't start arguing," Donny said. "We have enough to deal with. Now, let's just get through this."

"You're right, son." Mike rubbed Donny's leg. "Daneisha, it's settled then. Your mom will go with you to see this attorney. Then we'll get together afterwards and discuss the next course of action."

"Thank you. I feel so much better now. If I don't say it enough, I appreciate and love all of y'all." Tears welled up in Daneisha's eyes.

LeQuisha stood up and wrapped her arms around her daughter. "You know how I've felt about this relationship with Lamium, so I can't say I didn't expect it to come to this."

"Nevertheless," Mike interrupted, "we're going to help you get through this. And, there's no way on God's green earth you're going to jail. That's just not going to happen."

"That's right," Dante finally said.

Daneisha almost forgot he was in the room. A sense of relief came over her. She thanked God she had her family to support her through this crisis.

When Daneisha and her mom met with Vicki, she learned the FBI were in clear violation of her rights. Daneisha didn't have to meet with anyone unless she was called in for questioning. If Daneisha was contacted by an agent again, she was instructed to call Vicki at once. Vicki explained that Daneisha didn't have to meet with anyone without a legal representative present. Vicki took an extra step to contact the Special Agent in Charge, who was Roshanda's superior. If Daneisha wanted to file a complaint, Vicki would help her do that.

Tuesday morning, Evan called Daneisha's cell phone, and this time she decided to talk to him. He asked if he could come over to her apartment, and she agreed. Wanting to look good for her man, Daneisha changed out of her old clothes into a printed H&M minidress and knit leggings.

As Daneisha applied pressed powder to her face, she stared at her reflection in the mirror. She contemplated how much she should tell Evan about her problems with the FBI. Or should she say, Lamium's problems with the FBI.

Around noon, Evan rang the doorbell. Daneisha checked herself in the mirror before answering.

Daneisha didn't realize how much she'd missed Evan, until she saw his handsome face.

"Hello." Evan greeted her with a kiss on the lips.

"Hey." Daneisha smiled. She wrapped her arms around his shoulders. Evan lifted her up and gripped her on the butt.

"God, I missed you."

"I missed you too." Daneisha ran her fingers along his clean-shaven face. "Get in here."

Evan patted her on the butt and followed her inside.

They were kissing on the couch.

Evan sucked and licked every single inch from her breasts down to her navel.

Daneisha pushed him up when he tried to unbutton her jeans.

"Baby, what's up?" Evan asked. He licked his full lips, wanting to continue what he started.

Daneisha pressed both hands firmly on his chest. "I have a confession to make first."

Evan sighed. He pulled back and leaned against the cushions. "What is it?"

Daneisha sat up, gently finger combing her hair. "It's nothing bad. You know the other day when we had that fight?"

"Yes." Evan signaled with his hand for her to make it short. He was ready to get back to business.

"Well, I said that I didn't love you. But it wasn't true. I do love you." Daneisha pulled on his shirt. She unbuttoned the top two buttons then kissed him on the chest.

Evan's lips slowly curled into a smile. "You love me, baby?"

He moved in closer as his eyes lingered for a moment.

"Yes. I love you." Daneisha bit her bottom lip. She opened her mouth as his lips came closer. She felt his warm breath on her face and closed her eyes. His kiss sent a pulsating shock down her spine.

Chapter Twelve

Daneisha, Evan, and LJ completed the New Member's Orientation to become members of Bethel Baptist Institutional Church. It was the third Sunday in January, and the official induction was about to take place.

Nervously, Daneisha took a deep breath and straightened the sleeves to her crimson Chanel skirt suit. Her eyes scanned the sanctuary for her mother and stepdad. Evan found them in their usual pew and pulled Daneisha and LJ in that direction.

"Evan, you're pulling on my jacket," Daneisha whined as she quickly followed in his footsteps.

"I'm sorry." Evan reached the pew and hugged LeQuisha and shook hands with Mike.

"Hey, Daneisha." LeQuisha hugged her daughter. "I thought Dante and Donny were riding with you."

"No, Donny drove. They're upstairs."

"Okay." LeQuisha tried to hide her disappointment. "Just as long as they came to church. Did he bring that woman with him?"

"Yes, she's here, too."

LeQuisha held a tight-lipped grimace. "I can't believe it."

Daneisha grabbed her mother's hand and locked eyes with her. "Mama, let it go. Donny is a grown man."

"She's right," Mike chimed in. "You promised you wouldn't do this. Now, you're getting all worked up."

LeQuisha closed her eyes for a moment. "You're both right."

"I know." Daneisha smiled.

Evan, LJ, and Daneisha took their seats. They were all squished in like a pack of sardines.

Daneisha fidgeted with her hands.

"What is wrong with you?" Evan asked.

She whispered, "Mama doesn't know yet."

"You didn't tell her about the induction today?"

"No." Daneisha tried to sneak a glance to make sure her mother wasn't listening to them. "I wanted it to be a surprise."

LeQuisha was busy trying to tighten Mike's tie and straighten his collar.

Daneisha swung her head back and rolled her eyes. "Sometimes, she treats Mike like a child."

"Leave your mother alone," Evan ordered. "Obviously, he doesn't mind it one bit. I wish I could get my woman to pay me that kind of attention."

Daneisha looked him squarely in the eye. "Are you telling me you want me to fuss over you like that?"

Evan chewed on his toothpick. "Yes, I would."

"Then give me that." Daneisha snatched the toothpick out of his mouth. "It's a nasty habit, and I don't want you doing it anymore."

Evan put his arm around Daneisha and chuckled.

"See, that wasn't so hard, was it?"

Daneisha grinned. "No, it actually felt good."

While the announcements were going on, the music

played as the choir filled their seats on the far right. The new members' names flashed on the screen.

Daneisha gripped Evan's hand tighter. She had butterflies in her stomach when she saw her mother reading the long list of names. Then she said aloud, "Daneisha Harris and son Lamium . . . my eyes . . . Mike, did you see that?"

Pastor McKissick, Sr. took the microphone. "I want all the new members to please stand."

Daneisha, LJ, and Evan stood proudly, along with another thirty new members of the Bethel family.

The congregation clapped in their honor.

Pastor McKissick, Sr. shouted, "I know we can clap louder than that!"

LeQuisha opened her arms wide. "Welcome to the family!" She hugged and kissed Daneisha. Then she did the same for Evan and LJ.

"I'm proud of you," Mike said as he hugged Daneisha.

"Thanks." Daneisha blushed from all the attention.

Nicole Townsend, Daneisha's former Sunday School teacher, who was sitting behind them in the next pew, reached over to hug Daneisha. "Welcome to the Bethel family. I knew you would make your mother proud."

"Thank you, Ms. Nicole," Daneisha replied.

"Now, you know your mother is going to tear that aisle up today."

"I know." Daneisha rolled her eyes. "It's so embarrassing."

Nicole laughed. Her hair was perfect and her make-up flawless. "You should not be embarrassed by your mother at all. After everything your mother has been through, she has every reason to."

"You're right."

"Congratulations again," Nicole said before sitting down with her husband, Norris.

Norris shook hands with Evan. "Congratulations."

Evan shook his head. "Thank you. Thank you."

As predicted, when the choir sang the praise song, LeQuisha danced all the way down the aisle up to the stage.

"That's right, Sister Peeples," Pastor McKissick, Sr. said into the microphone. "We all have something to shout about. Ain't the Lord all right?"

"Yes!" the congregation shouted.

"Ain't He all right?"

"Yes!"

"Now shake three people's hands and tell them, 'The Lord is an all right God.'"

Daneisha happily obliged.

On the way back to her apartment, Evan was the one that seemed nervous.

"Evan, I was thinking that maybe you need a little help at the office."

"Sure. Are you offering your services?" Evan asked.

"Yes, I think I could help with the phones or something," Daneisha said. "That way I could learn the business before I start taking real estate classes."

Evan showed a surprised look on his face. "Wow. Are you sure about that?"

"Well, I want to be for sure, but I am interested." Daneisha gestured with her hands. "I have to find something better to do with my time than spend other people's money. I'm ready to start making some of my own."

"That's the right attitude," Evan replied. He wiped the sweat from his forehead.

"What's wrong with you?" Daneisha asked.

"Nothing. It's hot in here." He adjusted the heat on the driver's side. "What about you?"

"I'm cold." She stared back at LJ. "What about you, LJ?"

LJ held a satisfied look on his face. "Nice and toasty."

Daneisha laughed to herself. "I think I made Mama happy."

Evan shifted in his seat. "What did you say?"

Daneisha crossed her arms. "Are you listening to me?

"Of course, baby. I just missed that last part. Now what did you say again?"

"Nothing. Just forget it." Daneisha was agitated. She leaned her seat back and rested her eyes.

When they arrived at the complex, Evan picked up LJ and carried him upstairs, leaving Daneisha far behind.

Daneisha got an attitude. "Wow! What a gentleman!"

"I told you I was hot!" Evan shouted back.

Daneisha shook her head in disbelief. It was less than thirty degrees outside. She took her time climbing the stairs. When she opened the door, she couldn't believe her eyes.

Three huge floral arrangements sat on the table. Pink and white balloons were all over the living room.

"Oh my God." Daneisha clasped her hands on Evan's face. "It's so beautiful. I can't believe you went through all this trouble."

"It's no trouble when it brings a smile to your face. I thought this day deserved to be special for us as a family."

"Well, it is. Thank you, baby." Daneisha landed a wet kiss on his lips.

"There's one more thing to make this day complete."

Evan turned to face LJ, who was standing near the stereo, not paying attention.

"I said, there's one thing to make this day complete." This time his voice was louder.

"Oh, sorry." LJ giggled, his bottom snaggle tooth showing. Then he turned on the music.

It was Anthony Hamilton's song, "Can't Let Go."

Daneisha put her hands on her face.

Evan approached her. He kissed her on the cheek.

Then he got down on one knee. He reached in his suit jacket and pulled out a small black box.

Daneisha held a look of panic on her face. "No, you didn't!"

"Yes, I did." He opened the box.

Daneisha's eyes grew wide. "Evan." She took another deep breath.

Evan wiped his forehead with a napkin. "Okay, I got this."

Daneisha waited in anticipation.

"You are my life, Daneisha. I want to spend the rest of my life with you."

LJ cleared his throat.

Evan turned around. "I'm sorry. I want to spend the rest of my life with you and LJ."

"That's better," LJ replied.

"Will you marry me?" Evan asked, his voice scratchy.

Daneisha bit her bottom lip. "Yes, I will."

"Yeah!" LJ cheered loudly.

Evan put the ring on Daneisha's finger. It was no surprise that it fit perfectly. Evan stood up and held open his arms. "Can I have this dance, Ms. Harris?"

"You're a fool." Daneisha shook her head in amazement. "I can't believe you pulled this off without me knowing about it."

They slow-danced across the living room floor.

"Go, Mommy!" LJ clapped his hands to show his approval.

Evan and Daneisha laughed.

Then the doorbell rang.

"I bet I know who that is," Evan responded.

"You do?" Daneisha replied.

Evan opened the door.

"Is it okay for us to come in?" It was her mother's voice.

Evan winked in Daneisha's direction. "She said yes, so I guess it's all right."

Daneisha covered her mouth in embarrassment as her mother, stepdad, and brothers all came inside.

LeQuisha laughed. "I'm not the only one surprised today." She hugged her daughter.

"Mama, I can't believe you didn't say anything."

LeQuisha waved her hand. "I can't believe you didn't tell me you joined Bethel."

Daneisha grabbed her mother's hand. "Okay, so we're even."

LeQuisha's face lit up. "Congratulations, baby. I'm so happy for you."

Daneisha hugged her mother. "Thank you, Mama."

Evan treated the family to dinner at Copeland's.

The next morning, Daneisha went in the kitchen to fix a bowl of cereal.

"Put it back!" Evan ordered. He came in behind her and turned on the television. "I'm cooking breakfast."

"Oh, well you go right ahead. I will check up on LJ."

"Wait a minute!" Evan shouted. "Isn't that Lamium?"

Daneisha turned around to catch the news story. The headline read, NOTORIOUS DRUG DEALER ARRESTED.

"I can't believe this." Evan put his arm around Daneisha's waist.

"What is going on?" Daneisha tried her best to sound just as surprised as he was. Not sure whether she could trust Evan completely, she decided not to reveal her own personal involvement with the FBI.

The news reporter stated, *"Arrest warrants were issued to Lamium Jackson and all of the key members in his organization."*

"Awww, baby." Evan put his arms around Daneisha. "This is messed up. Are you okay?"

"Yes," Daneisha responded as she stared at the television, watching the playback of federal agents raiding Club Sensations. Lamium, Greg, and Rowan were dragged out with their hands handcuffed behind their backs.

Although she knew it was going to happen, she had no details as to when or where. It still seemed so unreal. Seeing Lamium's picture scattered all across the news made her feel horrible, but she knew she'd done the right thing by cooperating fully with the feds. She turned over all the documents she'd found in her bedroom months ago. Vicki struck a deal on Daneisha's behalf that she wouldn't have to testify in exchange. There would be no mention of her name.

Daneisha sat down on the couch with Evan's head on her lap. She ran her hand across his head. When LJ entered the living room, Daneisha turned the TV off. She wasn't ready to talk about his father's arrest just yet. When it came down to raising LJ, she'd learned the most important lesson of all. She was a mother first, and it was her job to protect her son.

About the Author

$\mathcal{L}$aTonya Y. Williams is the acclaimed author of **Mixed Messages, Make You Love Me,** and **Missed Opportunities.** LaTonya graduated from the University of Central Florida with a degree in education. She resides in Florida with her husband and three sons.

Stepping out on faith, LaTonya resigned from her teaching position to raise her family and write on a full-time basis. Her dream was finally realized in May 2004, when she signed a book deal with Carl Weber's *Urban Books.* Thought to be a thing of the past, her relationship novels have touched the hearts of many.

"It is my purpose to write what I know: women struggling to balance faith, family, and friends; while dealing with the harsh realities of life."

Currently, she is developing a project for television and completing her first inspirational novel (*Just Wanna Serve*).

My Little Secret

BY ANNA J.

Coming in September 2008

Ask Yourself

Ask yourself a question . . . have you ever had a session of love making, do you want me? Have you ever been to heaven?
—*Raheem DeVaughn*

February 9ᵗʰ, 2007

She feels like melted chocolate on my fingertips. The same color from the top of her head to the very tips of her feet. Her nipples are two shades darker than the rest of her, and they make her skin the perfect backdrop against her round breasts. Firm and sweet like two ripe peaches dipped in baker's chocolate. They are a little more than a handful, and greatly appreciated. Touching her makes me feel like I've finally found peace on earth, and there is no feeling in the world greater than that.

Right now her eyes are closed, and her bottom lip is

tightly tucked between her teeth. From my viewpoint between her wide-spread legs I can see the beginnings of yet
another orgasm playing across her angelic face. These are
the moments that make it all worthwhile. Her perfectly
arched eyebrows go into a deep frown, and her eyelids
flutter slightly. When her head falls back, I know she's
about to explode.

I move up on my knees so that we are pelvis to pelvis.
Both of us are dripping wet from the humidity and the situation. Her legs are up on my shoulders, and her hands
are cupping my breasts. I can't tell where her skin begins
or where mine ends. As I look down at her, and watch her
face go through way too many emotions, I smile a little bit.
She always did love the dick, and since we've been together she's never had to go without it. Especially since
the one I have never goes down.

I'm pushing her tool into her soft folds inch by inch as
if it were really a part of me, and her body is alive. I say
"her tool" because it belongs to her, and I just enjoy using
it on her. Her hip-length dreads seem to wrap us in a co-
coon of coconut oil and sweat, body heat and moisture,
soft moans and teardrops, pleasure and pain, until we
seemingly burst into an inferno of hot-like-fire ecstasy.
Our chocolate skin is searing to the touch, and we melt
into each other, becoming one. I can't tell where hers begins . . . I can't tell where mine ends.

She smiles . . . her eyes are still closed and she's still
shaking from the intensity. I take this opportunity to taste
her lips, and to lick the salty sweetness from the side of
her neck. My hands begin to explore, and my tongue en-
circles her dark nipples. She arches her back when my full
lips close around her nipple and I begin to suck softly as if
she's feeding me life from within her soul.

Her hands find their way to my head and become tan-
gled in my soft locks, identical to hers but not as long. I

push into her deep, and grind softly against her clit in search of her "J-spot" because it belongs to me, Jada. She speaks my name so soft that I barely hear her. I know she wants me to take what she so willingly gave me, and I want to hear her beg for it.

I start to pull back slowly, and I can feel her body tightening up, trying to keep me from moving. One of many soft moans is heard over the low hum of the clock radio that sits next to our bed. I hear slight snatches of Raheem DeVaughn singing about being in heaven, and I'm almost certain he wrote that song for me and my lady.

I open her lips up so that I can have full view of her sensitive pearl. Her body quakes with anticipation from the feel of my warm breath touching it, my mouth just mere inches away. I blow cool air on her stiff clit, causing her to tense up briefly, her hands taking hold of my head trying to pull me closer. At this point my mouth is so close to her, all I would have to do is twitch my lips to make contact, but I don't . . . I want her to beg for it.

My index finger is making small circles against my own clit, my honey sticky between my legs. The ultimate pleasure is giving pleasure, and I've experienced that on both accounts. My baby can't wait anymore, and her soft pants are turning into low moans. I stick my tongue out, and her clit gladly kisses me back.

Her body responds by releasing a syrupy-sweet slickness that I lap up until it's all gone, fucking her with my tongue the way she likes it. I hold her legs up and out to intensify her orgasm because I know she can't handle it that way.

"Does your husband do you like this?" I ask between licks. Before she could answer I wrap my full lips around her clit and suck her into my mouth, swirling my tongue around her hardened bud, causing her body to shake.

Snatching a second toy from the side of the bed, I take one hand to part her lips, and I ease her favorite toy (the rabbit) inside of her. Wishing that the strap-on I'm wearing was a real dick so that I could feel her pulsate, I turn the toy on low at first, wanting her to receive the ultimate pleasure. In the dark room the glow-in-the-dark toy is lit brightly, the light disappearing inside of her when I push it all the way in.

The head of the curved toy turns in a slow circle, while the pearl beads jump around on the inside, hitting up against her smooth walls during insertion. When I push the toy in, she pushes her pelvis up to receive it, my mouth latched on to her clit like a vice. She moans louder, and I kick the toy up a notch to medium, much to her delight. Removing my mouth from her clit, I rotate between flicking my wet tongue across it to heat it, and blowing my breath on it to cool it, bringing her to yet another screaming orgasm, followed by strings of "I love you" and "Please don't stop."

Torturing her body slowly, I continue to stimulate her clit while pushing her toy in and out of her on a constant rhythm. When she lifts her legs to her chest, I take the opportunity to let the ears on the rabbit toy that we are using do their job on her clit, while my tongue find its way to her chocolate ass. I bite one cheek at a time, replacing it with wet kisses, afterwards sliding my tongue in between to taste her there. Her body squirming underneath me lets me know I've hit the jackpot, and I fuck her with my tongue there also.

She's moaning, telling me in a loud whisper that she can't take it anymore. That's my cue to turn the toy up high. The buzzing from the toy matches that of the radio, and with her moans and my pants mixed in, we sound like a well-rehearsed orchestra singing a symphony of passion. I allow her to buck against my face while I keep up with the rhythm of the toy, her juice oozing out the sides and forming a puddle under her ass. I'm loving it.

She moans and shakes until the feeling in the pit of her stomach subsides and she is able to breathe at a normal rate. My lips taste salty-sweet from kissing her body while she tries to get her head together, rubbing the sides of my body up and down in a lazy motion.

Valentine's Day is fast approaching, and I have a wonderful evening planned for the two of us. She already promised me that her husband wouldn't be an issue because he'll be out of town that weekend, and besides all that, they haven't celebrated Cupid's day since the year after they were married, so I didn't even think twice about it. After seven years it should be over for them anyway.

"It's your turn now," she says to me in a husky, lust-filled voice, and I can't wait for her to take control.

The ultimate pleasure is giving pleasure . . . and man, does it feel good both ways. She starts by rubbing her oil-slicked hands over the front of my body, taking extra time around my sensitive nipples before bringing her hands down across my flat stomach. I've since then removed the strap-on dildo, and am completely naked under her hands.

I can still feel her sweat on my skin, and I can still taste her on my lips. Closing my eyes, I enjoy the sensual massage that I'm being treated to. After two years of us making love it's still good and gets better every time.

She likes to take her time covering every inch of my body, and I enjoy letting her. She skips past my love box, and starts at my feet, massaging my legs from the toes up. When she gets to my pleasure point, her fingertips graze the smooth, hairless skin there, quickly teasing me before she heads back down and does the same thing with my other limb. My legs are spread apart and lying flat on the bed with her in between, relaxing my body with ease. A cool breeze from the cracked window blows across the room every so often, caressing my erect nipples, making them harder than before, until her hands warm them back up again.

She knows when I can't take any more, and she rubs and caresses me until I am begging her to kiss my lips. I can see her smile through half-closed eyelids, and she does what I requested. Dipping her head down between my legs, she kisses my lips just as I asked, using her tongue to part them so that she can taste my clit. My body goes into mini-convulsions on contact, and I am fighting a battle to not cum, which I never win.

"Valentine's Day belongs to us, right?" I ask her again between moans. I need her to be here. V-Day is for lovers, and her and her husband haven't been that in ages. I deserve it . . . I deserve her. I just don't want this to be a repeat of Christmas or New Year's Eve.

"Yes, it's yours," she says between kisses on my thigh and sticking her tongue inside of me. Two of her fingers have found their way inside of my tight walls, and my pelvic area automatically bounces up and down on her hand as my orgasm approaches.

"Tell me you love me," I say to her as my breathing becomes raspy. Fire is spreading across my legs and working its way up to the pit of my stomach. I need her to tell me before I explode.

"I love you," she says, and at the moment she places her tongue in my slit, I release my honey all over her tongue.

It feels like I am on the Tea Cup ride at the amusement park as my orgasm jerks my body uncontrollably, and it feels like the room is spinning. She is sucking and slurping my clit while the weight of her body holds the bottom half of me captive. I'm practically screaming and begging her to stop, and just when I think I'm about to check out of here, she lets my clit go.

I take a few more minutes to get my head together, allowing her to pull me into her and rub my back. Moments like this make it all worthwhile. We lay like that for a while longer listening to each other breathe, and much to my dismay, she slides my head from where it was resting on her arm and gets up out of the bed.

I don't say a word. I just lie on the bed and watch her get dressed. I swear everything she does is so graceful, like there's a rhythm riding behind it. Pretty soon she is dressed and standing beside the bed looking down at me. She smiles, and I smile back, not worried, because she promised me our lover's day, and that's only a week away.

"So, Valentine's Day belongs to me, right?" I ask her again just to be certain.

"Yes, it belongs to you."

We kiss one last time, and I can still taste my honey on her lips. She already knows the routine, locking the bottom lock behind her. Just thinking about her makes me so horny, and I pick up her favorite toy to finish the job. Five more days, and it'll be on again.

COMING SOON FROM
Q-BORO
BOOKS

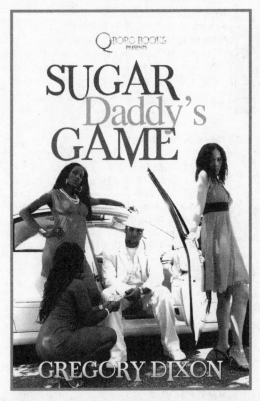

Jamell White is known as Sugar Daddy. Most of the people who know him assume that his nickname "Sugar" is a by-product of his cash-friendly habits with several beautiful, well known females. But they couldn't be more wrong.

MAY 2008
ISBN: 1-933967-41-2

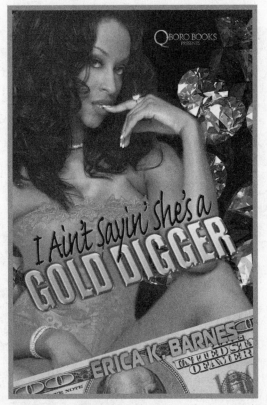

MESSIN'
UP